ABSOLUTE BRIGHTNESS

James Lecesne

ABSOLUTE BRIGHTNESS

Laura Geringer Books
HARPERTEEN

An Imprint of HarperCollinsPublishers

Though the town of Neptune, New Jersey, is a place both real and true, I have taken some liberties in terms of its geography and its character in order to accommodate my story. All the characters, however, are fictional, and any similarity to the actual people of Neptune is purely coincidental.

HarperTeen is an imprint of HarperCollins Publishers.

Absolute Brightness
Copyright © 2008 by James Lecesne
All rights reserved. Printed in the United States of America.
www.harperteen.com

Library of Congress Cataloging-in-Publication Data
Lecesne, James.
    Absolute brightness / James Lecesne. — 1st ed.
        p.   cm.
    "Laura Geringer books."
    Summary: In the beach town of Neptune, New Jersey, Phoebe's life is changed irrevocably when her gay cousin moves into her house and soon goes missing.
    ISBN 978-0-06-125627-1 (trade bdg.)
    ISBN 978-0-06-125628-8 (lib. bdg.)
    [1. Cousins—Fiction. 2. Homosexuality—Fiction. 3. Good and evil—Fiction. 4. Coming of age—Fiction. 5. New Jersey—Fiction.] I. Title.
PZ7.L483Ab 2008   2007002988
[Fic]—dc22   CIP
                                                         AC

Typography by Barbara Grzeslo
1 2 3 4 5 6 7 8 9 10
❖
First Edition

For Christopher Potter

This book would not have happened without the encouragement and support of Christopher Potter; he saw it before it existed and he believed in it. I'm also indebted to my early readers, who took the time to read this book as soon it was there and gave me the guidance I needed to complete it: Michael Cunningham, Eve Ensler, Katherine Deickmann, Michael Downing, Daniel Kaizer, Daniel Minahan, Adam Moss, Cy O'Neal, and Duncan Sheik. My special thanks to my friend and agent Bill Clegg for making the whole thing happen. And to my dear friends Gary Janetti, Armistead Maupin, and Ken Corbett, who are the best at being there for me. I'm so grateful to everyone at Laura Geringer Books, especially Lindsey Alexander, Jill Santopolo, Mary Albi, Cindy Tamasi, Amanda Lipnick, Dina Sherman, Martha Rago, Renée Cafiero, Barbara Grzeslo, and Jaime Morrell. But of course the lion's share of thanks goes to Laura Geringer herself, for seeing the goodness in *Absolute Brightness* and bringing it so perfectly into the world.

I flam'd amazement.

Ariel in *The Tempest*,
William Shakespeare

I was stalled in aisle 7 of our local supermarket, musing over the selection of potato chips and saying something like, "But really, don't you think thirty-seven different types of chips is a ridiculous number to choose from? I mean, how did we end up living in a country that makes a big deal over everything squeaky-clean and then at the same time makes you pay extra for chips called 'dirty'?"

As usual, Mom hadn't heard a word I'd said. Instead, she was standing in the middle of the aisle, smiling at nothing in particular and referring to her shopping list as if it were about to tell her something about her life that she didn't already know. My sister, Deirdre, was hanging the top half of her body over the shopping cart, letting her long, luxurious chestnut-colored hair touch the unpaid-for produce. She couldn't hear me even if she'd been so inclined; she was plugged into her iPod and humming along. If you happened to be passing by, you might have assumed that Deirdre was just some girl about to be sick into the cart, or you might have mistaken her humming for the kind of low moaning that is popular with television actors starring in telenovelas when they've just been fatally shot.

Deirdre has always been considered the great beauty in our family, so I made a point of keeping a certain distance from her. Someone might be forced to compare us, and I would only come up short. Literally. Deirdre is a full four inches taller than I am. Deirdre has always been the tall beautiful one. I was . . . well, I was Phoebe. I've also avoided lingering too long over her physical features, like her delicate bone structure, her glittery green eyes or the aforementioned full-bodied head of gorgeous, chestnut-colored hair. Compare and despair. It's true that I've never tried that hard in the beauty department. What's the point? That's Deirdre's territory. It was as if Deirdre had used up all the genetic coding in our family for beauty, and I got whatever was left over, the dregs. Everyone was always looking at her, admiring her, telling her how beautiful she looked, how perfect her outfit was, and asking where she got her shoes. From top to bottom she was Neptune's "it" girl. I was the also-ran. It's lucky I loved Deirdre as much as I did; otherwise I would have hated her guts.

It's not that I'm bad-looking. But my arms and legs have always been a bit too square, my hips are wide and I have a butt. I like my breasts. Once I got over the embarrassment of actually having breasts, I discovered that they gave me power over the boys at school when I wore a certain kind of top. My face is fine, but maybe it's a bit too flat and round to be considered anything other than just cute. Personally, I think my brown eyes are a little too far apart and they don't sparkle nearly as much as I would like, but I can see the world well enough with them, so I guess I shouldn't complain. I dye my hair;

I always have. It's my signature thing, my way to keep from being overlooked or forgotten altogether. As my mother has always reminded us girls, "Beauty may be in the eye of the beholder, but for god's sakes give 'em something worth beholding."

Mom poked Deirdre in the ribs and told her to stand up straight and take her earbuds out. Mom had an announcement to make. And then without any fanfare whatsoever, in the middle of aisle 7, she told us that our cousin Leonard would be coming to live with us.

"And soon," she added. "I mean, this Saturday."

"I didn't know we had a cousin," was the first thing out of my mouth.

Now normally, I don't like to hang out near the frozen foods. You can freeze your legs off if you linger too long in shorts by the Tater Tots and TV dinners. But we were stuck. Mom had decided that this was the time and place to tell us exactly who Leonard Pelkey was and why he would soon be living under our roof. By the time she had finished, my teeth were chattering and my fingertips had gone numb.

Apparently, Leonard was the son of Janet Somebody from Phoenix who had been getting beaten up pretty regularly by her husband. Finally, she ran off with baby Leonard and tried to piece together a life. Years later, when Leonard was about eleven, Janet met my mother's brother, Mike, in a bar. After noticing that he had a job, she started living with Mike in a low-rise apartment complex with a Spanish-inspired motif until she died of breast cancer the following year, which forced my uncle Mike to become Leonard's legal guardian. But Mike wasn't much of a father figure. He finally broke down, called my mother and cried long distance. He admitted that he couldn't handle the responsibility of raising a kid on his own. Mom asked him why this was the first she'd heard from him in two years. Uncle Mike explained that he had been traveling back and forth to Mexico and working on a scheme to raise some kind of cattle, which would later be sold for a ton of money. He wanted to know if Leonard could live with us—just until his cattle began to pay off.

After Mom finished telling us the story of

Leonard, we made our way to the checkout, where Mrs. Toucci rang us up. Mrs. T. took the opportunity to badger Mom; she wanted one of Mom's prime Saturday-morning appointment slots because, she said, she was going to a wedding in Atlantic City. Mom stood firm and explained to Mrs. T. that her beauty salon was not a fly-by-night joint, and her Saturday slots were sacrosanct.

"Oh," Mrs. T. said squinting through the tops of her bifocals. "What the hell's sacro-sacked mean?"

"It means forgetaboutit," Mom said as she handed over her credit card along with one of her signature smiles.

Deirdre and I stood on the sidelines, still reeling from the unexpected announcement. We tried to imagine what this unknown boy's arrival would mean to us personally. I looked at Deirdre and mouthed the words, "No way am I giving up my room." She mouthed back, "Don't look at me."

"Excuse me," I said aloud, interrupting Mrs. T. as she handed my mother back her credit card. Both women turned and looked right at me. To tell you the truth, Mrs. T. looked like she could've used some serious improvement. Her hair was the color of a paper bag and looked as though someone had ironed it flat against her scalp. I briefly considered offering her *my* services, which was something I sometimes did for Mom's customers when they were desperate enough to pay double to have someone come to their house and fix them up. But I decided I couldn't be bothered. We had much more pressing issues to attend to in our own backyard.

"How old is the boy? This cousin of ours?" I asked.

"Thirteen. But he's about to be fourteen."

I was fifteen at the time and Deirdre was seventeen, so we didn't have much use for a boy that age living under our roof. It wasn't as if Deirdre and I would be able to pick and choose P.B.F.s (Potential Boyfriends) from the gang of boys that our "cousin" dragged home from school with him. They'd all be way too young—and annoying.

"I have a very bad feeling about this Leonard situation," I said.

"Phoebe, don't start. I'm in no mood," she said

to me as she shoved her credit card back into her leatherette purse. "Grab those bags and put them in the cart. We have a lot to do."

I knew what was going on. I knew what Mom was up to. She was doing that thing she does when she forces life to go on as usual. She doesn't say anything, but her actions speak louder than words, and they all seem to be saying: *This is it. This is the way it's going to be from now on. Get used to it.* And that's how I knew we were going to be stuck with Leonard and there was nothing anyone could say or do from that moment forward to change the situation.

There are those moments in your life when you just know for sure that a major shift is happening right beneath your running shoes and you can feel that your world will never be the same again. That day I swear I felt as if the floor buckled and split and we were all suddenly standing at the edge of a giant abyss looking into God-knows-what. The weird thing is that on the surface everything seemed the same. It was just another Monday at the local supermarket; the PA system was pumping out a watered-down version of "Every Breath You Take," shoppers were loading up supplies for the week and Mrs. T. was badgering Mom for an appointment. Same ol', same ol'. But I wasn't fooled. Not for a minute. And neither was Deirdre.

"Where's he going to sleep?" Deirdre wanted to know once we were outside in the parking lot standing beside Mom's globally warmed Honda.

Mom was packing the groceries into the trunk. I noticed that her eyebrows were arched very high and her lips had been drawn tightly together in a little *O* of *No comment*. She slammed the trunk shut with a mighty thunk.

"Look," she said in the voice she only used with her customers who had complaints about the end result, "arrangements will be made."

Arrangements?

We lived in a two-story, three-bedroom, split-level house that was smack in the middle of nowhere along the Jersey shore. Ours was not a house where "arrangements" got made. We were more the type of family to whom things just happened. Fathers ran off. Parents got divorced. Grandmothers died.

Cousins moved in. Everything from the future just seemed to tumble into the present and take us by surprise. There was never any planning involved, and certainly no *arranging*. It was true that *appointments* got made at my mother's hair salon every day of the week (except Sundays and Mondays), and since the salon itself was attached to our house by a narrow breezeway, it was technically still a part of our home; but those appointments weren't *arranged*; they were *booked*.

Arrangements? Who was she kidding?

Because we didn't have a spare bedroom in our house and because both Deirdre and I had adamantly refused to give up our rooms to a total stranger, we were forced by my mother to spend the afternoon creating a suitable living space for Leonard down in the basement. We broke our backs clearing an area against one of the cinder-block walls and then stacking boxes five high to create a cozy cardboard corral just large enough to fit a twin bed, a small dresser and a milk crate that was transformed into a bedside table. We found an old floor lamp down there, the kind that has several conical shades sticking out of it, and we hooked it up in case Leonard was the type of kid who read books. Mom bought a wastebasket with pictures of trains embossed into it. She placed the thing on the floor, stood back to appraise it and then dismissed our objections by saying that we didn't know bubkes about what a boy likes. Judging from the look of the wastebasket, she didn't either, but we gave up arguing. To give the illusion of a doorway, we left an opening between two stacks of boxes; and then in a tragic attempt to provide the suggestion of privacy, Mom tacked up a piece of blue billowy fabric over the opening.

The fact that I ended up straining my back and having a bad attitude about our guest before he set foot on our property made no difference to my mother. When I complained about having to do all the heavy lifting, she said, "Well, having a boy around the house will change all that." She turned her back on me and continued to tape up a few tattered Sierra Club posters that had been rolled up and lying around forever. This was another one of her brilliant ideas. She said the posters would be like windows that looked out onto vistas more breathtaking and awe-inspiring than anything Leonard would be likely to find in Neptune, New Jersey. Her choice of views included the wide-open wilderness of Yosemite National Park, the moon rising over Massanutten Mountain in Shenandoah National Park, and an uninviting stretch of Arctic tundra that looked a little too frozen to be anything other than deadly. I refused to be impressed by any of it, mostly because the whole *arrangement* was the most obvious desecration of the memory of my dead grandmother.

Allow me to explain.

After my nana Hertle died, no one knew what to do with her stuff. The furniture was too good to put out on the street but not fine or fancy enough to sell for a profit on eBay. Her clothes were exceptional only because they had belonged to her; her knickknacks, potholders, inspirational books, crocheted vests, tam-o'-shanters, collection of cocktail swizzle sticks, Ouija board, yoga mat and electric juicer continued to sit there in her apartment gathering dust from one month to the next. My father still lived with us back then, and all the signs were that he was depressed. Who could blame him? His only mother had just died, and whenever someone (i.e., Mom) suggested that he drive over to Nana Hertle's place and box up her belongings, he claimed that it was too much for him. His short-term solution was to go to work, come home, watch TV game shows and pay the rent on Nana's apartment.

But paying rent on a dead person's apartment was, in my mother's estimation, the same as throwing money out the window. So one day, without any warning, she drove over to Nana's apartment, dragged all the furniture out onto the curb, priced everything, sold most of it and what she couldn't sell boxed up and moved into our basement. The empty apartment was then sublet to a Polish couple with a newborn baby, and that was that.

I was only eleven when Nana died, so I wasn't expected to figure out stuff like this; but then no one else in my family did anything about it either. As a result, the boxes just sat there, sagging, molding at the edges and smelling slightly of mildew. I think Mom was proud of herself for finally putting those boxes to good use while at the same time solving the problem of where Leonard was going to sleep. She kept repeating over and over that Leonard was going to love it, really love it.

For the next few days Deirdre and I lived in a state of suspended disbelief. Everything went on as it always had, and we tried not to think about the fact that life, as we had known it, was about to end. No one mentioned that a stranger, a boy, an uninvited guest was about to take up residence in our home, and no one uttered his name. We just went about our business. Looking back on it now, however, I realize that even if we had been ready to receive the imagined Leonard Pelkey into our midst with open arms, we still wouldn't have been prepared for the shock of that almost-fourteen-year-old boy who stood in our living room that first day.

Leonard was wearing Capri pants (pink and lime-green plaid) and a too-small T-shirt, which exposed his midriff. He wore a pair of shoes that were more like sandals set atop a pair of two-inch wooden platforms. Both ears were pierced, though only one chip of pale blue glinted from his left lobe.

He carried what looked like a flight attendant's overnight flight bag from the 1960s: The strap was hitched over his shoulder, lady style.

"Ciao," he said to me as he smiled and held out his hand.

I took hold of his delicate fingers and gave them a quick shake, while internally rolling my eyes. He was way too different. Don't get me wrong. I like different. I am different. But when different goes too far, it stops being a statement and just becomes weird. I made up my mind right then and there that he and I would not be getting that close, and as a way of making my point, I turned on my heel and got out of there as fast as I could without knocking anything over.

From the dining room I could watch Leonard's reflection in the large gilt mirror that hung over the sofa on the far wall. He didn't see me, not at first; he was too busy entertaining my mother, telling her stories about his journey, talking about what he had eaten on the plane, who he'd spoken to, pulling out the contents of his flight bag and then explaining where he got everything, including the bag itself. I thought he'd never shut up.

"They gave me the bag on the plane, because the air hostess said I was the most entertaining young person she'd met in a long while. It's vintage. I told her if she was any nicer, I'd have to do my Julie Andrews impression for her. She was like, Who's Julie Andrews? I was like, Are you kidding me?"

I was not in the least interested in what he was packing or what impressions he could pull off, but I was certainly intrigued by his appearance. He was like a visual code that was at once both a no-brainer to figure out and impossible to decipher. I mean, it wasn't just the fact that he was obviously gay. Please, I've watched enough TV to not be shocked by swish behavior. But there was something about Leonard that seemed to invite ridicule. Like he was saying, Go on, I dare you, say something, mention the obvious. The incredible thing was that no one said a word. Not Deirdre. Not Mom. And since I was out of the room, not me.

Leonard had a narrow face with plain Midwestern features. His mouth was tiny and unremarkable except for the fact that it was always in motion. A few freckles dotted the bridge of his nose and looked like they had been painted on for a musical performance in which he was to play a hillbilly. If it hadn't been for his eyes, two green pinpoints of flickering intensity, you might have missed him entirely. They were so bright, they made his whole head seem bright and biggish, sitting atop a narrow set of shoulders. His eyes were what held him in place, as if the sharpness of his gaze made him appear more visible to others, more present. The way those eyes could dart about the room and flit from surface to surface made it seem as though his life depended upon his ability to take in every single detail, assess every stitch of your outfit, calculate the distance to each exit and the time it would take to get there. He did have the most adorable eyelashes I'd ever seen on a boy, long and silky and dark; but then he may have been wearing some product.

"I see you," he said to my reflection in the mirror, which naturally made me crouch to the floor and then drag myself into the kitchen.

I had to warn my mother. I felt it was my duty

to tell her that I had a very bad feeling, the same feeling I'd had a few years ago when Dad took up with Chrissie Bettinger, an event which of course led to my parents' divorce and to the subsequent destruction of our entire family. Nana Hertle always tried to convince me that I possessed psychic abilities. I told her I didn't believe in such things. But when I realized that I might have prevented my father from running off if only I had heeded my nagging premonitions, I began to wonder if perhaps I did have a special power to foretell the future after all. If only I had said something at the time. So just to be on the safe side, after Leonard was settled into his makeshift basement bedroom and out of earshot, and Mom was back upstairs in the kitchen, I grabbed her arm and said, "Can't you see it? He's like a freak of nature. He's from another planet. I mean, what's he wearing on his feet?"

"Phoebe, let go of my arm," she said, narrowing her eyes and putting on a very cool voice. "They're a kind of sandal. I think they call them huaraches. And you don't know. Maybe they're popular with the boys where he comes from."

"Where? On Mars?"

My mother said I was pure evil, and she refused to listen to another word. To get me out of her sight, she instructed me to deliver a handful of fresh towels to Leonard.

He was lying on his new bed in his basement lair. The aforementioned huaraches were kicked off, and he was gazing up at the system of pipes and wires suspended from the rafters as though he was looking at a field of shimmering stars on a summer night.

"So cool. Right? I'm going to call it 'my boxed set.' Get it? Boxed. Set."

"Yeah," I said without the slightest inflection. "I get it."

"It's neato."

I felt I ought to explain to Leonard why "neato" was a word he needed to drop from his vocabulary. If he expected to make friends during his stay in Neptune, I told him, he couldn't talk like that. He just stared at me like I had something stuck to my face.

Finally I said, "What?"

"Nothing. I was just wondering if you've

considered a career in television news broadcasting. You have the 'on-air' face for it. Not exactly the hair, but definitely the face."

I couldn't believe my ears. He had puffed up his pathetic chest while making his brilliant diagnosis, as if to make himself appear larger or more important. But he had the puny rib cage of a kid who had survived early illness. If I had had the presence of mind, I would have responded right away by saying something brutally frank. I might have explained to him why I would never in a million years consider handing out bad news on a daily basis to an unsuspecting nation while wearing a cheerful face, a plunging neckline and a dated hairstyle. It was a hideous idea. The fact that my hair color at the time was magenta and my left nostril was pierced with a garnet should have convinced anyone with eyesight and half a brain that I had plans, and those plans did not include an "on-air" face.

But Leonard had just arrived from Mars, so perhaps he didn't understand the signals, customs and facial expressions of the inhabitants of planet Earth. I decided to let it go. I opted instead to stomp up the stairs and in so doing express my impatience with the whole conversation. At the same time, I could get as far away from him as I could manage in a house so small and cramped. I slammed the door and retired to my room to read *Madame Bovary*. As Emma Bovary went careening around the streets of Rouen in the back of a closed carriage, making mad and passionate love to Monsieur Léon, I silently made a vow to myself never to speak to Leonard again, because as anyone could see, he was a loser.

Our first meal together was a form of early-twenty-first-century torture. Over spaghetti and meatballs, Leonard tried to figure out the situation between my parents. Why were they no longer together? Where was Dad living now that they had separated? What happened to make him leave? Was it actually a divorce? Were they planning to get back together? Mom tried to deflect each one of Leonard's questions.

"He's a missing person."

"Don't ask."

"Could we change the subject?"

"More meatballs?"

"Enough."

When Leonard persisted, she decided to take another tack.

"You know the way a snail abandons its shell?" she said, spooning a second helping onto Leonard's plate whether he liked it or not. "Well, that's your uncle. Only he moved way faster than a snail. And he wasn't alone."

Whenever Mom talked about my father, she never mentioned the word "divorce"; it was against her Catholic religion. But then, it wasn't her style to say much about anything—for example, she didn't go around explaining to people why Chrissie Bettinger, a girl whom she had given every opportunity and had housed under her own roof, ran off with her husband. Not that she had to explain a thing to the folks in Neptune; everyone knew the whole story.

For a while, Mom was big news and the regular customers of Hair Today salon were privy to a ready supply of fresh details about the breakup. But even after all the screaming and the fighting, after that morning when we woke to find all Dad's belongings sitting in a pile out on the front lawn, after all the lawyers had served the legal papers and the whole thing was officially over, Mom fought against the idea that she was the type of person who could get a divorce. If asked, she said she was "separated." She once told Deirdre and me that if word got out about the divorce, it would ruin her as a hair stylist. But really, word was out, and she was in denial.

There are photographs of my mother from when she was a younger version of herself, and no matter what was going on, she always managed to smile for the camera. She smiled as she entered the room with the knotty-pine paneling; she smiled as she looked adoringly at her father, who was holding up a raw steak and wearing a KISS THE COOK apron; she smiled when she was caught with pink curlers in her blue-black hair and not a hint of makeup; she smiled in her wedding dress standing against an obviously fake autumnal backdrop; she smiled as she pointed to the Motel 6 outside Phoenix where she and Dad stayed on a cross-country road trip; and she smiled as she sat by the ocean with pint-sized versions of me and Deirdre playing in the background.

In each one of those pictures, it was plain to see she had no idea that her life would later become such a sad and sorry soap opera. Back in those days, when she was still drop-dead gorgeous and full of potential, she probably woke up each morning, put on her makeup, fixed her hair, got dressed, had places to go, stuff to look forward to and plenty of things to smile about. But by the time I came along, smiling was how she'd trained herself to meet every situation, no matter what. Smiling had become a habit. No, smiling was more than a habit for my mother; it was who she was.

I knew other mothers, mothers of girls my age, who had fabulous lives, working husbands, nice houses, clothes, cars, Cuisinarts and micro-waves, the whole split-level deal, and quite honestly they didn't smile half as much as my mother did. Even after my father announced that he was leaving us and taking up with Chrissie Bettinger, Mom kept smiling. And she smiled long after he was gone.

"It's okay, Aunt Ellen," Leonard said, leaning over and fingering the diamond center of her wed-ding ring. "I guess it kinda turned out different for all of us. How many carats is this, anyway?"

I can't remember the last time my mother cried, but right there at the kitchen table over a plate of spaghetti and meatballs, tears came streaming down her face. She was quiet about it. No sobs or choking back. It was as if Leonard had found the on/off switch to her tears. And no one was more surprised than Deirdre and me. We both sat there with our mouths hanging open. I think if I hadn't been chewing and trying to swallow a meatball, I would have burst out crying myself. But as it happened, I didn't want to add the Heimlich maneuver to our dinnertime activities, so I just closed my mouth and kept chewing as if nothing was wrong. Deirdre, on the other hand, excused herself from the table, went upstairs and didn't come back.

"I'm sorry," Mom said into her paper napkin. "I'm so sorry. I didn't mean to . . . It's just . . . I don't know. I'm exhausted. This week and all. There's been so much. I don't usually . . . Why am I explaining?"

"My mother used to cry at holidays," Leonard offered as a way of comforting Mom and making her feel like it wasn't anything to apologize about.

"Also anniversaries." And then as an afterthought, he added. "I miss her. A lot."

We all just sat there missing people who weren't there. Then Leonard sat straight up in his chair and let his eyes pop open wide. He had an idea.

"Hey, wait a minute. Is it like the anniversary of something between you and my uncle What's-his-name?"

Mom looked up, squinted and then blinked a few times like she was trying to see something very far off without her glasses. And then there it was, clear as if it had unexpectedly appeared on the horizon. We could see her seeing it—the date. Thirty years ago, almost to the moment, my mother had met my father.

Mom's eyes filled up with tears again, and she was unable to go on.

Leonard turned to me and in a voice that mixed urgency with unctuousness asked if we had any vodka in the house. Vodka? Why would we need vodka? I didn't get it. But then the next moment, I found myself standing on a chair in the dining room, turning the key of the liquor cabinet and pulling down a bottle of Smirnoff. *This better be good*, I thought.

When I came back into the kitchen, Leonard was standing at the kitchen sink with a head of iceberg lettuce in his hands. He was tearing away three of the large, crisp outer leaves and rinsing them under running water. He then laid these pale-green half-moons on the drainboard and tamped each one dry with a paper towel. He grabbed a few ice cubes from the freezer and plunked them one by one into the lettuce cups.

"Thanks," he said, grabbing the Smirnoff from my hand. He poured a couple of shots of vodka over the ice in one of the leaf cups and then handed it over to Mom. "I call it a Titanic, because of the iceberg lettuce. You drink the vodka, suck on the ice and then eat the lettuce. It's fabulous. *And* refreshing. Try it."

Mom looked incredulous as she pursed her lips to take the first sip. I thought the whole thing was insane, but I had to admit that the cocktail had already worked its first miracle—Mom had stopped crying. She was sitting there rolling around the taste of vodka and staring down at the little lake of spirits cupped in the lettuce while the ice cubes bobbed and clicked in the palm of her hand. Leonard turned back to the counter and began to fill the other two lettuce cups with water from the tap. When he was done, he handed me one of them and took the other for himself.

"Cheers," he said. "Yours and mine are non-alcoholic. For obvious reasons. Think Deirdre would want one?"

"Definitely not," I said.

All three of us sat there sipping our iceberg cocktail. I felt like something out of *Alice in Wonderland*.

But, of course, that was just the beginning.

Before the end of Leonard's first month with us, he started working at the salon. He said it had always been his dream to work in the beauty business, and he couldn't believe his luck when Mom asked him to sit at the front desk, answer the phones and make appointments. Since school hadn't started yet and Leonard hadn't made any friends in the neighborhood (and it was doubtful that he would), there was nothing to keep him from spending his free time at the salon, learning the customers' names and expanding his duties to include tasks that were, as he described them, "up-front and hands-on."

Right from the get-go, he acted as if he owned the place. He whistled show tunes as he cheerfully swept up the fuzzy, mouse-colored clumps of old-lady hair that littered the salon floor. He reached his fingers under the antiquated drying helmets and said with trumped-up authority: "Feels like you could stand a few more minutes, Mrs. Mixner." He took the money at the till and made change, coffee and small talk. He downloaded easy-listening versions of pop songs, burned CDs and piped them through a brand-new sound system that he himself installed. He even took it upon himself to listen to the long list of ailments, infirmities and family complaints from women five times his age.

I knew all of Mom's customers far more intimately than I cared to admit. If she was over sixty, lived within a fifty-mile radius and could still pick up a phone to make an appointment, I knew all about her—and not just the pitch and tint of her hairdo or the cut of her fancy housecoat. No. I could also tell you the cast of her ongoing personal drama, the make and model of her car, her date of birth, the last time she had sex, the name of the guy she last had sex with, her favorite TV program, her least favorite TV program, her movie star of choice, as well as the nicknames and habits of each and every one of her grandchildren. Despite the fact that I preferred to spend my spare time reading books and losing myself in the works of writers like Jane Austen and Charles Dickens, these old gals with their high hair and caked-on makeup were, for better or worse, the universe into which I had been born. They were my people.

Leonard was now ensconced in that world and had taken over the very job that I used to have at the salon, going so far as to wear my old smock and use my old telephone headset. Whereas I generally hated anything to do with the salon and couldn't care less about the women who came and went like clockwork, Leonard loved the whole scary scene and took to the customers like hair on fire. This was as close to his idea of dying and going straight to

Heaven as he was likely to find on this Earth.

To the average person I suppose the Hair Today salon would not seem that bad. It was just a run-of-the-mill beauty parlor outfitted in shades of dusty pink and slate gray and operating out of what used to be our garage. Nothing fancy, but not that shabby either. Back in the mid-nineties, after Mom had the place gutted, expanded, insulated and decorated within an inch of its life, it seemed the most natural thing in the world to connect the whole shebang to the house by a snazzy breezeway. To be able to dart back and forth between the main house and the salon on a rainy day without getting her hairdo mussed justified the added expense of jalousie windows and a shingled roof; and since we weren't exactly the outdoorsy types, not one of us missed having a backyard.

As you walk in the front door of the salon, right behind the reception desk there are three drying helmets. Elderly women, rolled tight and netted, get parked there so their hairdos can cook to a crisp along with their brains. Two beauty chairs sit smack in the middle of the salon—one operated by my mother, the other one reserved for the memory of Leslie Shilts, a woman with big hair and over-decorated fingernails who used to show up twice a week until she broke with Mom and opened her own place in Avon.

The décor of the salon is modern with a nod to the good old days. The atmosphere is businesslike but friendly. The overall effect, despite the ozone-destroying hair spray and the exposure to certain chemicals that could blind a lab rat, is always to the customer's liking. Our job is, after all, to make the customer's idea of beauty come to life right before her very eyes—no matter what. If she comes in with a picture of, say, Nicole Kidman and begs us to make her look like that, Mom nods and directs her to the shampoo station. Mom never mentions the fact that Nicole is thirty years younger and still has hair to work with. She never says, "Lady, have you looked in the mirror lately?" She just smiles and gives it her best shot. That's what she's paid to do. Usually the customer leaves there satisfied even if she doesn't end up looking anything like Ms. Kidman. Everybody loves to be fussed over.

Originally the place was a beauty parlor known as The Beauty Spot. Then in the late nineties Mom came back from a big convention in Las Vegas with the bright idea to refer to the place as a "salon" and call it Hair Today. For a few weeks, everyone oohed and aahed over the neon signage out front and Mom's new leatherette smock. But soon enough life went back to the way it had always been. The only change seemed to be the way we answered the phone, which went something like this:

"Hair Today. How can I help you?"

"What?"

"I said, Hair Today. How can I help you?"

"I musta dialed the wrong number. Wait. This The Beauty Spot?"

"We used to be The Beauty Spot. We're Hair Today now."

"Why? What's wrong with The Beauty Spot?"

"Nothing. We just changed names . . . Mrs. Bustamante? That you?"

"Yeah. Who's this?"

"It's me. Phoebe."

"Well, honey, why didn't you say so up front?

I'm just calling to say that I'm gonna be late for my three o'clock."

After a two-year stint as Hair Today's receptionist and part-time shampooer, I decided that the time had come for me to move on. I was sick to death of being an accomplice in destroying the ozone layer with a can of hair spray just so Mrs. Weinstein could feel secure beneath a hardened helmet of hair for her granddaughter's bat mitzvah.

I also had to admit that my idea of beauty had evolved to the point where I could no longer stand being exposed to frosted tips, perms, bouffants or hair dyes with names like Autumn Mist and Champagne Moments. I wanted to live a different type of life and mix with a different sort of person. It wasn't that I disapproved of people who teased their hair and wore a plastic rain bonnet even when the sun was shining; I just wanted to expand my horizons. After too many hot tears, big fights, shouted ultimatums and slammed doors—behavior that is, in my opinion, as far from personal beauty as you can get—I came to the conclusion that Mom and I were no longer compatible and Hair Today wasn't worth the trouble. So I quit.

After that, if my hair was in need of some kind of attention, I ended up at Supercuts in Asbury Park, a plate-glass palace where they played loud music and someone closer to my own age, who didn't bother with the blow dryer because I was only going to wash my hair when I got home anyway, presided over me with a who-cares attitude. If I wanted to dye my hair (something I've done regularly since I was about twelve), I just took care of it myself in the upstairs bathroom.

Deirdre's relationship to the salon was more complicated than mine. She never actually worked at the place, and I think she always held a little contempt for the business because she had come by her hair beauty so naturally. Her long, shiny, chestnut-colored hair hung down past her shoulder blades and gently flipped under in a V. Like a prize-winning dog that needed constant grooming and a special diet, but at the same time delighted the judges and brought home all the blue ribbons, her hair was everybody's favorite. As a result, her duties on behalf of Hair Today were more in the line of advertising. If, for example, Deirdre happened to be walking down the street minding her own business, it wasn't all that unusual for her to be stopped by a woman who felt the need to compliment her hair. Naturally, the woman would ask Deirdre how she got her hair that way. Deirdre would simply smile and say, "Oh, my mom owns a salon, so y'know, it's just in the family, I guess." Next question: "What's the name of your mom's place?" That was Deirdre's cue to flip her hair back over her shoulder and casually say, "Hair Today," before being distracted and moving on. The woman, hoping to somehow look just like Deirdre, would make a mental note, and sure enough, the following week she would show up.

Of course, no one ever talked about this. I once mentioned that I found it inconceivable that a mother could use one of her own children as a shill.

"Whaddaya, crazy?" Mom asked me with hands on hips and her jaw set hard. "You think with my schedule I got time to think up stuff like that? Who do you think I am? Proctor and Gamble?"

• • •

The first thing I noticed when Leonard started working in the salon was that Mom began walking around the place wearing a thoughtful expression. This was unusual, because it was more her style to appear harried and overworked and, on occasion, hysterical. Her day generally started at nine A.M. and then snowballed into avalanche proportions by noon. By three P.M., she was so busy problem solving and disaster averting, she rarely had a minute to herself. If an actual thought occurred to her, it was likely to get crowded out by the demands of her customers.

Once Leonard was on the scene, however, Mom somehow found the time to pause before a mirror and quietly appraise her looks. She seemed no longer satisfied with the person staring back at her. She began to consider changes, like flattering shades of lipstick, new outfits, fad diets and even face-lifts. Was it just a coincidence that she started entertaining these ideas and following through with a few of them shortly after Leonard arrived? I don't think so. As everybody within a twenty-mile radius soon discovered, Leonard was a major fan of the personal makeover.

On the blank pages of his spiral notebook, Leonard drew the faces of generic girls and boys and ladies and gentlemen; and then, using nothing but a ballpoint pen and his overactive imagination, he transformed their faces into something fantastical. This was more than just a hobby, more than merely doodling; it was like his full-time job, his obsession. He could spend hours lengthening eyelashes, smoothing brows, shaping hair, making lips more fulsome, sculpting cheekbones, making a nose less pronounced, an expression more vivid and alive. I think he was trying to convince some unsuspecting idiot to be his guinea pig; but no one ever took the bait.

Once, he tried to sign Mom up to be a contestant on a TV show where they gave total strangers a new look and then redecorated the stranger's home to match. Mom kept saying that she was way too busy and couldn't even dream of doing such a thing. But Leonard kept after her. He reminded her that we all had a responsibility to improve ourselves or else we could become hopelessly outdated, or worse, extinct. He didn't care whether the makeover involved a person or a footstool, he believed in upgrade and overhaul. He had plans for everything and everyone—including himself. I once overheard him saying to Mom, "There's nothing wrong with you that a new do and a fresh Amex card couldn't fix."

Of course it's possible that Mom might have found her way to changing her look on her own. Being the same old disappointed person day after day for the rest of her life might eventually have worn thin. But there is no denying the fact that Leonard's presence and his mania for the makeover goosed her along the path. In any case, within a month, my mother was a new woman. She had tossed aside the pair of powder-blue Reeboks that she'd been wearing to work for the past 150 years, and she was suddenly zipping around the salon in a pair of cute candy-colored mules. She also stopped putting on just any old pair of slacks before going to work. Instead, she wore a short skirt, so short that her legs seemed like they had a mind of their own and could go walking off at any moment without her. She began applying lipstick, eye shadow, and blush. She looked like a shelf item that had been reissued and priced to move. And the worst part? No one was supposed to notice.

"What's with you?" I asked her.

"Whaddya talking about?" was how she side-stepped the issue.

When I found her collection of dowdy, loose-fitting leatherette smocks stuffed into a garbage bag out by the curb on trash night, I wanted to know what it all meant. She told me to mind my own business, but if I must know, she said, she had ordered a whole new supply of pink jersey smocks with an entirely different cut, a style of smock that she considered "more slimming." She had a proto-type, which she had been wearing for a week. "I like it," she declared. "It's just so much better." And to prove that this was true, she modeled it for me, twirling in the middle of the kitchen with the words Hair Today dramatically embroidered across her breasts.

Customers began to stare at Mom, and it was clear by the way their eyes followed her around the salon that they wanted whatever she was having. I don't mean they wanted her smock or her new mules. No. They wanted their old lives back, their legs, their breasts, hair, skin—the works. If someone like my mother, a woman who was not so crazy about change to begin with, could effect a transformation so dramatic over a few weeks' time, then it must be available to anyone. And it wasn't that hard to see that Leonard was the mini-mastermind behind it all.

"Whose idea was the smock?" they asked my mother nonchalantly.

"Leonard's. He had a catalog," she told them, pretending it was no big deal.

"What'd you do to your hair?" they wanted to know.

"Leonard's idea. Pretty wild, huh?"

Soon our phone started ringing off the hook.

"Is Leonard around?"

"Mrs. Ladinsky?" I said, my voice rising with surprise. I wanted her to understand that I considered it highly unusual for a sixty-seven-year-old woman, who had hair the texture of cotton candy and an estranged husband living in Tampa, to be calling my fourteen-year-old girly-boy cousin at ten P.M. on a school night.

"Yeah, it's me. Honey, lemme talk to Leonard, will ya?"

"Hold on," I said, and then I pressed the receiver against the front of my nightgown, took a few deep breaths and waited for a decent amount of time to pass. When I was finally good and ready, I said into the phone: "Sorry, Mrs. L., but Leonard's in the bathroom right now. I'm not sure, but I think he's masturbating and I don't want to disturb him."

"I'll call back."

Click.

I never told Leonard. Really, they shouldn't have been telephoning our house at all hours of the day and night and treating me like his personal assistant. It wasn't right.

Of course, the question we *should* have been asking was Why did Leonard have so much influence? I'd been trying to get Mrs. Cafiero to stop coloring her hair Sunset Mist since I knew what hair dye was all about. Why hadn't she ever listened to me? Suddenly there was an orphan in our midst who had a power over Mrs. C. that no one could dispute. At his suggestion, Mrs. C. walked into the salon one sunny Tuesday and ordered Mom to "Chop it all off. I'm goin' au naturel!"

In fact, Leonard was so busy making everybody over, encouraging everybody to be herself, or rather to become his idea of who he thought she ought to be, that before long all the women were checking out their hair, their hemlines, their crow's-feet, and their bustlines in front of the full-length mirror at the salon. They spent hours trying to figure out if they should indeed go blond, jog, shop, tweeze, exfoliate, go online, learn to drive, or do any one of the 1,001 things Leonard suggested they do in order to improve their lives. Leonard was the go-to guy all our clients had been dreaming about, the guy who noticed them, the guy who wanted what was best for them.

I, however, wasn't fooled for a second. I suspected that Leonard was just trying to get on everybody's good side so that Mom would find him indispensable and then eventually ask him to stay forever. Because let's face it, he had nowhere else to go. We were the end of the line for him, and he was desperate. I just didn't see why *we* should have to be the ones responsible for him, why he had come to live at *our* house, or why people kept telling us it was such a perfect match. The mere thought of living with Leonard for the rest of my life, or even for another year, was more than I could stand. So for the next several months I devoted myself to the task of exposing Leonard's character defects and revealing his true manipulative nature to my mother. Once he had done something inexcusable, Mom would certainly make other "arrangements" and send him packing. Of course, I had to be crafty. I was so busy devising a plan, I never considered the possibility that Leonard might do it himself. And that was exactly what happened. I didn't even have to lift a finger. It was almost too easy.

THREE

"Don't you like it here?" Mom asked as she freshened her lipstick and looked into her little illuminated compact mirror. It was Thanksgiving Day, and Mom had decided that she couldn't possibly wrestle a turkey into the oven on her day off, and so we had ended up at the Fin & Claw restaurant.

"Well, I thought you girls liked it here," Mom said. "Look. They have that nice cranberry sauce from a can like you like. We don't have to stay here if you don't want to. I thought it was your idea."

Mom then pressed her lips into a tissue and took one last look at her corrected face before snapping the mirror shut.

"Wasn't it *your* idea, Deirdre?" she asked.

That's when Deirdre lost it.

"*No!* It was *not* my idea. It was Leonard's idea, okay? You *know* that. And really, Mother, you shouldn't do that at the table! It's very—"

"Do what?"

"That!" Deirdre snapped back and took a quick look at the compact.

"Oh, stop it, Deirdre," my mother said as she tucked the compact back into her purse and out of sight. "There's no one here."

I looked around the room. It was a sea of old folks, the kind of people who eat dinner before the sun goes down, the kind who don't count.

"Thanks a lot," said Deirdre, making it seem as though Mom was saying that *we* didn't count either. She stared off into an imagined distance as if the whole world meant nothing to her and there wasn't a single thing worth discussing.

"I wish I'd never been born," Deirdre said in a very tired voice.

"You know," Leonard began with an overly

· bright gleam in his eyes, "I read somewhere that to be born into this life is as rare as a one-eyed turtle rising to the surface of the ocean once every hundred years and he just happens to come up with his head poked through a hole in the center of a piece of wood that just happens to be floating right there where the turtle comes up."

All three of us looked at him like he was one of those people at the bus terminal who try to hand you leaflets about the afterlife—which is to say we tried *not* to look at him at all.

"Anyway, that's what they say. It's pretty rare."

Deirdre groaned, grabbed her purse and got up from the table.

There was a time when behavior of this sort was out of the question where Deirdre was concerned, because once upon a time, Deirdre was happy. She got all A's in school, laughed at everything, talked to everyone and made up clever songs about Mom's customers on the spot. She smiled at strangers, and she had a way of making the people we knew feel as if they actually mattered. When she was nine and signed up for junior cheerleading, she became squad

captain within six months, not because she was par-
ticularly good at splits or high kicks, or looked good
in pleats, but because she knew how to rally the
girls. It's a shame she didn't pursue her cheerleading
in high school, but by then the light in her had
dimmed a bit. No one really knew why. At the time,
I just figured that she was going through stuff and
that Mom and Dad's divorce had taken its toll.
Puberty could have also explained it. Everybody
knew that puberty could cause all kinds of unexpected changes; it was just a matter of degree. For
Deirdre, the degree had been extreme.

"I think she needs a new look," Leonard said,
sipping his Diet Coke through a slim, red cocktail
straw. "Something sassy. Something that says,
'Hey, get a load of me.'"

Even Mom rolled her eyes at that one.

"And just for the record," I interjected, "this
was Leonard's idea. The restaurant. Not Deirdre's.
Not mine. His."

A word about the Fin & Claw: The Fin & Claw
is basically a summer business, but it serves the
community throughout the year as a tragic

backdrop for birthday parties, anniversary and reunion celebrations, dinners in honor of graduating seniors, newborns, bank presidents and the Elks club. Every family within twenty miles has contributed to its success. We never had much choice, really. It was one of the few places in Neptune where you could celebrate Thanksgiving Day in public. The place was described on the front of the menu as "a Neptunian lair fit for a king," but really it was just a lot of cheap souvenirs and seaside frippery designed to inspire the summer trade into believing that they had traveled far from home. Starfish, palm fronds and life preservers were tangled in swags of fish netting, all of it draped dramatically from the rafters and crossbeams. Stuffed sea game and fishing tackle hung on the walls. Large seashells (*not* native to the Jersey shore) were arranged along the ledges of the room. The salad bar had become a big draw long before they installed the see-through sneeze guard.

But the décor was not the only reason I'd hated the Fin & Claw with such a deep and abiding passion. The problem was that no one in Neptune could step foot in there without suffering from a severe attack of remembering. My family was no exception. The last time I was there, I turned to Deirdre and whispered to her that from now on we were going to refer to the place as "the tomb of our passed youth." It was as if everything that had ever happened to us as a family was dead and hanging up in the rafters. My seventh, eighth and tenth birthday celebrations, as well as Deirdre's sweet sixteen. My dad was up there too (though I tried not to look at him). Every prayer I ever directed toward that beamed roof of the Fin & Claw during those endless Sunday dinners was hanging alongside those horrid plastic lobsters and the splintered oars.

Josh Mintern, who was posing as a busboy in a blood-red jacket that clashed with his bright-red hair, delivered a basket of dinner rolls to our table. No wonder he couldn't look me in the eye—the rolls were so stale, they clicked against one another when he set them down in front of me. He had a golden trace of a mustache on his upper lip, and I thought, *My God, we're all growing up, and in about ten minutes we'll be old people ordering the early bird special and complaining about lumps in the gravy.*

"Hey, Josh," said Leonard, and he flashed a bright smile up from the table.

We were all stunned that Leonard was on a first-name basis with anyone in town, let alone someone a grade above him. Josh seemed surprised as well. He just stood there, looking as if he had just been hit on the head with one of his dinner rolls.

Once Josh had loped across the room and disappeared into the kitchen, Leonard leaned over and looked toward the entrance as if he was expecting someone. A person would have to be blind not to notice that Leonard was acting weird, even for him. Mom shot a glance at him.

"Leonard, I don't know what's up with you, but you're acting very queer."

"Mother!" I said, using my restaurant voice. "We have told you six trillion times that 'queer' is not a word you should be using."

What I didn't tell her was that "queer" was a word I had stopped using anywhere near Leonard—not in the same sentence, not in the same room, not in the same thought. Words like "faggot," also "fruit loop" or "poofta," "fairy-pants," "sissy," "girlyboy," "freakazoid," "nellie," "big Nell-box," "Nancy," "Mary" and "Margaret Anne" were, for the time being, also off-limits. I had forbidden myself to even consider what these words meant—especially since the kids at school had started using them in broad daylight.

Leonard, on the other hand, never seemed to mind. Whenever I happened to be walking with him and someone lobbed a word bomb like "queenie-boo" in his direction, he acted as if there was a faint electrical buzzing in the air, one that had no discernible source to bother complaining about. Once, Leonard just looked at me, sighed and then drew my attention to the shine coming off his new oxblood penny loafers.

"Do you think these shoes make my feet look small?" he asked, oblivious to the threat that was breathing down his neck.

At moments like that, I couldn't tell whether I wanted to hug him or to step all over his new shoes. I suppose if I had been a better person, I would have found the nerve to stand up to the local bullies. I would have told them to their faces that they couldn't go around terrorizing people who were posing as my cousin. But the last thing I needed was to get a reputation as a smart-mouthed do-gooder and defender of the local queenie-boos.

"Stop turning around in your seat," my mother said to Leonard.

"I know. But I really shouldn't be sitting with my back to the door," Leonard said.

Whenever we went out to a restaurant, Leonard insisted on a seat facing the front door of the restaurant. He claimed that it was an old Italian custom.

"You never know who could walk through the door," he told us.

But that night at the Fin & Claw, my mother put her foot down and made him sit across from her with his back to the door.

"You aren't even remotely Italian, Leonard," she told him, "so don't start."

He raised his little eyebrows (I swear he plucked them) and said, "Haven't you ever heard of it happening? Middle-aged men in sweatsuits get shot over a plate of spaghetti all the time. They forget to watch their backs."

"Leonard, you've been watching way too much TV," was all I had to say on the subject.

Just then all the blood drained from Mom's face and her features seemed to disappear. She looked as though she had just spotted a hit man toting a machine gun the moment before he opened fire. We all stopped breathing.

When you are connected to a person by blood or by the force of love, it's as if you have some kind of internal Geiger counter that begins to tick quicker, louder, whenever that person gets close to you. At that moment, mine was ticking like crazy, and even without turning around, I knew my father had just walked into the restaurant and he was coming toward us.

"Go get Deirdre," my mother said without looking at me directly. "We're leaving right this minute."

I got up from the table, raced across the dining room toward the ladies room and bumped into Aunt Bet (who is not our actual aunt); her small, compact body was right in my path, and it didn't look like she was going anywhere fast. Aunt Bet had an apple-shaped face and a pear-shaped body; her hair, which had been permed and tinted a pale champagne color by my mother, always looked a little crooked on her head. She locked me in her gaze and then shot me a smile that was entirely false.

"Ho there. Where's the fire, young lady?" she asked, putting on her people-pleaser voice and taking hold of my arm. "Slow down. We don't want to be rushing you to no emergency room, not on Thanksgiving Day."

Just then Deirdre came out of the ladies' room and stopped in her tracks. She was trying to figure out what was going on between Aunt Bet and me. But when Aunt Bet let go of my arm, Deirdre focused her gaze beyond us and saw what was happening over at the booth. She saw Dad, large as life.

"Come on," I said to her. "We're going. Mom said we're outa here."

Mom was making a beeline toward the front door of the restaurant. Deirdre and I decided to fall in behind her, though I had made the decision for both of us by grabbing hold of her sleeve and pulling her along with me. We'd almost made it to the exit when Mom came to an unexpected halt. She just stopped like a woman in a dream who suddenly realizes she's forgotten her clothes but is too afraid to look down and find out that she really *is* naked. Because Deirdre and I were literally right on her heels, there was a pileup.

"Our coats," Mom said, realizing that we were about to leave without essential outerwear. It was November, after all. The next thing I knew, Mom was headed back to the booth, where Leonard and my father were sitting.

"Uh-oh," I said to the back of Mom's pumpkin-colored pantsuit as I tried to get my shoe back on. "Mom? We ought to be leaving here. We ought to be leaving this minute."

But Mom was already standing beside the booth and glaring down at Leonard and my father as if they were felons. It's a good thing she didn't have a gun handy.

"Hey, look who's here," Leonard said to her

as he pointed to my father. "How about that? Something, right?"

I looked Leonard hard in the face and tried to control his brain with my thoughts, but he was very dense when family matters were involved, so it didn't work. He merely straightened in his seat and said, "It's him. It's your father," as though there had been some confusion about the identity of my own flesh and blood.

I always thought of my father as a handsome man. I once admitted to my best girl friend, Electra, how I thought he looked like a more golden version of George Clooney. She laughed out loud and then caught herself when she realized that I was being serious. "I guess, sort of," she conceded, and then added, "but not really." In any case, there was a resemblance—at least to me. He had pale, freckled skin and coarse, ginger-colored hair. His features were all sharp and to the point, his lips were thick and cushy, and the fine yellow hairs on his forearms glistened. Whereas I had inherited all the darker traits of our mother's southern Italian clan, Deirdre had inherited the good looks, bright tones and green eyes from our dad.

That afternoon, he looked older than I remembered, and tired. He was sitting with his fists on the table, wearing a pale-green plaid short-sleeved shirt and looking over at us as if we were insane. We just stood there. He didn't say a word. Nothing. His mouth tried to smile, but his eyes were sorrowful, and they began to fill with tears. I looked away. I couldn't stand it. Deirdre was staring up at the fish netting as though she had just located some lost thing up there. She looked hopeless and utterly alone in the middle of the crowded restaurant. We all were.

Meanwhile, Aunt Bet was flitting around the room from one table to the next chatting up the customers. She had her eye on us; she knew enough about the situation between my mom and dad to know that this could be trouble, but she was playing it down and pretending not to notice our unscheduled stop at what was now my father's table. It was obvious that something was wrong.

"Everything's fine," I heard her say to three old women with sweaters draped over their shoulders and hair the color of their dinner napkins. They were craning their necks to see what was going to happen next. Something was obviously up with us; but Aunt Bet just said, "It's nothing. Just family matters."

The idea that the previous three years and everything we'd been through—the separation, the divorce, living without my father, watching Mom trying to make ends meet—amounted to *nothing* in the minds of other people made me crazy. I wanted to scream or scratch somebody's eye out, but instead I just stood there like everybody else, waiting for the next thing to happen.

"Come on, Leonard," Mom said. "We're going home."

"Ellen . . . ?" My father's voice came as a surprise. We all looked at him. He took a heavy breath, as if he was about to make a big speech and appeal to my mother's sense of fairness.

"Don't. Okay?" Mom said to him. "Just don't."

And then she stretched her left hand flat out for emphasis. I noticed that she wasn't wearing her wedding ring. When did that happen? I wondered. Maybe she never put it back on after that night when Leonard touched the diamond chip and introduced her to the Titanic cocktail.

"Coats," Mom said to us over her shoulder, which was her way of ending the possibility of a conversation and getting us out of there as fast as she could.

Leonard got up. We all tried not to look at one another as we put on our late-autumn, early-winter outerwear, but I could see that Leonard was a nervous wreck.

Then I heard my father say, "I'm sorry." But he said it low and into his chest and not quite loud enough for it to do any good.

Mom said, "Excuse me?"

He looked up at us and then in a louder voice he repeated himself. "I'm sorry. Believe me, this never should've happened. It's my fault. I'm . . . I'm so, so sorry."

The words came out of his mouth, but each syllable sounded cheap and flat. I suppose these were the words that we all wanted to hear from him. We had wanted him to be sorry, to cry; to see him squirming in his seat and then begging for our forgiveness. But as it was happening, I felt like it wasn't really enough.

Aunt Bet came over to the table. She was slightly stooped over, and she was wearing the most pitiful expression.

"Girls, please," she said, "let's not block the aisle."

We all looked at her as though she was an alien creature as she moved on toward the kitchen. That's when Deirdre seemed to come back from whatever far-off planet she'd been visiting. She blinked a few times and laughed. It was not a happy laugh. It was low and smoky and slightly menacing.

Then she reached over and grabbed a handful of lettuce from the salad bar beside her. She tossed the lettuce at my father lightly, almost as if she was showering him with rose petals. The individual curls of lettuce landed on his shoulders and in his hair, a few fell to the floor and onto the table. I heard one of the nearby diners gasp in horror. Everyone was stunned—my father, too. He just sat there examining the mess in front of him.

Deirdre reached behind her again, but this time I was ready for her. I was able to grab her arm and stop her. But then she pivoted her whole body and got a hold of a handful of lettuce with her other fist. This time her aim was off, and the stuff flew wildly through the air, hitting no one in particular but everyone in general. It landed in water glasses and dessert flutes.

Aunt Bet came rushing back. She was looking at the lettuce scattered on the carpet like it was broken dishware. She was really upset. She had had it, she was saying as she pushed Deirdre and me and Leonard toward the door. Under her breath, she threatened us with police action, and said over and over that we would *not* be allowed in her restaurant anymore because of our outrageous behavior. We were, she hissed, a disgrace.

Deirdre and Leonard and I stood in the parking lot for at least twenty minutes wondering what to do next. We waited for Mom to walk out the door, get into the car and then drive us away so we could all sulk at home as a group; but she kept not coming out. We discussed going back inside to rescue her, but none of us wanted to risk another scene with Aunt Bet. Leonard agreed to investigate. He walked around to the side of the building and peeked through the window like a spy. When he came back, he reported that Mom was seated across from my father in the booth. They were chatting.

"Like old friends," he said cheerily. The shreds of lettuce had been picked up from the carpet and everything looked pretty normal.

"We should go back in," Deirdre said.

"Why would we ever want to do that?" I said.

"To get Mom."

"No way. Personally, I plan to never set foot in there again. I will certainly not eat there. Ever. In fact, I might not eat another meal for the rest of my life. I don't know about you, but I could die over this. I could literally die. For real."

That was it—my big speech.

"I think it's kind of funny," Leonard said.

"Funny?"

"Yeah. Isn't the Fin & Claw where your parents first met?"

"Yes," Deirdre said. She was perched on the hood of Mom's car in her hat and scarf, looking like a bundled-up beauty queen after the parade had passed by. "What's that got to do with anything?"

"Nothing," Leonard replied. "I'm just saying."

As I whipped my head around, I happened to catch him smiling, more to himself than to anyone in particular. When he saw me looking at him, he dropped the smile, raised his plucked eyebrows and said, "What?"

When I didn't respond with anything other than a mean, all-knowing look, he added, "Wha-at?"

Mom came striding out of the restaurant and made her way across the parking lot. Her keys were in her fist, and she looked as if she might hit anyone who tried to stop her from getting into the car. For once, she wasn't smiling. We all hopped down from our perches and waited for her to unlock the doors, but instead of aiming her keys and giving the car the beep, she walked straight up to Leonard and grabbed him by his coat collar.

"If you ever, *ever*, pull anything like that again, I will personally kick your sorry ass back to wherever it came from and be done with you. Do you hear me?"

Leonard just dangled there, unsure of what to say.

"Do you hear me?"

"I hear you," he replied. And that smile, which had rarely left his face since he had arrived on our doorstep, entirely disappeared.

FOUR

The holidays were bearing down on us, and every customer had an appointment scheduled. Like all red-blooded Christians, Leonard and I had a responsibility to get our shopping done before the twenty-fifth of December, so even though Mom was booked, she agreed to drive us to the mall and then pick us up afterward. I knew from past experience that if I wasn't waiting outside Sears and in plain sight at the appointed time, she would leave without us and we'd have to find our own way home. That was the deal.

I've always considered myself an expert at the timing and execution of my weekly expeditions to the mall. I would make the usual rounds, stopping at Sam Goody's, The Gap, Foot Locker, Banana Republic, Victoria's Secret, Borders bookstore, the Candle Castle, Dollar Bob's and still have time to get a slice and a Coke at the cheesy Pizza Hut that was built to look like someone's idea of an authentic Italian villa. I could be in and out of those places like a mad bee flitting from flower to flower, ready to sting anyone who got in my way. But Leonard had insisted on coming along with me, and though I did manage to lose him in a surge of shoppers going through a revolving door at Stern's, my shopping clock was off and I was running late.

Leonard was the kind of person who always stood out in a crowd; but that day he was pushing it, sporting a cherry-red beret, pink-and-purple-striped jeans and a white patent-leather belt. I had almost forgotten how outlandish he looked in plain daylight. But when I rounded the corner of the Bagel Boutique and saw him standing there wearing those ridiculous six-inch platform sneakers, I stopped in my tracks.

Right after Thanksgiving, Leonard made up his mind to find a pair of platform sneakers. He felt that these were about to become a major thing, the big featured item of the next fashion wave, and he shopped for them as though they might actually be out there, an undiscovered item just waiting for the right person to appreciate them publicly and thereby start the trend. When he couldn't find a pair for sale anywhere within a fifty-mile radius, Leonard made up his mind to create his own. He bought a dozen pairs of flip-flops at Dollar Bob's, cut off each thong part that fits between the toes and then glued the rubber slabs of flop to the bottoms of a pair of purple Converse high-tops. When he had added six inches of rainbow tread to each sneaker, he proudly modeled them for us in our living room.

Hideous.

I tried to warn him, but he wouldn't listen. Wearing rainbow-colored platform sneakers, I informed him, would put him in physical jeopardy. They were a definite fashion hazard. Finally, I had to explain to him in plain English that if he intended to go out in public wearing those things on his feet, he would soon be running for his life.

He claimed that they were entirely safe for

walking, and to prove it he pranced around the living room several times.

"You've *got* to help me!" he said in a desperate voice that is usually reserved for actors when they find themselves in an action movie. "They're after me."

Under normal circumstances I would have stayed out of sight until my mother showed up, but Leonard was waving and calling to me as if he was in real danger. He called out my name several times and then clomped quickly toward me.

"What's the matter now?"

"Travis Lembeck and that Calzoni kid with the pig face. They cornered me outside Payless and took all my money. Okay, so I don't care about the money. They can have the money. But they took my gold-plated Yves St. Laurent money clip, the one my mother gave me, and it's all I have left of her in this world."

Travis and Curtis (that Calzoni kid) came striding out of Sears, pushing the doors hard and looking very satisfied with themselves. Both of them were toting hefty shopping bags.

Travis and Curtis were a grade ahead of me, and you could tell just by looking at them that they were trouble, the kind of boys who had too much past and no future. As a result they had a power over everyone in town. People were speechless around them. Nobody called them "poor white trash" to their faces or made fun of them for having parents who couldn't care less. Nobody offered to tutor them in algebra. Nobody bothered them about their SAT scores, asked them what they did over spring break or where they planned to go to college. The fact that Travis's eyes were a little too far apart and had an evil slant to them never came up as a topic of conversation either. Curtis's badly bowed legs, which caused him to walk with a conspicuous waddle, were also not discussed. No comments were ever made about their clothes; no one said, "Why do they wear those matching black down parkas? It's May for god's sakes." And as far as I know, nobody had ever asked them point-blank if they carried firearms.

Something had to be done. Leonard didn't look like he was capable of anything other than a flood of tears at that moment, and there was no one else around. It was up to me to step up to the plate.

"If I don't get that money clip back right now," I told them, "both of you are dead meat."

Anyone with half a working brain cell could tell you that threatening Travis Lembeck was not a smart idea. Not in public. Not anywhere. Ever. But I couldn't just stand by and let him and his hench-man, Curtis, walk away with Leonard's lousy clip.

"That's right, Lembeck," I said, moving closer to where he and Curtis were standing. "I'm talking to you." And then I added. "Now."

I reached out my hand expecting him to fork over the clip. I could almost hear him thinking, "Who does she think she is?" When nothing happened, I realized that he was in shock. He never would have predicted that I had it in me to do such a thing. Then the right side of his face resumed its usual sneer, and he looked at me out of one narrowed eye.

"Really? And what if I don't feel like giving it up?"

"No problem. I just report it stolen and give the police a couple of names."

There was a moment when everything just hung in the air between us. I thought Travis might haul off and hit me in the head. Curtis kept looking back and forth from Travis to me, from me to Travis. This was making me very nervous, because I knew that Travis was going to have to do *something* in order to prove to Curtis that he was still the alpha idiot.

"Tell you what," Travis finally said. "How 'bout I give you the clip and then *you* get to be the one who's dead meat. How's that?"

"Whatever."

I was suddenly a cartoon superhero with cartoon superhero powers. I felt that I was able to see through the cloth of Travis's down parka and into his sorry little pocket—some stray lint, a few bits of loose tobacco, coins, an old butterscotch-flavored LifeSaver and a pack of matches were all nestled up against Leonard's money clip. I just knew it was there and I wanted it.

I had no way of making Travis give it to me. Not really. Leonard's sob story about how his mother had given him this useless thing would never sway the likes of Travis and Curtis. I just kept thinking, What next? What next? And then a new thought occurred to me. What if I had miscalculated my move, what if I was in the middle of leaping a tall building in not quite a single bound, what if I didn't know what I was doing? I wasn't sure if it was the fright, but my legs began to wobble beneath me, and my shoes felt like they were shrinking as I stood there for what seemed like forever.

"So, you queer too?" Travis asked me.

"Excuse me?" I heard him all right, but I needed some time to think about how to answer.

"You heard him," Curtis piped in. "Wants to know if you're a lesbo."

And then Curtis let out a squeal of girlish laughter that shook his middle and forced tears to his piggy eyes.

That's when I made my move. I'm not even sure how it happened; I was just there, attached to Travis's mouth. Leonard gasped with surprise, or maybe it was horror. Curtis lost control of his shopping bag, and it landed with a clank on the pavement. He had stopped laughing and just stood there watching me kiss his friend. Travis went rigid for a minute and tried to pull away from me. But his mouth had developed a mind of its own, and I could feel him kissing me back. His tongue, small and darty and fully alive to the possibilities, was busy leading him forward, into the future and closer to me. He tasted like an aluminum measuring cup or those old canteens from our camping days with my dad. I also caught a whiff of tobacco that clung to his hair and skin, and the smell of him, a surprising mix of chocolate milk and hard candy.

"Whoa," I heard Curtis mutter in the background.

When I stepped back, Travis looked like a totally different person to me. All his usual hard edges had been smoothed. He seemed like someone I might want to talk to once in a while, someone who could take a joke. I wondered if I looked different to him too. It was probably just a lot of hormones getting released into my bloodstream, causing me to see things in a whole new light.

The honk of my mother's car horn broke the spell.

"Come on, let's get out of here," I said, grabbing Leonard and pulling him along toward the car.

"But—"

I was not about to let him finish his sentence.

"Just get in."

I took the front seat. Leonard climbed into the back.

"Who are those two boys?" my mother asked as she checked out her hair in the rearview mirror.

I rolled the leftover taste of Travis around in my mouth, savoring my success.

"That's her new boyfriend," Leonard chimed in from the backseat. "That one. The one on the left."

"Shut up, you. He is so *not* my boyfriend. And you of all people should know it."

"I hope not," Mom said as the car pulled away from the curb. "Neither of them look much like boyfriend material to me."

I sat there in the front seat of Mom's car, fingering Leonard's stupid money clip inside my coat pocket and feeling that little lift that comes when I've scored. As someone who has had some experience in the world of shoplifting, I've learned that the release of endorphins is definitely one reason to take the risk and pocket merchandise. I mean, for people like me, it's rarely a matter of actually *needing* the stuff. It's the high I'm after, the lift.

When I was good and ready, I reached over into the backseat and presented Leonard with my balled-up fist. Then slowly, really slowly, I opened my fingers one by one until the money clip was visible in the sweaty center of my palm.

"Here," I said.

Leonard's mouth literally dropped open.

"But how . . ."

Even after he had grabbed hold of the clip and then sat there staring at it, I could feel the ghost of the thing still in my hand. When I looked, there was a deep impression in the middle of my lifeline.

Leonard looked at me as if I was the Blue Fairy in the Pinocchio story, the one who had the power to turn him into a real boy. There were actual tears in his eyes, and he mouthed the words "Thank you."

Jeez, I thought, *I'll never get rid of him now.*

And that's when I burst out crying.

Don't ask me why. Maybe the wiring of my deep inner emotional life had gotten crossed and I had lost the ability to tell the difference between happiness and sadness. Maybe crying was just a new form of laughing, and vice versa.

When we got home, I marched Leonard out behind the house, sat him down on the trash bin and told him the story of Winona Ryder. Because I had once been a huge Winona Ryder fan, even going so far as writing letters to her and sending them to her talent agency, I knew her *E! True Hollywood Story* by heart and had no difficulty working it into our conversation. Even though she had already had a whole career by the time I was old enough to appreciate her and had gone into semiretirement when I was about ten, she still held some kind of fascination for me. Her story was enough to inspire anybody.

"Winona was like eight or nine years old and living in Petaluma with her family. She was a total tomboy, and the first week at her new school, these kids attacked her, called her a wuss and worse. Then, for good measure, they gave her a beating. And you know why?"

Leonard was engrossed in the story; he stared at me and didn't seem to realize that the question was, in fact, directed at him. So I repeated it.

"Do you know why they beat her up?"

"Um . . . I dunno. Because her last name used to be Horowitz?"

Frankly, I was surprised as hell that Leonard knew this. But that was not the reason she got beat up.

"No," I told him. "The reason they beat her up was because they thought she was a sissy boy."

Leonard blinked at me as though he was determined to send me an encoded message by opening and closing his eyelids. I didn't know the code, however, so it had no effect on me.

"Thank you for getting my money clip back," he said.

I felt that it was important to tell him the rest of the story; he needed to know that following the beating-up incident Winona's parents took her out of school, gave her home study and enrolled her in the prestigious American Conservatory Theatre in

San Francisco, where she was later discovered and given a screen test for the role of Jon Voight's daughter in *Desert Bloom*. And even though she didn't get the part, it did lead to her being cast as a poetry-loving teen in *Lucas* (a movie I've seen seven times).

But telling Leonard this was obviously a big mistake, because he smiled too brightly and said, "Wait. Are you saying I should take acting classes?"

"No," I said, because in fact I was not saying that and he was totally missing the point. "I'm saying that you can't go around looking like a big sissy or you'll get the shit beat out of you just like Winona did."

"But it turned out okay for Winona Ryder, didn't it?"

"Look," I said to him, lowering my voice and trying a different tack. "I don't care one way or the other if you're gay or if you're not gay. I'm just saying do you have to be so obvious about it all the time?"

"Obvious? How do you mean?"

"The shoes? The beret? The pants? I mean, just for starters."

"But I like the way they look. They make me feel good."

"Good?" I asked. "How can they make you feel good? You look ridiculous and everybody's laughing at you."

He glanced down at himself—his pants, his shoes and the parts of himself that he could see. Maybe he was trying to get an idea of how he looked from someone else's point of view. He shook his head.

"I'm just being myself. I mean, obviously."

That was pretty much the end of our discussion. I left him sitting there and went inside the house to do something that at the time I considered important but now can't even remember. About an hour later, when Mom called up the stairs to tell us it was snowing, I looked out my bedroom window to see for myself. That's when I noticed Leonard; he was still sitting there on the trash bin, leaning back, dangling his stupid platform sneakers and singing like a girl in a high soprano voice.

"Girls in white dresses with blue satin sashes,
Snowflakes that stay on my nose and eyelashes,
Silver-white winters that melt into springs—
These are a few of my favorite things."

I couldn't believe my eyes—or my ears. And I remember thinking, *If he doesn't understand that being himself in the world is a complete and total liability, then he deserves whatever comes down the pike to bite him on the ass. The kid's an idiot. Obviously.*

FIVE

My best friend, Electra Wheeler, had her hands around Leonard's throat and she was pressing her two big thumbs into the hollow areas on either side of his Adam's apple. His wind was cut off, which would explain why his face had gone bright red, his lips were turning blue and his eyes were bugging out of his skull. He was gagging.

"Careful you don't kill him," I warned from my place on the sideline.

My job was to stand next to Electra and hold her dreads behind her neck. We didn't want them to swing down in Leonard's face and distract her from the business at hand. I refused to be the one who actually did the choking. I couldn't trust myself to not go too far and accidentally murder Leonard.

Ever since school started, he had been making my life a living nightmare. Everyone knew Leonard was my cousin by marriage, and as a result random schoolmates were always approaching me to ask me what was up with him. As if I could explain. By spring break, Leonard had become famous because of the way he dressed, because of the way he walked, because of the way he talked and because he sang show tunes in the school corridors. He just couldn't see how far outside the bounds of normal behavior he had strayed, and so he kept acting more and more outrageous. His name had even appeared in *The Trident*, our school newspaper, when the senior class jokingly nominated him for queen of the Christmas Cotillion. Everyone on the committee was hoping that he would accept the nomination, go on to be crowned and make history at Neptune High. For weeks, the talk in the cafeteria was all about what Leonard might wear to the cotillion. Leonard, in his usual style, pretended that it wasn't happening. Christmas came and went, and just when I thought the whole thing had blown over, rumors started to circulate that Leonard's name was being put forward as a possibility for queen of the prom. When he was confronted with the news, he said he had other, more important things on his mind.

The choking game was Leonard's idea. He wanted to give it a try after he'd heard about it from several girls in his class who had recently gotten very good at it and had lived to tell the tale. I was against it from the start. But then Leonard offered Electra and me actual money to do the honors, and how could we refuse? Forty dollars could buy us each a movie with all the extras, like a combo popcorn, Twizzlers and maybe even an order of nachos. We decided that there was no harm in providing Leonard with his idea of a good time.

Electra could have been beading a necklace or hemming a skirt; she was that into it. Her brows were furrowed, her eyes neatly focused, her mouth shut tight, her lips sucked into her mouth. Her cocoa-colored skin was flush with excitement, and I could see a natural blush blooming on both cheeks.

Some people think that black people don't blush, but that's because they probably never knew a black person or maybe they never really looked at one closely enough. If they had, they would have discovered that African Americans not only blush, but they also can get sunburned pretty badly too.

Mom liked to embarrass me by telling a story about the first time I saw an actual black person. It was years ago, before Neptune got all mixed up racially, and folks hadn't yet moved beyond the bounds of what was considered *their* area and into what was known as *our* area. There were still little enclaves of Asian families or Hispanics or whites or blacks, each of them separated by the invisible barriers that were only understood by each respective group. This is *ours*; that is *theirs*. People pretty much stuck to their own areas for reasons that made sense only to themselves. The weird part is, the areas weren't that big; they could extend for maybe a half a block on one side of the street, and once you crossed over to the other side you could be in a whole other area, populated by a different race of human. But it wasn't as though people were being forced to live within their assigned areas; people just naturally stuck to their own.

Then in the mid-nineties it all just broke down and everyone started moving all over the place. Money became the primary factor in determining where a person chose to live. If you had the bucks to buy a big house, no sweat, you could move in and no one was going to give you a hard time or even raise an eyebrow—at least to your face. After a while, we even started to consider Neptune a progressive town because we had all these ethnic groups living smashed up against one another and pretty much everyone got along. We even forgot the fact that only ten years earlier everything had been completely different. My mother often told the story about me, not with the intention of embarrassing me but rather to make the point that the situation in Neptune had changed for the better.

As the story goes, I was about three or four years old and playing with my dolls on our front steps. A black man came walking down our street. I don't remember this, but Mom says I started yelling to her, telling her to come quick, because there was a chocolate man in front of our house. She said I was frantic with excitement.

When I first told this story to Electra, she and I were sitting on her canopied bed in her bedroom, confessing the secrets of our youth to each other. It was my turn, and I figured if I told her the chocolate man story myself instead of her hearing it later on from my mother, I might not come off seeming like a pint-sized racist. As I set the scene for Electra, I was careful to include all sorts of caveats, like "What did I know? I was only three or four years old," and "Hey, I'd never seen a black person up close and personal; what could you expect?" She listened to the whole story and then stared at me for an eternity. I thought she was going to hit me, but then, finally and very unexpectedly, she burst out laughing and fell back onto her bed. The idea that she herself could be chocolate seemed to delight her no end. When she had pulled herself together, she held out her forearm and said, "Lick it, bitch." We howled and then fell back onto her bed together. After that, whenever anyone showed any kind of racial prejudice or disrespect toward her and I happened to be around, she would hold out her arm to the offending party and say, "Lick it, bitch." Eventually, all she had to do was hold out her arm and we would both understand and laugh.

"Ohmygod, ohmygod," said Leonard, trying to catch his breath and looking all excited, like he had just seen Jesus. "That was . . . ohmygod, that was . . . wow. I'm like . . . wait. . . . Okay, it's still . . . no, it's done. That was fabulous. You guys . . . you guys should totally try it."

Electra and I looked at each other and began to laugh out loud. We didn't need to have the oxygen cut off from our brains and then restored in a sudden rush just so we could have a good time. We went in more for watching movies or doing our nails.

"Right. Like I would ever let you put your hands around my throat," I said to Leonard. "And anyway, you wouldn't do this if you saw your face. You looked gruesome."

"Totally," Electra concurred. "Nobody oughtta give themselves over to ugly like that 'less it's gonna save lives or get you on *Oprah*."

Leonard was massaging his neck and examining himself in the mirror, gingerly fingering the bright-red marks that Electra had left around his throat. I wondered if at home I would get blamed for the telltale bruises and forced to say how it had happened, but then I noticed Leonard putting on his turtleneck and figured that maybe no one would ever find out.

"So when do we get paid?" Electra asked him.

Leonard looked at her and then tilted his head to one side. I knew what was up. He was quietly assessing her look, wondering how he could improve her, make her over, and he was about to offer his services.

"You know, Electra . . . ," he began.

"Forget it," I told him before he could go any further. "We're going to the movies. Fork it over."

"I'll pay the money. It's not *instead* of the money. I'm just offering to . . . I don't know . . . like the dreads. How important are they to you?"

Electra just stood there and gave him deadeye. She wasn't even going to discuss her look with him. She had witnessed what had happened to Deirdre's hair; and even though the cool kids had revised their thinking and begun to treat Deirdre like one of their own again, Electra didn't want to take any chances. She had worked too hard to find her style, and she wasn't about to give it up for the likes of Leonard.

"Uh. No," said Electra with imperious finality. "No touch-ee the dreads. Okay? These are my girls, and they ain't goin' nowhere."

"No prob," he replied.

Leonard held to his position that the barber had simply chopped off too much of Deirdre's hair, and we all needed to just chill until it filled in. "Wait a week or two," he kept telling us. "You watch. You'll see."

And he was right, of course. But right after it happened, Deirdre's just-cut hair was all anyone at school could talk about, and the salon was buzzing with the news as well. Mom hadn't reacted nearly as badly as we thought she would. Everyone knew she was shaken to her core by so unexpected a change, but whenever a customer commented on Deirdre's new look, Mom simply *tsk*ed, checked herself out in the nearest mirror, smiled and said, "Honey, things change." No one bought it, but everyone was grateful she wasn't making more of a scene.

Deirdre announced right away that the cut had been Leonard's idea, and maybe that was why Mom wasn't too upset. So many of Leonard's innovations for the salon and his improvements of my mother's look had worked out perfectly despite her initial skepticism. So maybe this was just another case of wait-and-see.

We watched, we waited and sure enough in time, we saw Deirdre's hair grow back. Soon she began to look "cutting edge" instead of "skinheaded." The beauty of her features, her eyes, her ears, her cheekbones, which had been eclipsed for too long by the outstanding and overriding beauty of her hair, were suddenly revealed for all the world to admire.

Mom started getting requests from customers who had seen Deirdre's do and wanted to copy it even if it didn't fit the shape of their heads. Mom tried to talk them out of it, fearing that this new shorn look would put her out of business altogether. But once again Leonard stepped in and made it clear to my mother that if she planned to survive as a hair stylist into the twenty-first century, she might want to learn a few new skills. They shopped for a handheld buzzer and then got some helpful hints from the sad-faced barber, Mr. Fallston, who had a shop on Main Street. Mr. Fallston was the guy who'd given Deirdre her look, and though he had been happy to do the honors, he wasn't that interested in expanding his business to include the fairer sex. He said that his customers counted on an all-male environment so that they could feel free to sit back and relax. Mom said the same went for her customers.

And so Mom expanded her business to include the shorn and buzzed, Deirdre began hanging out with the cool kids again and Leonard's disgrace turned out to be a triumph.

But before the happy ending was in place, something happened that allowed me to see how much it mattered to Leonard to be right.

I had come home from school, and all I wanted to do was go straight to my room and lose myself in *Mansfield Park*. The reality of Deirdre's haircut had been revealed to the entire school that day, and it was all anyone could talk about, but really what

I wanted to know was whether Fanny Price would, in the end, marry Edmund Bertram. Added to that, I was sick of answering questions that involved Leonard and Deirdre. I just wanted to be alone.

I was relieved to find the house empty. But as soon as I threw my backpack into the corner of the kitchen, I heard a weird sound coming from downstairs. My heart began to race and I stopped breathing altogether. The noise could've been someone with a slashed throat gasping for his or her last breath, or it could've been the washing machine backing up, choking suds and about to explode. In either case and despite my worst fears, I ventured down the stairs.

"Hello?" I croaked.

The sound, as it turned out, was Leonard; he sat huddled in a corner of his "room," his knees drawn up to his chest, his arms tightly wrapped around himself. He was sobbing. Hard. I knocked on the side of one of the boxes to announce myself, and he looked up at me. His eyes were red rimmed and brimming with tears; his face looked hot and swollen. The shape of his mouth perfectly imitated that

cheesy mask of tragedy that hung on the wall outside Ms. Deitmueller's Drama Club, except that in
Leonard's case, a thin string of dribble was dangling
from the gaping hole. As soon as he saw me, he
sprang up from his position on the floor and threw
himself facedown on his bed. It was a dramatic
move, but one I recognized from my own dramatic
childhood; it was the kind of move designed to signal that there was really no hope to be found in this
cruel and heartless world, and the only solace was
being able to block out everything in sight. He
buried his head in a pillow, and even though his
sobs were momentarily muffled, it was clear he
wasn't going to stop any time soon.

"Leonard . . . ?"

"Go away."

"What's the matter?

"*Go. A. Way.*"

I stood there letting my presence convey what
my words couldn't. I wanted him to know that he
wasn't alone, and whatever it was that was causing
him such grief (I suspected it was The Deirdre
Debacle), it couldn't be *that* bad, not really, and even

if it was that bad, the whole thing would probably blow over soon enough and be completely forgotten.

"Well," I finally said, "*something* must be the matter."

He popped up, swung around and stared at me with real hatred.

"Well, let's see," he began, infusing his voice with venom and mock curiosity. "Could it be maybe that my father never did much for me except be a jerk? Or wait, maybe it's that my mother's dead and I'm now forced to live in a stupid cellar surrounded by crappy cardboard boxes and people who secretly hate my guts?"

He fell back onto the bed and started up a whole new jag of crying. I wanted to say something, something like, "Hey, no one hates you here," but it was such an obvious lie that I couldn't utter a single word of it.

"You don't know how hard it is," he mumbled into the pillow. "You can't even imagine." And then he let out a loud, mournful wail that made me actually take a step back in horror. I so wished he was a backed-up washing machine. Anything but this.

"If you're crying about Deirdre's hair . . . ," I began.

There was more wailing, followed by a noisy intake of breath. By this point, he had worked himself into a pitch of hysterical proportions. I knew the signs; I'd exhibited them myself often enough during my adolescence and childhood. Once you got going with a performance like that, there was no stopping until exhaustion set in. I decided to sit on the edge of the bed and wait it out with him. Seemed like the least I could do.

Finally I managed to offer this: "I thought you liked it here?"

"I *doooooooooo!*" he howled. He lifted his head to wipe his nose on the pillowcase. Gross. "It's not . . ." Another gasp for breath. "It's not . . ." For a moment I thought he was saying *it's snot*. "It's not"—he motioned all around him with a gesture that was theatrical to the extreme—"*here* that's the problem. It's *here!*" And to make his point, he began pounding his head with his two clenched fists. "It's my brain, my mind. *It's me!*"

Poor kid. It was hard not to feel sorry for him.

He'd been through so much and he wasn't even fifteen. But then, when he started to literally pull his hair out, I knew I had to do more than pity him; I had to intervene. Grabbing hold of his spindly wrists, I pushed against his strength, which as it happened was something to be reckoned with for a kid so slight and swish.

"Don't. Okay?" I said. "You're scaring me."

He looked up at me and tilted his head, and in that moment all his resistance fell away. He just sat there, staring at me, scanning my face and clothes and hair, assessing it all and calculating the cost of change. I felt for sure that he was a heartbeat away from making some pronouncement about my look or offering a suggestion about how to style my hair or rearrange my outfit. I could see that all his attention was suddenly focused on me and he had stopped crying. I figured, hey, if this was his way of coping, the least I could do was to hear what he had to say.

"Go on," I said.

"What?"

"Go ahead. Say it. I know what you're thinking."

"I'm not thinking anything. Honest. I'm just looking."

Unable to stand the pressure of his gaze another moment, I glanced around the room looking for I-don't-know-what. I happened to notice that one of the boxes had been opened and there was a small stack of books on the floor. I walked right over to the pile and picked up one of the books.

My grandmother, Judy Hertle, had a collection of books written by people who had died and then come back to life, people who could see into other dimensions, people who spoke to spirit beings on the other side, people who wrote automatically. She was into that kind of thing back when she was still alive and living in Bradley Beach. I never actually read these books, but I had poked around in her boxes of stuff enough to know what they were about and to know they were not for me. I also knew them well enough to recognize them sitting beside Leonard's bed.

"You've been going through these boxes," I said as I brandished a copy of Edgar Cayce's *Channeling Your Higher Self* in Leonard's face. "You know you're not supposed to. This is not your stuff."

"I couldn't sleep." He was suddenly done with the crying; all of his attention was focused outward— on me. "I wasn't snooping. Honest. I was just looking for something to read."

I started furiously packing the books back into the open box.

"She must've been something. Your grand-mother."

Nothing from me. He wasn't getting a word.

"I don't remember what book it came from, but I read this thing all about how the whole world is actually a pulsing, glowing web of invisible fiber optics that connect one person to another."

I turned and stared at him hard. "They don't belong to you."

He was now up, kneeling on his bedspread, and even though his face was swollen and puffy from crying, he was lit with excitement.

"But still," he went on, "it said that the stronger and truer the bond between two people, the brighter the strand between them becomes. The more strands there are, the brighter the overall glow. Not everyone can see this, of course, because not everyone is looking, but certain people—the guy who wrote the book, for example—could see it all the time. He said sometimes he was blinded by it."

"Anything else?" I asked, giving my voice as much edge as I could without actually drawing blood.

"Actually, yeah. A lot," he said, ignoring my tone. "Like sometimes the glow got so dim, he worried it would completely disappear. And I was thinking maybe that's why you shoplift. Maybe you steal stuff as a way of making more connection. What I mean is, maybe you *want* to get caught so that—"

"What're you talking about? I do *not* shoplift. Are you saying I *steal* things? What've I stolen? What? Name one thing."

He just knelt there staring at me. He didn't need to name anything. I was busy doing a complete mental inventory, trying to recall every item I'd ever stolen, while forcing my face to adopt the most innocent expression I could manage under the circumstances.

The phone rang. It was Mom calling to find out

what all the howling had been about. She said she'd heard it over the sound of the hair dryer, for god's sakes. When I told her what had happened, she immediately left her station to be by Leonard's side. Even though the crisis had passed, Mom cradled Leonard in her arms and talked softly to him while Mrs. Ferrante was kept waiting in the salon with a wet head and a fashion magazine. That kind of coddling never happened to me when I was Leonard's age and I happened to fall into a pit of despair about the sorry state of my life. I returned to my room to read the last of Fanny Price. She and her new husband "had removed to Mansfield Park," and soon those people who had caused Fanny "some painful sensation of restraint and alarm" began to seem "thoroughly perfect in her eyes." Lucky for her. Of my makeover nothing more was said.

A month later, as I sat perched on the edge of Electra's bed pretending to have trouble with the zipper of my sweatshirt, I couldn't help wondering why Leonard had never gotten around to at least suggesting some improvement to my person. Was I too far gone? Did he think I wasn't worth it? Had my personal glow completely disappeared? He had zeroed in on almost everyone in town. Either he had made substantial changes to each of them or he had had a plan. Even if they point-blank refused to change their hair color or have their faces peeled or their tummies tucked or any of the 1,001 things he had in mind for them to do, they seemed to blossom simply because someone had them in mind and was willing to think of them as more than what they were. In this way, my mother had become someone else, and my sister was now unrecognizable. Surely I *had* to be next. But when? After so many months of waiting for Leonard to propose a plan for my improvement, I was beginning to see that I might be mistaken. I just wasn't in the running. He had no interest in me. Whenever I saw him coming at me, I ducked into my room and prayed he wouldn't find me. He usually walked right by. If he came upon me while I was doing my hair or putting on makeup, he stared at me hard but never made a suggestion. And Lord knows I could have used some suggestions. You might think that I'm putting myself down when I tell you this, but I'm not; it's just something I've learned from experience. I'm just not the type of girl a guy like Travis Lembeck kisses twice.

"What's wrong with *me*?" I asked Leonard, blurting out the question that had been rolling around in my brain for the past several weeks.

Electra and Leonard stopped discussing the merits and failings of various modern movie stars and their respective current hairstyles and upcoming projects. They both turned their attention on me, a non–movie star.

"I mean, how come I never get a makeover?"

I was looking directly at Leonard, though I gave a sharp, quick look over to Electra. I wanted to let her know that this was not some sort of practical joke that I was playing on Leonard. I wasn't setting him up for a fall like we sometimes did just so we could watch his shoulders slump and his mouth turn down the moment when he discovered we were actually putting him on. No, this was serious. I wanted to know once and for all.

"Everybody else seems to get some kind of program, while I'm just left to sit on the bed and play with my zipper."

"Pheebs," said Electra with real hesitancy in her voice, "for real?"

"Yes, for real. But hey, it's not like I would do what he says, or anything. And I'm not going around thinking anything's wrong with me, like I *need* fixing. I'm fine. But after a while, when no one's paying attention to you . . . I dunno. It makes a person wonder is all."

"I pay attention to you, Phoebe," Leonard said in the most pathetic voice imaginable. Then he tried to take hold of my hand in a tragic attempt to comfort me. I swatted him away, smacking the back of his freckled wrist with surprising force.

"Get off me."

Leonard just stood there, stung. He held his hit hand in his other hand and looked at me. Electra fell into an overstuffed chair and threw her legs over the arm. She gave her head a couple of quick shakes to indicate that she didn't know what the hell was going on. Who could blame her?

"I don't know," said Leonard, looking up toward the ceiling and literally sticking his neck out to offer his opinion. "Maybe you'll hit me again for saying it, but as far as I'm concerned, you're the one person around here who doesn't need a makeover. I mean it. To me, you're like my total ideal. You're kinda perfect."

Electra's face registered the shock first. She blinked and then nodded her head once real fast, as if she was trying to wake herself from a dream. Her mouth opened, but she didn't say anything. She started to laugh and then pointed at my face.

"What?" I said to her.

"You. Your face. Man, if you could see your face right now."

I turned back to Leonard, and it was clear from his expression that he wasn't playing me. He meant every word.

was sitting in the brightly lit auditorium of Neptune High School, surrounded by a hundred other girls. In my hand I held a pink piece of paper, a pledge I had just willingly signed. I, Phoebe Margaret Hertle, agreed to abstain from sexual intercourse until the day I became a married woman. There was other stuff too, about how I planned to conduct myself as a woman of unlimited self-esteem. None of the girls who had signed along with me actually took the thing seriously, because it was invented and introduced to us by a young woman wearing a pink sweater with a scoop neck, pressed jeans and a pair of Puma running shoes. She said that she was a former Miss New Jersey contestant.

I instantly felt sorry for her, less on account of her pitiful claim to fame than because of her hair. It was all wrong—triple processed, crimped and invented for softer lighting than a high school auditorium. She admitted that the computer-generated document would not be binding in any court of law, but she hoped that before any of us "compromised our virginity," we would stop and think about the consequences, and consider how a simple act performed in the heat of passion could change the course of our whole entire lives.

She told us that even before she had become a professional beauty contestant and a former Miss New Jersey runner-up (she came in third), she had been trained to use her good looks, feminine charms and power to please as a means of getting ahead. She didn't come right out and say it, but I interpreted this to mean that she had slept around. Whatever she was up to, her behavior had cost her an unwanted pregnancy, heartbreak, STDs, abortion, disgrace, low self-esteem as well as the Miss New Jersey crown. At the mention of the crown, her eyes watered up and the tip of her nose turned a pretty shade of red. She pressed a finger to each of her lower lids in an effort to keep the tears from brimming over and ruining her mascara.

"Oh, phoo," she said, when a single teardrop snuck through.

Her name was Bethany, and though she had the highly polished look of a J.Crew catalog model, the moment she opened her mouth, she seemed somehow less than camera ready.

"So I'm not out to win souls for Jesus or anything like that. And I'm no party pooper, okay? I like to have as much fun as the next person, believe me. Ask my friends. But I wouldn't be able to sleep nights if I wasn't out here trying like crazy to keep each one of you from giving yourself away to the first guy who comes along with a plan to get into your pants."

She wore an ankle bracelet and it peeked out below her pant leg, shining like real gold just above her sport sock. I was sitting in the front row, so whenever she jiggled her foot nervously or shifted her weight from one leg to the other, I could watch the bracelet catch the light. I imagined that her new boyfriend had given it to her. I imagined his name was Brad, and when he presented it to her, I imagined, they had made a promise to each other to abstain from sex until their wedding night. I imagined that the bracelet represented a kind of chastity belt or a little ball and chain.

Bethany handed out a number of brightly colored pamphlets with cartoon drawings of teens of all races in jazzy outfits and with arms akimbo. Block letters spelled out what was on their minds. HOW DOES SAYING NO PROTECT ME FROM HIV? DOES ABSTINENCE WORK? STDS, ORAL SEX & US. THE CONDOM QUIZ.

One of the pamphlets, "No Is a Complete Sentence," outlined possible scenarios between a girl and a boy in which sex was the desired outcome for one but not the other. Another pamphlet ("How Do I Know I'm Ready?") listed fifty telltale signs that might indicate that I didn't really want to have sex even if I said I did.

Bethany instructed us to go around the room so that each of us had a chance to read one of those fifty reasons aloud. Number 24 was mine; but when I opened my mouth to speak, I choked on a blob of spit that suddenly caught in my windpipe. I began to cough uncontrollably. Courtney Chaykin clapped me on the back, but that didn't work. Finally Bethany stepped forward, wafting her perfume in my direction, and offered me a sip of her Poland Spring. That shut me up. I shook my head no and abruptly stopped coughing. As soon as everyone was satisfied that I wasn't going to require medical attention, the litany continued.

"We may be animals," Bethany told us after the list had been read straight through to the end, "but unlike animals, we have a choice. We don't have to give in to every feeling, every instinct. We can't let our animal natures lead us by the nose wherever it wants to take us. Part of being a human being is being able to see the consequences of our actions. Can anyone give me an example of how they made a choice in their own life and then they saw the consequences? What I mean is, something you did and then saw how it wasn't such a good idea after you did it."

No one moved. In fact, it seemed as if everyone had made the choice to stop breathing.

"It doesn't matter if the consequence was good

or bad. Okay, just think of a situation where you made a choice and something happened as a result?"

More silence.

"C'mon, guys. Think."

It was no use. There were no points to be had for speaking up. No one would go to the head of the class or get to skip P.E. We all knew how it worked— there were no takers, no raised hands, and no "pick-me-pick-me-pick-me" people waving their arms from the unpopular back rows. We were all too old for that. If grades K–8 had taught us anything at all, it was that Bethany would not be able to stand the silence. In two seconds she would lean forward, trying to read someone's printed name off their sticky HELLO MY NAME IS name tag, and that person would be elected to participate against her will. And no one in her right mind wanted to be that person.

"Phoebe?"

I knew it. I knew she was going to pick me. I can always tell when something like this is going to happen, because just seconds before, I am praying so hard that it *won't*. A nanosecond later my blood rushes up to my head, a wall of white sound fills my ears, my brain is flooded with adrenaline and I'm making all kinds of brilliant connections about the nature of life itself. But I can't say a word. In fact, I can't move. To bide my time and avoid looking like a total retard, I play dumb.

"Huh?" I said.

"Why don't you start us off? Tell us an instance where you made a choice and there were consequences."

Everyone was looking at me. I could feel their eyes on the back of my hair. They were all totally relieved that they weren't chosen by Bethany to prove her stupid point about cause-and-effect. They were all feeling superior. Oddly enough, I suddenly felt smart. I decided to go with it, ride the wave. I knew exactly what to say.

"Yeah, okay," I said, straightening in my seat so I seemed responsive to the opportunity Bethany had offered me. "Um. Well, my cousin came to live with us a while ago, and right off the bat he drove me nuts. In fact, I hate his guts. Don't ask me why. I just do. So I thought to myself, how hard would it be to murder him in his sleep? I mean, really. But I haven't done it. Not yet anyway. So now I'm living with the consequences, which totally suck."

Everyone laughed out loud. But the success of my performance relied on my ability to *not* play to the crowd. I had to make it look as though I had chosen this particular example without any idea of how funny it was, or how mean. I had to look all wide-eyed and innocent in order to put it over. Bethany just held my glance until the tittering died down, and then quickly, as though she was grabbing at the Miss New Jersey crown before it was snatched away from her forever, she reached for her bottle of Poland Spring and took a swig as if it were something stronger.

"Good," she said to me.

She had decided to go with it. She probably figured that since no one else was going to volunteer, she might as well take my lame example, turn it around and use it to make her point.

"So in your case, Phoebe, it was by *not* taking an action that you saw the consequences. If you had murdered your cousin, for instance, well, you'd be living a very different life. Don't you think?"

"Maybe not," I replied. "Maybe I would've gotten away with it."

More giggling from the peanut gallery. Bethany held herself in check. I saw the little twitch of a smile at the corner of her mouth. She was going in for the kill. I could tell.

"But even if you didn't end up in jail for his murder . . . what's his name?"

"Leonard."

"Even if you weren't put in jail for murdering Leonard, even if no one ever suspected you of killing him, don't you think there'd be consequences? More personal ones? Don't you have a conscience, Phoebe? Just 'cause no one catches you doing something wrong, well, that doesn't mean you won't suffer consequences, does it?"

Point made. Score one for Bethany. Class dismissed.

As we were filing out of the auditorium, I saw Leonard leaning against the back wall. He was wedged between two well-known theater geeks. I had no way of knowing how long they'd been there, but it was entirely possible that Leonard had overheard the exchange between Bethany and me. I waved tentatively in his direction, just to gauge his reaction, but he just stood there, like a lump, staring straight in front of him at the empty auditorium stage. I could clearly see the hurt in his eyes; or rather I could see the effort he was making to cover up the hurt in his eyes, trying to prove that I was dead to him.

It was only after I was outside the school building that I began to wonder what the hell Leonard was doing with the theater geeks, waiting to take over the auditorium. That he was involved, even peripherally, with the Drama kids was news to me, and I began to wonder if maybe he hadn't overheard me after all. Maybe he was trying to go unnoticed, hoping I wouldn't see him and then report to everyone back home that on top of everything else he had become a thespian.

Every summer Ms. Deitmueller pulled together a group of misfits and freaks who had aspirations to be Gwyneth Paltrow or Tom Cruise. She called it Drama Camp, and for the theatrically inclined, it was a must. To be chosen for this grueling, six-week course that promised a sharpening of talents, a firm grasp of acting technique and a featured role in an actual (though abridged) Shakespearean classic was an unparalleled honor. Kids I'd known who had been tapped to go through the summer camp program reported that there had been a lot of jumping around on stage, some hooting and hollering, a fair amount of pretending to be trees and bugs and machine parts, but it all came down to memorizing lines that basically made no sense unless you really thought about the words one by one. The boys got to wear tights and carry swords. The girls wore gauzy gowns with cinched bodices and hair extensions and were often killed, though not onstage.

The fact that Leonard was in the auditorium was proof that he was hoping to be chosen for Drama Camp. What else would he have been doing there at tryouts? I suppose if I'd thought about it, all the signs had been obvious from the start—he loved makeup, gestured broadly, sang like Julie Andrews. Somewhere inside him he had been harboring the dream of becoming an actor, and now he was pursuing his dream. Ms. Deitmueller began the tryouts after Christmas break and extended the process over the course of several months. By the end of it, those who had the guts, the glamour, the stamina and the pizzazz to be onstage in one of her productions got chosen for the camp. According to Ms. D. she herself didn't have the proper training to direct one of the summer classics. So she left that part of the business to her old friend and former acting colleague, Mr. Buddy Howard. Everybody knew that Mr. Buddy was a big gay who lived in New York City and had once been in an actual Broadway musical. Rumor had it that Ms. D. and Mr. Buddy were once lovers; but when they starred opposite each other in a college production of *A Funny Thing Happened on the Way to the Forum* and the reviews stated that, as a couple, they had "negative chemistry," Mr. Buddy realized that this held true offstage as well. He broke down crying and confessed to Ms. D. that he had been having same-sex sex with one of the toga-wearing chorus boys. Ms. D., who was known at the time as Sally Dietz, also cried and confessed that she was having an affair with the bisexual lady costume designer. Somehow their friendship survived their senior year. Buddy went on to become a successful director of TV soap operas, while Sally got a job teaching English at Neptune Senior High as well as heading up the Drama Club. Occasionally, the two would meet in New York for dinner and a show. And it was during one of those meals that they stumbled upon a plan to recapture the wonder of their youth by making their own ad hoc summer theater in Neptune.

Whether or not the stories about Ms. D. and Mr. Buddy were true or just made up by Drama Club insiders who circulated them throughout the school was anybody's guess. What we did know was that Ms. D. never married. She had a small head and tiny features that were all crowded into the center of her face as if each one wanted to take center stage. Her dyed-black hair was cut in a pixie style with mental-hospital bangs, and she always wore bright-red lipstick and a crisp, white, man-tailored shirt. If she happened to wear a skirt (a rarity), it somehow looked, on her, like a pair of pants. Her shoes were formidable and could be heard as clear as Frankenstein's when she walked. Her annual freshman production of *Spoon River Anthology* was legendary. When we were freshmen and it was our turn to speak the words of the dead Emilys and Benjamins in our own production of *Spoon River*, we cried our eyes out as we took our final curtain call and believed in our hearts that Ms. D. was a kind of goddess.

About Mr. Buddy we knew less. He was off of our radar for most of the year. If you were ever sick enough to stay home from school but well enough to flip between channels, you might get a glimpse of the name Bud Howard as the end credits of a certain TV soap scrolled by. Even though Mr. Buddy wasn't (thank God) you, or (God forbid) a friend of yours, seeing his name on TV made you feel as if you were connected to the WBN—the World Beyond Neptune.

Mr. Buddy himself was a big, bald-headed man with a baby's face. His look was what a mother might call cherubic, but according to Electra, who called things as she saw them, he seemed more than a little pervy. His beady little eyes were quick to size up the boys, his fat cheeks turned candy-apple red whenever he was confronted with a swimmer's build and his large, sweaty brow worked overtime whenever he actually had to speak to a senior heartthrob.

Anyway, I had been hanging around by the side of the school building and waiting for Leonard to make an appearance. I wanted to find out whether he had actually heard what I said about murdering him or if he was just embarrassed to be spotted at tryouts. All I would have to do was take one long look in his eyes to know the answer. But after an hour he still hadn't come out, so I decided to go in and find him myself.

There were about five or six kids standing in the hallway; each of them had a book in hand and they were all mumbling to themselves. They looked like insane asylum inmates who'd been let out of their rooms and told not to wander too far. Leonard was among them; he was facing the wall and speaking to the tiles. I came up behind him, and when I said his name, he literally jumped.

"Oh," he said. "What're you doing here?"

"I guess I could ask you the same question."

"I know, I know," he said, scrunching up his shoulders and trying to make himself invisible by covering his face with his hands. "It's so totally embarrassing. You won't tell anyone, will you?"

Not a word about my fantasy life as his murderer. I felt instantly relieved and decided to go with what was happening right then and there.

"Tryouts for Drama Camp?"

"Yes."

"Please, Leonard. You're bound to get in. And then your name'll be on a list for everyone to see. The whole world's gonna find out sooner or later."

"I know, I know," he said, peeking at me through his fanned-out fingers. "But nobody knows *now*. And I mean, what if I *don't* get picked? How humiliating would *that* be? What would I tell your mom? Or the ladies? They'd be so disappointed."

I don't know which I found more pathetic, Leonard caring what the ladies of the salon knew or didn't know, or me agreeing to keep his secret. In any case, I was so thrilled to *not* be discussing my homicidal tendencies that I would have gone along with pretty much anything.

Just then a fat-faced theater geek poked his head through the crack between the auditorium doors.

"Pelkey. You're up."

Again Leonard jumped, but this time he wasn't taken by surprise; he was ready. He instantly twirled around to face me, bobbed up and down on his toes and exclaimed, "Ohmygod. Ohmygod. I'm so nervous. Quick. Tell me to break a leg."

"Break a leg," I said as if I really meant it.

He leaned in and gave me an unexpected kiss on the cheek. Before I could even react, he had scampered away and disappeared into the auditorium.

"Can I go in there?" I asked a pale, redheaded girl who was standing nearby. I was pointing toward the auditorium, and I think she had an idea that I wanted to audition, because right away she checked me out from head to foot.

"There's only one girl character in *The Tempest*," she said, nervously chewing the ends of her hair, "so you'd probably only get to be a sailor or something. I mean, unless you're expecting to just walk away with the lead part. And no offense, but Miranda's supposed to be drop-dead gorgeous."

"And besides," added a lumpy boy with mean eyes and a noticeable lisp, "there's a sign-up sheet.

Some of us have been waiting for like our whole lives."

I rolled my eyes, grabbed the door handle and let myself into the auditorium. The place was black except for a shaft of golden light that fell on the stage and cut a perfect circle on the blond wood floor. Leonard was standing in the center of that circle, clasping his book tightly to his chest and peering out toward the audience. With all that light in his face, I was sure he couldn't see me, so I decided to take a seat and watch. *This ought to be good,* I thought. And then I heard, but did not see, Ms. Deitmueller shouting.

"And what are you reading for us today, Leonard?"

"Ariel. Act 1, scene 2. The scene where Ariel tells Prospero how he did what he was told by totally freaking out everyone on board the ship and creating this huge thunder and lightning—"

"Okay, just . . . why don't you go ahead and do it for us. Mr. Buddy will read Prospero from here. Okay?"

"Okay."

Leonard didn't need the words in front of him;

he'd memorized his speech. And so he set the book facedown just outside the pool of light and then stepped back to take his place stage center. He planted his feet and steadied himself, but at the same time he seemed to be reaching down inside himself to find something. Slowly he made his body seem like it was half the size; he crabbed his arms and legs so that he looked like something not quite human; and finally he worked his face into a hobbity grimace, rendering him completely unrecognizable. When he opened his mouth to speak, I was so surprised, I gasped. It wasn't just that he'd been able to create the voice of some unknown species from a parallel dimension; it was that his sound matched exactly the condition of his body, and suddenly the Leonard I'd known was gone. In his place, standing in a spill of light up on the stage, was a wizened spirit creature. Then, as he spoke, he began to flit all over the place, jumping from one spot to the next like a mad grasshopper on crack. He rolled on the floor and hopped up onto a black box that was pushed back into the shadows, and then leaped forward and landed like something amphibious and crazed.

And the whole time he just kept gabbling the memorized text in that voice:

> "All hail, great master! grave sir,
>   hail! I come
> To answer thy best pleasure; be't to
>   fly,
> To swim, to dive into the fire, to
>   ride
> On the curl'd clouds. To thy strong
>   bidding task
> Ariel and all his quality."

From out of the darkness, Mr. Buddy's voice boomed. I think even he would have admitted that his performance was less convincing and committed than Leonard's, but he carried out his duties well enough to keep the momentum of the scene going and allowed us all to see how perfectly Leonard could respond to another actor. "'Hast thou, spirit, performed to point the tempest that I bade thee'?" he read. Which I think meant "did Ariel make the storm happen as Prospero had commanded him?" Leonard responded as if Buddy Howard's voice were indeed Prospero's and the whole thing made perfect sense to him:

> "To every article.
>   I boarded the King's ship; now on
>   the beak,
>   Now in the waist, the deck, in
>   every cabin,
>   I flamed amazement: sometime I'ld
>   divide,
>   And burn in many places; on the
>   topmast,
>   The yards and bowsprit, would I
>   flame distinctly,
>   Then meet, and join."

When he was finished, the hall was silent. What was there to say? Even though I'd only understood every third word, I had to admit I was impressed. And so, it seemed, was everybody else. No one stirred. Despite the overt theatricality of his gestures and the almost ludicrous intonation of his spritelike self, Leonard had managed to convey the poetry and drama of the situation. In other words, the kid could act. But with no response coming back at him, he mistook the quiet for the opposite of encouragement, and I watched him visibly deflate. As he leaned over to retrieve his book from the floor, he shrugged it off and all traces of Ariel were extinguished. He was done for the day.

Mr. Buddy came galumphing excitedly down the aisle toward the stage. He parked himself at the apron and motioned to Leonard to come forward. Once Leonard stepped out of the light, I could only guess at what was being said; the two of them spoke softly to each other, and I could only make out the shadows of their heads nodding and nuzzling like horses in the dark. I suspected that Mr. Buddy was quietly praising the boy's talents, and then assuring him that no matter what happened between now and the summer, he would have a leading part in Ms. D.'s production of *The Tempest*. And I imagined that, for the first time in Leonard's life, he didn't say much, because he was as surprised as we all were that day to discover that he had a talent for much more than survival.

SEVEN

Spring happened in Neptune, and just like always the tang of ocean brine came drifting ashore to mix with the sweet scent of blossoming linden trees. It was a heady scent, nature's perfume designed to make everybody long for what they didn't have. It was a complicated thing that got into your nose, then traveled to your brain and ended up making you crazy. For Leonard, however, who had never even *seen* the ocean until he came to live in Neptune, spring in our town came as a first-time shock, and it stirred up in him a restlessness he never knew he had. About once a week, he would blow off his shift at the salon by telling Mom he had stuff to do and then disappear.

"Stuff?" she wanted to know. "What kind of stuff?"

"Nothing really," he told her, as he breezed out the door of the salon. "Just stuff."

Finally, my mother, who was never very good at allowing people in her charge to go wandering off on their own, wanted to know what was going on. She cornered Leonard one afternoon right outside his "boxed set." I was folding laundry, and because the dryer was quietly tumbling delicates, I happened to overhear the whole thing.

"You have to tell me where you're going, Leonard, and what you're doing. And don't tell me *stuff*. You'll have to do better than that."

"Okay," he said, lowering his voice as though he was about to give away trade secrets. "It's the *weltschmerz*."

"The what?"

"*Weltschmerz*. Translated from the German, it roughly means 'world sadness.' Sometimes I get it kinda bad. What helps is to just sit on the beach and watch the ocean roll in. I don't know. It, like, sorta soothes me."

Maybe because Leonard was an orphan, my mother didn't argue with him. She started letting him go off by himself without much of an explanation, and she gave up the need to keep tabs on him every minute of the day the way she did with Deirdre and me. I was pretty sure *weltschmerz* wouldn't have worked nearly so well as an excuse where I was concerned. Plus, if I had tried it, Mom would've accused me of being a smart aleck and then punished me for eavesdropping.

Whether Leonard actually went to sit by the ocean that spring and summer, and whether he observed the uninterrupted boredom of waves rolling in, I don't know. I never followed him to find out. But not long after his audition, the cast list for Ms. Deitmueller's summertime production of *The Tempest* was posted on the wall right outside the Drama Club, and Leonard's name appeared on that list, so naturally I figured that *weltschmerz* was just his cover-up for after-school Drama Camp business.

It was a Tuesday evening and Mom had just locked up the salon for the night. I was making vegetarian sloppy joe sandwiches in the kitchen.

Deirdre was, as usual, up in her room, keeping to herself and out of the way. Mom sat hunched over the kitchen table, her glasses slipping down her nose, intent on putting a pile of receipts from the previous month in order. Suddenly Leonard came banging into the kitchen; he was seriously out of breath and he didn't have his backpack with him. He quickly shut the door behind him and then stood against it as if barricading it with his body. Mom and I stared at him.

"Hi," he said. "Sorry, I'm late. Um . . . I'll be in my room. 'Bye."

As a performance it wasn't convincing.

"Leonard?" Mom said.

He stopped dead in his tracks and turned around. From the wide-eyed, who-me look on his face, we knew right away that something was up. Something not good.

"What's going on with you? Where's your bag?"

"Um . . . it's . . . I left it in . . . Wait. I have to pee so bad."

He made a run for it, leaping across the kitchen, racing up the stairs and disappearing into the bathroom, before anyone could object. Mom and I looked at each other.

When he finally came back downstairs, Mom had already pushed aside her paperwork and we were seated at the table eating our sloppy joes. As usual, I had set the table for four. Even though Deirdre hardly ever joined us anymore for a sit-down meal, Mom felt that it was important to make a show of including her. Most of the time Deirdre came down late for dinner, made herself a plate and then took it back upstairs to her room. She preferred to eat while i-chatting with people who had interesting profiles and made-up names. Oddly, Mom never made an issue over Deirdre's eating patterns. In fact, she only ever acknowledged the situation when Deirdre failed to return the used dinnerware too many nights in a row and we were forced to go hunting for spoons and cups.

Anyway, Leonard slipped into the room, took his seat at the table and tried to pretend as if Mom and I suffered short-term memory loss.

"Oooo," he intoned, like a backup singer for an R&B recording artist. "Sloppy joes. My total fave."

It would be too painful to fully recount the interrogation process that followed. I watched my mother inch Leonard slowly toward a full confession. Leonard never had a chance. He was no match for Mom. Eventually he put down his napkin and cried into his lap. Mom had broken him.

Leonard explained that he was coming home from yet another after-school session of Drama Camp, minding his own business.

"Phoebe?" Mom said to me. "Did *you* know about this? Were you aware that he was involved in Drama Camp?"

My silence was enough to damn me forever in her eyes.

"Go on," she said to Leonard. He told us that he'd just made the turn onto our street when he realized that he was being followed. He turned around and saw a boy he didn't recognize. Leonard quickened his pace. But then so did the boy. He turned around again and saw that the boy was about a year older than him, maybe two. His hair was scruffy and his bangs hung down over his face. The boy tipped his chin up as a signal. "Wait up," he said. Leonard froze. He knew he wouldn't be able to outrun the boy. Why? Because strapped to each of Leonard's ankles was a two-and-a-half-pound weight.

"Wait a minute. Hold on," Mom said as she closed her eyes and pressed the tips of her fingernails to her temples. "Ankle weights? Why?"

He told us that he had not only been cast in Drama Camp's production of *The Tempest*, but he had actually been given the part of a fairy. I think my groan was audible when he announced it, because Mom shot me a glance that I recognized; it meant *shut it*. Right away, Mr. Buddy had taken an interest in Leonard, because after all, he was going to be one of the stars of the show and he had real talent. Leonard would need plenty of personal training such as movement, speech and possibly jazz dance classes. Mr. Buddy's first suggestion, however, required no special training. Leonard was presented with the weights and told that a time-tested method of preparing for the part of a sprite involved keeping the weights attached to his ankles right up until the actual performance. He was to go about his daily routine with the added weight, and then, on opening night, when he removed them, voilà, he would be amazed to discover that all his movements were much easier, more fluid, more fairylike.

I couldn't believe my ears. Mom looked equally dumbfounded. Perhaps Leonard thought we were having trouble believing him, because at this point he extended his left leg, leaned over and peeled down his tube sock. There was a slim blue canvas pack that weighed two and a half pounds secured to his ankle.

"Go on," Mom said for the second time. "What happened with the boy?"

Since Leonard suspected that the boy's intention was to beat him up and leave him for dead, he felt that running not only would be futile but would also be a bit like showing red to a bull. So he decided instead to stand his ground, not because he was brave, but because he knew he was going to need all his strength and breath to fight back. He waited as the boy caught up. They stood there on the sidewalk and talked.

"What's up?"

"Nothing."

"Where you off to?"

"Home."

"Why don't you come behind this house with me?"

"Huh?"

"I won't hurt you. Honest. It'll be fun."

"No. I mean, I have to go home. I'm late."

"Two minutes."

"I can't."

"Come on. Please?"

"Um . . . okay."

Leonard waited for the boy to turn toward the house and lead the way around to the side where it was dark. He couldn't see anyone, but he was sure there was a gang waiting to jump him and pummel him to death. He listened to the sound of his own feet crushing the just-mowed grass. He smelled the musty sweetness of the daffodils. Where was everyone? he wondered. Why were all the nearby houses dark? Who was going to save him?

Right then, he dropped his backpack on the sidewalk and ran like bloody murder. He ran and ran and ran and never looked back. He was only half a block from home, but it felt like forever to the front steps. The door was locked, so he sprinted around to the back of the house. His leg muscles burned, his lungs stung him from the inside out and his heart pumped harder than it should have. By the time he made it to the back door, he knew he was in the clear.

But there was Mom to deal with.

"And you say you never saw this boy before?" Mom wanted to know. She had stopped eating her sloppy joe a long time ago; it sat there on the plate, getting cold as she went from exasperation to concern. She was no longer mad at Leonard; now all her anger was focused on the mystery boy.

"No. He's definitely not from around here, or from our school. I would've remembered him."

"Did he . . . did he touch you at all? Anything? Any kind of—"

"No. I told you, he was going to beat me up. I got out of there."

After Leonard had eaten his dinner, Mom made him get in the car and drive around town looking for the boy. They never found him. They did manage to retrieve Leonard's backpack, which was still sitting beside the darkened house with the daffodils, exactly where he had dropped it. Mom wanted to file a complaint with the police, but Leonard pleaded with her not to make a big deal over it. In the end, she felt he'd been through enough, so she let it go.

My job, while they were out being vigilantes, was to do the dishes and clean up the kitchen. I had just finished scrubbing the stove, mopping up the sloppy part of the sloppy joes, when Deirdre appeared in the doorway.

"Where's Mom?" she asked. She placed her dirty dish in the sink and ran the water over it.

"Out with Leonard," I told her. "He got jumped by some kid and they've gone looking for him."

"Jumped?"

"I don't know. He cried. Mom's all up in his business now. She says that if he's going to do the Drama Camp thing, from now on he's got to get a ride home."

Deirdre sat at the table in her seat. It was just like the old days, me doing the dishes and her fiddling with stuff on the table, us talking. Except now with her hair so short, she looked like an imposter of her former self and we didn't have as much to say to each other. Over the past several months, she hadn't really taken an interest in Leonard at all. She had demonstrated that she couldn't care less about his comings and goings, his outfits, his ideas and how he was influencing Mom and the women of the salon. She had other things on her mind, though what those things were, I couldn't tell.

She pulled a stack of scrap paper from the plastic holder that I had made for Mom at sleepaway camp about a gazillion years ago. She laid one of the pieces of paper out flat and then quickly and expertly folded it origami style into a tiny crane. Then she made a duck, an elephant, a camel and a pig. In a matter of minutes, the table was littered with a small paper menagerie. I'd forgotten that she could do this. Years ago she checked a book out of the local library; it was written in Japanese, but by carefully following the diagrams, she had been able to teach herself how to make things.

"Well, I hope she's not planning to make him ride in a car alone with Buddy Howard. That would be a mistake. I mean, considering."

She held up a paper bird, and by gently manipulating its tail, she made its wings flap up and down. We both smiled, and then, as a kind of peace offering, she handed it to me. My hand was wet, which caused the head of the thing to instantly bloat and go limp. I'd ruined it. Deirdre laughed, grabbed it back and bunched it into a ball. She shot it across the room and, like an ace player, landed the wad bingo in the garbage pail.

"Considering what?" I asked.

"Are you kidding? Mr. Buddy and Leonard? Alone? Think about it, Pheeb. No. Never mind. Don't. It's too lurid."

As she made the last of her origami animals (a rabbit), Deirdre could tell I didn't have a clue.

"Sex, Phoebe. Leonard is like walking bait for a perv like Buddy Howard. And don't look so shocked."

I have to admit it had never occurred to me that Mr. Buddy had designs on any of the boys who took part in Drama Camp. The idea that he was after sex, and sex with a minor at that, was, well, it *was* lurid.

"But you don't think . . . ," I began weakly.

"Please, Pheebs. Where have you been living?"

She crumpled up her collection of paper napkins and tossed them one by one into the garbage. She hit her mark every time. Then she got up and checked out her reflection in the side of our old-fashioned chrome toaster. She gave what little hair she had a few quick brushes forward with her fingers, but it didn't really respond, so she moved in close to inspect her eyes.

"I'm thinking of doing kind of a Goth thing," she announced without pulling back. She assumed I was still watching her and listening to her every word. And she was right; I was. "Not the outfits. I mean the outfits are a big don't. But the eye treatment could work. Y'know, dark lids and some underliner. Whatdaya have in the way of shadow? Anything?"

We went upstairs and I gave her what I had. She experimented while I watched her and waited for her to ask my opinion. I told her what she wanted to hear and she rolled her eyes at me. I didn't care if she knew how desperate I was to be her friend. I didn't care if I appeared to be a suck-up. I was just grateful to be standing in front of the mirror together like we used to, talking, and I didn't want it to end.

But then I heard Mom and Leonard enter the house.

"*Phoebe . . . Deirdre?*" Mom called out from downstairs.

Deirdre and I just looked at each other. She gave me a sad smile and then gently touched my cheek with the blush brush.

"Don't listen to me, Pheebs." She whispered the words just loud enough for me to hear her, but soft enough that Mom wouldn't. "I don't know Buddy Howard's story. I just know that there are bad people in the world. And bad things happen to people. You just gotta wake up, is all I'm saying."

"*Phoebe!*" Mom called again; this time she expected a response.

"*We're up here,*" Deirdre called out. "*We'll be right down.*"

She wiped her eyes clean with a pad, removing any trace of her new look. I guess she wasn't ready to unveil it yet. She plopped a J.Crew bucket hat on her head, and together we clomped down the stairs into the living room. Mom and Leonard were sitting sadsack on the sofa. Deirdre announced that she and I would be serving ice cream parfaits in a matter of minutes. We went into the kitchen, whipped up the parfaits and served them in beer glasses, and then we all sat together in the living room. Instead of turning on the TV and tuning in to news about the bad things that bad people were up to that day, Deirdre and I entertained everyone with scandalous stories about Mom's customers. Sometimes we even got up from our seats to act out the dramatic parts. We were hilarious.

"Stop!" Mom cried, practically choking on her parfait. "You girls are so bad."

"No, no, Aunt Ellen. Please?" Leonard begged. "Don't make them stop."

At that moment it was hard not to at least *like* Leonard; he was, after all, trying so hard. Perched on the edge of his seat, clapping at our antics and egging us on, he was making it plain that all he really wanted in this world was to be included. This, he seemed to be saying, is all I need to be happy. But unlike the rest of us, he didn't care that his need showed; he wasn't embarrassed by his ridiculous desire to be liked.

That was a good night for us. For all of us. And I'm glad that I have it as a memory to look back on, because a week later everything changed.

EIGHT

Officer DeSantis had a red face and a big neck that pressed against his shirt collar. His chest was huge. As he jotted down the information about Leonard into a logbook, I watched the buttons of his shirt strain against the fabric and thought for sure that one of them was due to pop at any minute. He told us that if experience had taught him anything, it was that when a kid like Leonard disappears, he usually turns up several days later with a long story about how he just needed some space so he went and spent a night or two with some friend.

"Leonard doesn't really have friends," my mother pointed out. "Just the kids from Drama

Camp. Other than that, he doesn't know anyone."

Officer DeSantis looked up at her and said, "That's what I'm saying. Every kid knows someone."

When I pointed out that Leonard had also become pretty chummy with plenty of Mom's customers, Mom cut her eyes at me and then sighed as if I didn't know what I was talking about.

"He's very tight with some of them," I explained. I felt it was best if the authorities had all the facts to work with. "Leonard even convinced Mrs. Cafiero to let her hair go natural. Stuff like that. Oh, and there's also Mr. Buddy. Buddy Howard."

"Who's he?" asked Officer DeSantis, jotting down the name.

"He's the guy who sort of runs Drama Camp. We telephoned him last night when Leonard didn't come home. Usually Mr. Buddy gives Leonard a ride, so naturally . . . But Mr. Buddy said that Leonard didn't want a ride last night after rehearsal. Said he was going to meet a friend."

"A friend," said the policeman as if to prove his point. "See what I mean?"

None of us was convinced. Deirdre, who had been standing patiently behind me, sighed heavily and said, "Could you just, y'know, look for him?"

Officer DeSantis took all our information and assured us that he'd check out every lead. Then he suggested the idea of making a poster. He said it had worked for cats and dogs and once for the unhappy owner of an escaped parakeet. People see the missing whatever on the poster and it jogs their memory. They call. We'd be surprised, he said; and then he suggested that we might try posting the information on the Internet as well. The plan sounded pretty desperate to me. But clearly it appealed to my mother, because there she was, within the hour, sitting at our kitchen table, affixing Leonard's picture to a piece of paper.

It was a Polaroid photograph that I had taken myself almost a month ago at my mother's picnic for her regulars. Every Memorial Day she throws a picnic, and every year she swears that it's going to be the last time. After it's all over, she collapses onto her bed and does a monologue about how it's all just gotten to be too much trouble, deviling eggs, cutting crusts off sandwiches, lugging coolers, buying paper tablecloths, plastic dinnerware, party favors, setting everything up just to show some appreciation. "Next year," she says when it's over, "I'm giving out free rain bonnets and that'll be the end of it." But then by the following May, she's forgotten all about her promise and we are stuck dragging stuff to the same old picnic area.

This past year was a little different because Leonard had decided to set up a booth and offer Mom's customers before-and-after Polaroid portraits. He said that for some of the women it would be their "before" photos and for others it would be "after." His marketing ploy was to let each woman decide for herself where she fell on the time line. For those who felt that the best part of their lives was still in the future, he labeled their photos "before"; for those who held to the idea that they were living the best of their lives today, he labeled their photos "after." Five bucks a pop.

At the time, we all thought the scheme was pretty lame. But even Deirdre, who said she wouldn't be caught dead at one of Mom's picnics, admitted that the booth was a stroke of genius. At the end of the day, Leonard had pulled in real money—$225—and no one was about to argue with a fistful of dollars.

After the shindig was over and everyone had left the fairground, Leonard plopped himself down on the milk crate in front of his crudely painted backdrop (a tropical beach motif) and demanded that I take his picture. I told him I'd do it only if he paid me. He handed me a crisp twenty-dollar bill, and we went to work.

Snap. Grrr. Snap. Grrr. Snap. Grrr.

"So, wait," I said as we watched the three perfect squares develop in the palm of my hand. "Is this your 'before' or 'after'?"

"Both," he said. "I'm right in the middle."

The picture showed him wearing a striped T-shirt, his hair going every which way and one eye looking a little bigger than the other. Almost all of his teeth were exposed, demonstrating his eagerness to please just about anyone who cared to look at him. Except for the hint of a macramé choker that was peeking out from under the collar of his

T-shirt, he looked like the kind of kid you might just walk right by in a bus terminal somewhere in the Midwest. There was nothing in the picture that made him seem as different and unusual as he was in real life. Nothing crazy like those insane platform sneakers, which he insisted on risking his life to wear. I mentioned this to my mother when she showed me the Missing poster, but she simply moved her hands as if she was fanning gnats away.

"We have to do something!" she said. "We can't just sit around not doing anything!"

The finished poster read:

MISSING
14-year-old boy

LEONARD

Light Brown HAIR

HAZEL EYES

4' 11"

Last seen wearing

WHITE T-SHIRT, BLUE JEANS, BLUE NYLON

JACKET

My first reaction was to imagine Leonard's horror at being described so drably. His hair, as he often reminded us, was *not* light brown but dark blond. His eye color of choice had always been green ("What the hell is hazel?" he used to say. "Hazel's not even a color. It's an old lady name.") As for his outfit, not a word was said about the embroidered sunburst, which he had painstakingly stitched onto the white T-shirt just over his heart, using every available color in my mother's sewing basket. He was so proud of his handiwork and the fact that he had taught himself how to thread a needle, I knew if he found out, he'd be mad as hell we hadn't mentioned it. And, excuse me, a blue nylon jacket? I don't think so. Leonard was more likely to refer to that article of clothing as "an aqua-colored Windbreaker" or "a turquoise sailing jacket."

Not a word about his platform sneakers.

After making five hundred copies on bright yellow paper at the copy place, Deirdre and I were mobilized. We were given a stack and sent forth to cover a grid of streets, even cul-de-sacs, which had been meticulously mapped out and sectioned off by my mother. Mrs. Landis, Mrs. Manotti and Mrs. Kavanaugh pitched in, and they were given hand-bills and areas as well. We taped copies of the poster on telephone poles all over our assigned neighbor-hoods and pasted them in some of the store win-dows, and whenever we passed someone on the street, we forced a flyer into their hands and explained the situation. Within hours, Leonard had become a local celebrity.

It wasn't just our regular customers, however, who called on the phone at all hours to register their concern, their worry, their predictions and escalat-ing hysteria; we also heard from crank callers who pretended to know something about Leonard's whereabouts and then asked for ridiculous amounts of ransom money (anywhere from five dollars to a cool million). These calls usually ended in a fit of adolescent giggling and then a click. We didn't even bother to *69 them. We were too tired.

Some of our customers felt it was their duty to stop by and weigh in with their opinions and their stories, which inevitably involved missing children, dead babies and student nurses who had been tortured and then dumped in shallow graves by maniacs. They talked as if they had known the Lindbergh baby and little JonBenet personally. They were experts at the unsolved mysteries of this world, and thanks to TV, each of them had an encyclopedic knowledge of murderous motives and evil deeds. To be honest, I wasn't in the mood to hear these stories; they caused me to question just how good or evil human beings were at heart and how important a part God played in their dastardly acts.

If I had been a big believer in God, I would have chosen a moment like that to strike a deal with Him or Her. The deal would have certainly involved a solemn promise to be a big sister to Leonard when he was returned to us. In other words, I would have promised to be good, to introduce Leonard to my gang (as soon as I belonged to one) and to stand up for him when someone called him a sissy in the school parking lot. In return, God would have been expected to deliver Leonard back into our midst safe and sound.

But the thing I've learned about God is that He/She doesn't really respond that well to vows,

threats, bargaining or promises, because He/She
either:

1. *Is above it all;*
2. *Really doesn't exist;*
3. *Has a plan that involves heartbreak
   and misery for everyone.*

If it is 1 or 2, there is no point making promises
and swearing to do things. It's all just praying into
the wind.

But if it turns out to be 3, then I have to suppose there is some hidden value in the heartbreak
and misery, and my job as a human is to figure out
what it all means before it's too late.

We returned to the police station the following
day, and Mom cried right after she signed her name
to the missing persons document. Deirdre didn't
come. It was just me sitting with her in the waiting
area of the police station as she wiped her tears and
reapplied her makeup. When she raised her lip-
gloss applicator to her face and realized that this
was the last item that Leonard had bought for her,

there was a rush of fresh tears.

"Leonard told me that my Avon frosted pink had outlived its shelf life. Then he goes out and buys me this—Glossimer with high-beam gleam by Chanel."

More tears, and then, "What am I going to do without him?"

At first, I thought she meant what was she going to do without Leonard to advise her on her choice of makeup. But when she sighed and said, "Oh, Phoebe, why does everything always go wrong for us?" I realized that this went much deeper than just blush powder and lip color. Later, when we got home, she was to put the official "missing" document in her brown purse-size accordion-file folder along with her divorce papers, the yellowing newspaper obituaries of her favorite customers, and several bad reports from our school. In the future, whenever her thoughts darkly turned toward depression, whenever she was convinced that things never worked out for the Hertle family, she could just take down that accordion-file folder from the shelf in her closet, thumb through the evidence and come to the same sad conclusion: Everything always goes wrong for us.

But at the moment we were still in the police station. And the next thing I knew, my arms were wrapped around my mother. Her White Diamonds perfume by Elizabeth Taylor was mixed together with the familiar odors of the salon and my entire childhood. I pressed myself into her. I could hear the actual beating of her heart loud and clear through her rayon blouse.

"You're crushing the air outa me," she said, pausing in mid sob to clutch my shoulders. "Ease up."

Finally we broke apart, but only because the contents of her purse had crashed onto the just-mopped linoleum floor and everything went sliding every which way. I reached under the chair for her mascara and heard myself saying things like "Don't worry." I felt around for her little mirror and repeated, "Everything will be all right." I said, "It'll all work out, you'll see," like I really meant it. I was suddenly spouting a stream of comforting expressions that my mother had used on me in the past when things were *not* all right, *not* working out, and the situation remained just plain awful.

"I know," Mom said, sniffing back her tears and forcing one of her smiles. "I know, I know."

We were, the two of us, like amateur actors in a bad play, forced to recite lines and affect emotions that were way beyond our abilities to convey convincingly. In other words, we were a mess.

A drunk was seated in one of the plastic chairs opposite us. Our audience. Not yet ten A.M. and the guy was already hammered. He wore a Duke University T-shirt and satiny purple running shorts, an outfit that clashed stylistically with his black nylon socks and leather-soled loafers. His face was the color of a dirty gym sock, and not that attractive to begin with. As he came to life, he pointed his scruffy chin and tequila-soaked eyeballs up toward the ceiling and said in a voice way too loud to be ignored, *"In touch or indifferent! Get it? In touch! Or in different!"*

I looked away. Another bad actor, I said to myself.

"Let's get out of here," I said to my mother.

When we got back to the house, the last of the sunlight was draining from the kitchen curtains and Mom announced that she was going to call Uncle

Mike in Mexico. Mom had a crazy hunch (or maybe it was just a crazy hope) that Uncle Mike might know something of Leonard's whereabouts. When she got him on the phone, Uncle Mike said no, he hadn't heard from Leonard, not at all, not since getting a postcard of a bikini-clad blonde holding a beach ball over her head and standing on what is supposed to be one of Neptune's fun-filled recreation areas. That card had been in the racks at the drugstore since before I was old enough to read the lazy hot-pink inscription: HAVING A BALL! As if such a thing had ever been possible in this town. According to Uncle Mike, Leonard wrote to him saying that he loved his new home in Neptune, the salon, the people, Aunt Ellen, Deirdre and especially me.

I practically screamed into the receiver.

"What!"

All three of us were on various extensions around the house. I had the old wall phone down in the basement, Mom was in her room and Deirdre was listening in on the kitchen phone.

"Yup," Uncle Mike continued long distance. "Says you and him was as close to best friends as he was liable to get."

There was a pause as everyone let this lie soak in and take hold. No one offered a contradictory statement. I hated myself.

Finally Uncle Mike told us not to worry, because Leonard had spunk. And then he added, "That kid can smell shit in the wind from forty friggin' miles away." I assumed this was an expression he had picked up from his new life in Mexico, spoken by his new cronies, who probably had a lot of experience with both shit and wind.

Uncle Mike also told us about his cattle and said that he probably had two more seasons before he went to slaughter. I gagged. As a vegetarian, I am opposed to the slaughter of cattle. Right then and there I canceled out Uncle Mike's ranch as one of Leonard's possible runaway destinations. A home on the range where cows are routinely slaughtered and where the smell of shit is always in the wind didn't sound like much of a refuge for him. Leonard was more the type to be heading toward a place like Oz, as in The Wizard Of. In any case, as far as I was concerned, Uncle Mike was a dead end.

After that, Mom announced that the time had come for us to go rifling through Leonard's things. We needed a clue, she said. Though reluctant at first, Deirdre joined us downstairs and together we pulled and jostled stuff from various hiding places around Leonard's makeshift room. I felt like the Gestapo on a suburban house tour. We unrolled socks, shook change loose from pants pockets, found a collection of men's muscle magazines and ogled the pictures of overly cheerful guy-guys in teeny-tiny bathing suits and flexed biceps, tried to decipher the doodles that appeared in the margins of schoolbooks. We found a list of names of all Mom's customers with sketches of their hairdos penciled in beside them. There were no real surprises; everything was just as we expected. But when we came across several packages of condoms stuffed in a crevice between Grandma Hertle's boxes, Mom grabbed her hair and let a little shout escape from her.

"Ew, ew, ew," Deirdre exclaimed, as she chucked the packets clear across the room.

"Everyone get a grip," I said, and then suggested

that maybe Leonard's condoms were evidence of wishful thinking. "I mean, they haven't been opened."

"Still," said Deirdre, and then she shuddered theatrically just to let us know that she couldn't bear to think of anything sexual connected to Leonard. "It's totally gross."

My own surprise came later, when I pulled a floor plan of the American Museum of Natural History from beneath Leonard's mattress. Who knew that Leonard had an interest in natural history—or in anything natural, for that matter? He was more the type who went in for artificial everything—sweetener, hair color, flavors. The idea that he might have been interested in dinosaurs, moon rocks or semiprecious minerals made me pause and reevaluate the person I thought I knew as Leonard Pelkey. Were there other aspects to him that I had failed to notice? Had he actually *been* to the American Museum of Natural History in New York City? And if so, with whom?

From the moment Leonard came to live with us, I did everything I could to *not* pay attention to him, his interests, his whereabouts, his history. As far as I was concerned, he was an unwelcome stranger in our midst, white noise, dead air. Other people fell for him left and right, they felt sorry for him, they wanted to know what he was up to, what he was thinking about and how he was getting on. But I had no intention of signing up for The Leonard Pelkey Show, and nothing he did or said, no bribe offered or prize promised, could change my mind.

Leonard occupied about 2.5 cubic feet of space, but once he was gone, he became a much bigger deal. By the time we finished putting up the posters (as far east as Long Branch and as far west as the Turnpike), he was covering vast distances. Everywhere I went during that first week, I saw him smiling back at me. He was hanging from telephone poles and grinning at me from store windows. You just couldn't get away from him and his crazy like-me-like-me-please-like-me smile. Even if I had wanted to, I wouldn't have been able to forget him for more than a block in any direction. Once he had disappeared, he was everywhere.

Then, just when the posters were really beginning to do a number on me, the sky went dark over Neptune, and everybody's cellar flooded from the heavy rains. Most people didn't know what had hit them. The TV weather forecasters, wearing brightly colored outfits and professional expressions of mock surprise, kept insisting that they couldn't have known such a deluge was on its way, and then they promised us a cool air mass that would blow the whole mess offshore and far out to sea. When their version of the future failed to materialize, actual facts were dredged up and broadcast. They told us that the Jersey shore hadn't seen so much rain during the month of June since the year 1903. We weren't all that impressed. In fact, we couldn't have cared less; we just wanted the rain to stop. When the sun finally did come out again, our posters were soggy reminders of our faded hopes; many of them had been washed away completely.

In their place, however, we found new posters. But instead of Leonard's picture, it was Larry Wheeler's face staring at us from every surface. Larry was Electra's brother. Six months earlier he had signed up to liberate Iraq with the help of the United States Army, and now he was coming home a hero. He had been shot at, along with his entire battalion. And this was weird, because at the time of the shooting, everyone in Neptune was sitting around thinking that the whole Iraq thing was finished and that we had won the war on terrorism. Apparently the situation was more complicated than that, and according to Electra, the war was far from finished, especially in certain places south of Baghdad where renegades got it into their heads to shower Larry and his fellow desert rats with what she described to everyone as "mortal fire."

"Mortar, I think it's called," I explained to her, as we all crowded around her down at the video store where she worked.

"Whatever. He's wounded," she told us. "He lost a part of his leg."

Thanks to Larry's quick reflexes and loud mouth, the rest of his guys were all saved from certain death. He managed to warn everyone and get them out of harm's way before the second explosion. Larry was thrown thirty feet by the blast, he lost his

Ray-Ban sunglasses as well as the lower portion of his left leg, and he was awarded a Purple Heart for his bravery. The *Asbury Park Press* ran a full account of the incident on the front page along with a pre-explosion picture of Larry wearing his helmet, a big grin, the sunglasses and both his legs. I couldn't help feeling skeptical.

A week earlier a big news story featured an alleged war hero who had survived "mortal fire" and then was miraculously rescued from the enemy by Special Forces. The girl soldier who had been saved looked like a high school cheerleader wearing the wrong costume. She seemed almost too good to be true, and in fact that's exactly what we later discovered. The story of her rescue turned out to be mostly made up by the government in order to allow the American public to feel proud of our troops in Iraq. Was it any wonder I was doubtful?

"He's my brother!" Electra insisted.

"I know, but still, he could've been paid off or something by the government. I'm just saying."

After I saw Larry, however, there was no denying the fact that he was actually missing a leg. You can't make something like that up, and I was doubt-ful whether there was enough money in the world to make someone give up a leg just so they could be part of a publicity stunt. But even though Larry was really wounded, even though he was an actual hero, I couldn't help feeling a little pissed off because his situation had so totally eclipsed Leonard's. The new posters announced that a parade would be taking place in Larry's honor and then a picnic afterward with lots of prizes and free stuff. The idea was to celebrate Larry's safe return and allow Neptune the opportunity to thank him for risking his neck and losing his leg in the fight against terrorism. We hadn't offered anything like that on *our* posters, no free soda, no picnic, no parade, games or valuable prizes. Leonard didn't stand a chance.

Electra couldn't have been more thrilled that her brother had become the new focus of local concern. She began to act as though he had suddenly become best buds with the president of the United States.

I was grateful that school had already let out for the summer, because otherwise I would have had to watch her working the hallways, taking in everyone's compliments, reigning in her unruly dreadlocks and generally presiding over everything.

In spite of Larry's sudden celebrity and Neptune's fascination with the story of how he'd lost his leg, there were a few people who remained steadfast on Leonard's behalf. They were mostly oldies, folks who understood what it was like to be entirely forgotten by most everyone and then end up totally invisible. They knew how to remind people of Leonard in subtle ways—wearing a scarf that he had given them, carrying his poster in their purses, casually dropping his name into the conversation. And even if these were the same people who couldn't tell Monday from Wednesday or me from Deirdre, you had to love them for hanging in there.

"You know what you ought to do, Deirdre?" Mrs. F. told me as we waited on line together in the pharmacy. "You oughtta get Leonard's picture on them milk cartons." She was poking at her hive of dyed-black hair with her pointy, brightly polished nails. I knew she didn't want me to ask her why she hadn't been to the salon lately or what was up with all the dangling bobby pins. Mrs. F. was on a fixed income, and the less said about her home do, the better. So instead I said: "My mom's got a new prescription for Zoloft. Personally, I'm against anti-depressants. I think the pharmaceutical companies are controlling everyone's brain chemistry in this country. Pretty soon we won't be making our own decisions. We'll be like robots. And just for the record, Leonard's a little too old to have his picture on a milk carton."

Mrs. F. just nodded while I turned toward the selection of flavored breath mints and pretended to be interested in what chemicals they put in them.

Ms. D. from Drama Camp was also on the case. She called us every day to express how absolutely positive "everyone" was that Leonard would be returned to us safe and sound. Naturally, we assumed that "everyone" included Mr. Buddy. But when we heard that Nathan Kutholtz had been cast to play the part of Ariel in *The Tempest*, and that Nathan had been seen driving around with Mr. Buddy, we began to wonder how sincere and positive "everyone" really was.

Officer DeSantis (or "Chuck," as we had begun

to call him) was also among the small band of believers, those who continued to place Leonard's situation above that of Private First Class Larry Wheeler. And though he wasn't one of my mother's regular customers, he stopped by our house often enough. He came to discuss the details of Leonard's case, gather information, drink my mother's coffee, ask questions and use the bathroom. When he wasn't in uniform, he looked handsome in a rugged sort of way. His hairstyle, which was almost identical to Deirdre's, made him look like a football coach for the winning team. He had a big face with very small features, and delicate ears that stuck out a bit too much, positioned perhaps to catch clues.

Chuck spent the better part of a week interviewing most of Mom's customers to find out if Leonard had ever mentioned a desire to run away or if he had ever discussed people, places or things that were unknown to us. The interviews resulted in a long list of exotic locales that the ladies wished to visit someday and a list of names we'd never heard of, names that corresponded to the out-of-state friends and relatives of those being interviewed. A less exacting detective might have dismissed all this as the useless chatter of old women who didn't have a clue, but Chuck was nothing if not exacting. He wrote everything down and kept the information in a black binder that sat on the front seat of his metallic-blue Subaru. He called this phase of the investigation "casting a wide net," or "trawling for clues," or "Phase One." If any place or person was mentioned a second time during the course of the investigation, he transferred the detail into his blue binder, which he also kept on his front seat. I anticipated, with a kind of dread excitement, the moment when Chuck reached for that blue binder and we knew for sure that we were headed into the thick of "Phase Two."

NINE

"**D**on't wait to call. If you find a clue, call. If you think of something we forgot, call. And for god's sakes, if you hear from Leonard, call."

Unfortunately Mom took her own advice and carried it way too far. She called so many times that after a while I no longer bothered to say "Hello" when I answered the phone; I just said, "Minutes, Mom." This was my way of reminding her that if we went over our allotted minutes per month, we would have to pay extra. Most of the time she didn't have anything to report. I didn't either. As a result, our conversations were brief. But they were frequent.

Before Leonard came into our lives, Mom was

dead set against the idea of Deirdre or me owning a cell phone due to the possibility of brain cancer. She also objected to the expense and could do a ten-minute monologue on why she considered it outrageous for phone companies to give you the actual phone almost for free and then have the nerve to charge you for waves that a person couldn't see with the naked eye. But because she wanted us all to keep in constant contact during the search for Leonard, she broke down and got us all Nokias. Mine was magenta to match the color of my hair at the time.

It was the Fourth of July and I was standing outside the VFW. I was holding my phone a little away from my ear, because my mother hadn't yet learned how to talk like a normal person into a cell; she seemed to think they were constructed of tin cans and strings and required plenty of volume. She was giving a lecture on matchbooks.

"Mom, stop. Okay? Just stop. I don't know what you're going on about. I'm honestly not listening."

Then she asked again. Had I ever noticed Leonard collecting matchbook covers from fancy restaurants, because she'd heard stories about boys who collected matchbook covers and if Leonard happened to be one of those boys then we could find his matchbook collection, track down those restaurants and ask the waiters if they had seen him. The whole scheme seemed kind of nutty to me, but I couldn't say I was giving it much thought. Not really. Instead, I was staring hard at the VFW building and wondering how a building so neglected and forlorn could have escaped the bulldozer and made it into the twenty-first century. This was a place as hopeless as my mother's latest plan to find Leonard.

"Good-bye, Mother," I said, and then turned off my phone.

VFW stands for Veterans of Foreign Wars, and let me just say that the VFW meeting hall in Neptune can bring to mind every unfortunate association with the words *veterans*, *foreign* and *war*.

1. *The place is ancient.*

2. *It is far from home (way on the other side of town).*

3. *Everyone was fighting. They weren't fighting with guns; they were mostly just arguing among themselves. But still.*

After finishing up my call with Mom, I noticed an old guy wearing a jaunty little blue cap and a tired sash with gold fringe that dangled across his chest. He was yelling at the barbecue, declaiming in a very loud voice that it wasn't placed correctly and it definitely had to be moved. His grievance seemed to be with the barbecue itself. But then a younger guy with a bandana and a belly came bounding out of the meeting hall and told the old guy with the cap and sash to cut it out; he kept saying that the old guy didn't know what the hell he was talking about. I wandered inside and began looking around for a familiar face.

Mrs. Lewis, a tall African-American woman who worked at the library, was there, wearing a flowered-print top and bright-blue slacks. Her hair had been blow-dried for the occasion and then curled under at the ends, probably with a hand iron.

I hung back and watched her having an animated argument with a short, blond lady with squinty eyes and sharpened eyebrows.

"I just think the streamers will look more festive if we twirl them from floor to ceiling, then anchor them with tape at either end," Mrs. Lewis said in her library voice, the one she usually used on the first graders who didn't understand how to use a library.

"No," the squinty woman replied as she grabbed the streamers from Mrs. Lewis's hand. "We want to swaaag them. Like bunting."

"We got plenty of bunting already. And nobody likes to swag."

I was on Mrs. Lewis's side; I thought it was only fair that she had a say in the matter due to the fact that she had a son in the armed services at the time. Also, I didn't like the look of the blonde, or her attitude. I was just about to step forward and offer my opinion when I heard a voice from behind me.

"Hey."

I turned around and saw someone standing there who resembled Travis Lembeck. In fact, it *was* Travis Lembeck, except he looked as if he had just received an extreme makeover. Everything a person might have ever wanted to improve about him had been improved. He had washed his hair. He was wearing a white T-shirt that was actually white, jeans that fit him, and black New Balance running shoes that looked as if someone cared enough to buy him a brand-new pair. But most astonishing of all, he had lost the black parka. Without it, the shape of his body was visible, and as it turned out, his body had a definite shape. I could see the sharp rise of each upper arm muscle before it disappeared into his shirtsleeve. The indentation of his breastbone was clearly visible through the shirt, and the sight of his clavicle just above the collar nearly made me swoon.

"Hey, yourself," I said, as if his whole body was no big deal and not worth losing sleep over.

"You're here early. You here t' help or . . ."

"No. God, no. I mean . . . no. I just have these . . . It's my mother. She wants me to put up these posters. About Leonard."

He didn't saying anything. He just looked at the pile of yellow paper I was cradling in the crook of my arm.

"Guess you heard," I said.

"Yeah. Sorry." He looked away like he might, if he concentrated hard enough, see Leonard standing a long way off on the far side of the room.

"Listen," he said without looking back at me.

"You wanna, I dunno, get outa here? Go for a ride w' me? I got my car."

I started to panic, because I realized, Oh my God, this guy wants me to get in his car and go somewhere with him. And to tell you the truth, if something hadn't suddenly taken hold of me (guilt, I guess), I would've turned the panic into excitement, dumped the posters and taken off with him in a second.

"Maybe later," I said. "I've got to do this. But later for sure."

After he left, I could have kicked myself. This is so my life, I thought. I seem to be forever hanging out with old farts with bad hair instead of making out in a parked car with an actual boy. Added to this, Mrs. Rivera, who was in charge of the festivities, had refused to allow me to hang the posters. She felt that it would put a damper on the atmosphere. But she assured me that it was a free country with First Amendment rights, so I was free to discuss anything with anyone as much as I wanted. Nobody would stop me.

The party, once it got under way, was a real

blowout. Since the idea was to combine the occasion of Larry's heroism in Iraq with the Fourth of July, everyone's spirits were very high. Folks chugged beer, downed soda and got food all over themselves. They carried their children on their shoulders, yelled at one another to be heard above the piped-in music, waved American flags and wore costumes with a stars-and-stripes motif.

Larry arrived in a wheelchair. He was dressed in regular clothes—shorts, sandals, a Mets baseball cap and sunglasses. His lower left leg was missing, and in its place there was a shiny, new prosthetic device with a hinge. Everyone cheered loudly, and they waved their flags as he was wheeled up the ramp to the building's porch. As soon as he was positioned beneath an arc of red, white and blue balloons, he was rushed by a bunch of freaks with video cameras. The whole event took on shades of MTV's *Real World*.

Electra was right there in the center of everything, beaming and wearing an OUR HERO T-shirt that featured the same picture of Larry that we had been staring at all week. Her brother saluted and then waved to the crowd; he smiled and said things into the microphone that no one could hear over the racket.

Just because I had nothing better to do, I waited in line to say hey to Larry. It took forever, and I was stuck behind old Mrs. Kurtz. She smelled like sweat and was blind as a bat. One of her bra straps was showing, and she carried a blot rag with her.

"He'll turn up," she said to me as she touched my arm with the hand that held the rag. "You watch. God looks after us in Neptune."

"Leonard's been gone for almost ten days," I reminded her, shifting my weight to my other hip and taking another baby step forward in line.

"Look at Larry," she said, which I considered hilarious since she was pointing a little too far to the left of where Larry was actually seated. "He came back to us. What're the chances? And he came back a *hero*."

"Right," I said. "And without a leg."

We were almost up to Larry at this point, except I could see that the guy who had Larry's ear was going to bend it for a good long while. He was going on and on about how when *he* came back from Vietnam, nobody threw *him* a party, nosiree, and *he* could have rotted in a gutter for all anyone cared, and also stuff about war being hell, actual hell. He even spelled it out. H-E-L-L. He was following up with details when old Mrs. Kurtz wiped her face one last time with her trusty rag and said to me, "Oh, by the by, I've got one of Leonard's notebooks and his copy of *Great Expectations*. Maybe you could stop by sometime. He'll want them when he gets back."

Then as an afterthought she added, "And maybe you'll read to me when you come over. Leonard had such a nice voice. I could listen to him all day."

"Has," I said to Mrs. K. very pointedly. "He *has* a nice voice. And I'm not a great public speaker. I throw up if I have to read aloud."

"Oh," she said, and then turned to greet Larry.

How Leonard ever managed to sit in Mrs. Kurtz's musty old house every Friday afternoon reading aloud while she blotted herself and sighed because Pip or whoever was in a Dickensian bind I'll never know. Maybe *our hero* was, after all,

Leonard Pelkey and no one ever really knew it.

Except for a wisecrack that Larry made about my former obsession with Winona Ryder, my interview with him was pretty dull. I lied and told him that Winona and I had struck up a very lively correspondence, which I hoped to publish someday in book form. He shook his head and laughed. Then I said stupid stuff I didn't really mean about how proud we all were of him. I tried to look at his fake leg without being obvious about it, but he caught me looking and told me I could touch it if I wanted to.

"I'm what they call 'baloney' now," he informed me.

"What?"

"Baloney. That's what we're called. Those of us without a leg *b'low the knee*. Get it? Below knee."

I couldn't laugh. I just stood there, slightly stunned while he laughed hard enough for both of us.

"Does it hurt?" I asked him.

"Like hell. But tell ya the truth, I got pills. Pills for everything. Pills t' dull the pain. Pills t' keep me from getting too bummed. Pills t' do something for my kidneys. Pills t' help me sleep. Sleep is tough, man. Sleep's the worst."

Suddenly I remembered the old days right after Dad ran off with Chrissie Bettinger. I slept over at Electra's house, ate dinner there, watched movies on their big-screen TV; and sometimes Electra and I would make brownies and drink milk out of martini glasses. We painted our nails in matching colors, wrote letters to Winona Ryder, gave each other peanut butter facials. And eventually I would forget I had a home of my own. At the time, I loved that old house and Electra's whole nutty family. They were always yelling at one another from separate rooms. They'd have whole conversations, calling from floor to floor, as if it was the most normal thing in the world. Sometimes they'd laugh at me because my voice didn't carry as well as theirs did and they always had to say, "What?" in a way that made everyone laugh out loud. Especially Larry. That guy could really laugh. Sometimes when Electra and I horsed around with him, he called us "crackheads."

"You two are a coupla crackheads," he'd say. "Yup, that's what you are."

That was our cue to crack our heads together, which made Larry lose it every time. Never failed. We could always make him laugh. Once we snuck into his room in the middle of the night and watched him sleeping. We sat there snapping our fingers louder, then louder, trying to see if he would wake up. He never did. We could have lit a fire in the room and it wouldn't have disturbed him. He could really sleep, that guy.

"I've got to go."

I wandered over to the food table, where I ate too many pickles. Then I happened to notice Carol Silva-Hernandez, the reporter from NEWS 5. You couldn't miss her, with her shiny, dark-brown bob. She was carrying a microphone with a NEWS 5 logo on it and being followed around by a big burly guy and his camera. Together they were trying to interview random people about Larry, but from the looks of it, they kept striking out. Not one of the folks who were approached knew Larry for real. I mean from before he was a hero. They just stared with their mouths full of chips and shook their heads whenever Carol asked a question.

Finally she snagged Electra, who instantly lit up at the prospect of appearing on TV. Carol couldn't believe her luck. As she fussed with her hairdo and straightened the synthetic fabric of her shell top, she practically screamed at her cameraman to "Roll tape! Roll tape!" And he did.

Carol didn't look like much—just a short-waisted woman in her mid-whatevers with a tiny nose, big eyes and better-than-average diction; but once that camera got rolling, she really came to life. Suddenly everything about her seemed broadcast quality—eyes, nose, teeth—and even her chintzy red, white and blue pantsuit fell into place.

"I'm here in Neptune, New Jersey, talking with the proud sister of war hero Larry Wheeler. Electro . . . Shoot. Can we take that again, Gary? I'm here in Neptune, New Jersey, talking with Electra Wheeler, sister of recently returned roar hero. Shoot. One more time."

She got it right eventually. She was a very determined lady, a professional all the way. But

Electra wisely used the extra time to get her dreads under control, and I could see her trying to adopt a suitably humble expression for the camera. That's when I got my big idea.

I strolled up to them, very cool, very self-assured, and politely said, "Excuse me. Can I talk to you for a minute?"

Electra woke up from her humble little dream and stared at me—hard.

"I'm busy right now," Electra said to me.

"Not you," I replied, a little too coolly. "I want to talk to your reporter friend here."

The silence was momentarily broken by the sound of an exploding firecracker out in the parking lot, which caused several neighborhood dogs to start yapping their heads off. Time seemed to stand still as Electra just turned away, leaving me standing there.

"So I'm wondering if you can do a story on my cousin, Leonard Pelkey," I said to the reporter from NEWS 5. "Maybe you heard of him. He's famous around here. Or was. He's been missing for—"

"*Phoebe!*" Electra said, biting into the air in

front of her. "This is so *not* the right moment, okay?"

That's the exact thing about Electra that really bugs me the most. She thinks she knows just what sort of thing should happen and when. It's as if she received a manual in the mail that explains what is appropriate and what is not. Then she acts surprised as hell because apparently I didn't get the manual or I got it and didn't bother to read it. Of course, Rule Numero Uno in this manual is *Now is not the right moment.* Manual or no manual, I made up my mind that right then was the exact right moment, because when, I reasoned to myself, would I ever again be near a TV reporter? And besides, as Mrs. Rivera had said, it's a free country.

"You have to do a story about my cousin. You *have* to."

Carol smiled at me like I was a suicide bomber with a strong will to live. Maybe reporters for NEWS 5 are forced to attend classes in conflict resolution, because our gal-on-the-go took a deep breath and said, "Phoebe? May I call you Phoebe?"

I nodded noncommittally.

"How about you let us finish up here and then you and me, we can have a talk about your cousin. How's that?"

She was smooth and, like I said, professional, but she didn't fool me for a second. This was just a more professional way of saying, "This is not the right moment."

The next thing that happened shocked me. I carpe diemed the moment and began screaming something like, *"You people! You're all proud of ol' Larry here because he was off fighting evil in Iraq. But do any of you* know *what evil looks like? Evil is here—right here in Neptune, New Jersey!"*

By this time, just about everyone within earshot was staring at me. I'm sure they thought I had flipped out. Maybe they thought I was pre-menstrual.

"I dunno what's wrong with you, Phoebe," Electra shouted, interrupting me. "Leonard's just missing, that's all. Nothing bad's happened."

I suddenly remembered Deirdre throwing lettuce at my father at the Fin & Claw, I remembered how Aunt Bet told her customers that our family problems amounted to basically nothing. And then it occurred to me that people like Electra and Aunt Bet just *want* things to add up to nothing, so they say it over and over and thereby make it nothing, when in fact it is definitely *something*.

I grabbed the pile of Leonard's posters from my shoulder bag and threw them. The air exploded in a burst of yellow. It was a beautiful sight. To tell you the truth, after a day filled with so much red, white and blue, all that yellow came as an enormous relief. But once the pages settled to the ground and Leonard's face was staring up at us from all over the pavement, there was really nothing left to say. I had made my point. So I ran into the parking lot and as far away from everyone as I could get.

I tried to call Deirdre on my cell, but the illuminated readout informed me that I was out of range. This made me so mad, I screamed and threw my brand-new phone into the bushes with all my might. I was disgusted with myself, because then I had to go traipsing into the bug-infested underbrush and crawl on my hands and knees to find the stupid thing.

"Is it later yet?"

I heard the voice before I recognized where it was coming from. His car was parked haphazardly, and waves of heat were rising from the hood. There he was—Travis—lying across the front end of his very dented, burgundy-colored Nissan Sentra, like a perfect desert mirage.

"What?" I said, making my way out of the woods. "Sorry. What'd you say?"

"The ride. You said maybe later. Is it later yet?"

"No," I told him. "It's now."

"Get in," he said.

TEN

Over breakfast Mom informed me that our pal Chuck would be stopping by at two thirty, and she wanted me to be present. She actually said the word "present."

"Present?" I said, repeating her.

I made my eyebrows rise as high as they would go, but she didn't see them because she was busy dumping the last of her morning coffee down the drain.

"Yes," she replied. "I want you here. Two thirty."

Even though it was Monday, her day off, she acted as though she had a schedule.

"Deirdre too?" I asked.

"No. Just you. And me."

"Why not Deirdre?"

"Because."

"Because why?"

"Because she doesn't need to be here."

Mom started going through her purse, doing her ritual inventory—keys, lip gloss, mascara, blush, shopping list, money, Advil. It was what she did when she got nervous.

"Who decided that?" I asked her.

"Who decided what?"

"Who decided me and not Deirdre?"

"Whaddya mean?"

I waited for her to close her purse and look up at me so I could see the blank expression on her face; it was perfect.

"Did you decide this or did Chuck? Am I going to be interrogated? Am I a suspect?"

"Don't be ridiculous. He wants to talk with us."

Us used to mean Deirdre, Mom, Dad and me. Then Dad left us, and *us* meant the three people he left behind. For a while Leonard tried to become a part of *us*, but I think all parties have to agree to the deal if it's going to work and that never happened, because mostly I was never up for it and Deirdre had resigned from *us*, including the *us* that was just her and me. Apparently *us* had been whittled down and somehow had become just Mom and me.

As Mom stood in front of the mirror, poking and prodding her hair into place, I thought I might tell her about what had happened between Travis and me the other night in his car out on Beach Road. I thought for a moment that a confession of this kind would solidify our *us*ness and make us buddies; but every time I tried to imagine her reaction, all I could see in my mind was her face going white with anger. Wouldn't she freak when she found out that the boy from the mall had kissed me hard on the mouth? She might even scream when I described how he had pressed his lips against my neck, waggled his tongue in my mouth, and jiggered his hand up inside my blouse. Of course there was always the possibility that she might just hear me out and do nothing other than make a small, strangled sound at the back of her throat and smile.

I decided if I told her, she would be bugging me for weeks, searching my face, my clothes, trying to figure out if I was still a virgin. She wouldn't care about how softly Travis said my name into my ear, or how he found a way to climb smoothly on top of my thighs in that front seat, or how gently he slid his left hand down between my jeans and abdomen or how long he was able to keep his fingers positioned there without moving a knuckle. She would merely want to know if I'd said "no" to him and at what point.

"Deirdre! C'mon! Now!" Mom yelled up the stairs. Then she turned to me and without really seeing me, she said, "I'm driving Deirdre over to Mina's for an overnight. Help me out and clean up a bit around here."

Poor Deirdre. She didn't have anyone kissing her in the front seat of a Nissan Sentra. She still didn't have a car of her own, and there was no boyfriend in sight. She had passed up our father's offer of a new car when she graduated and she had even turned down a possible date with several irresistibly gorgeous seniors. On both counts, everyone thought she was crazy or at least in a state of clinical depression. Meanwhile, she hadn't been accepted into a single college, mostly due to the fact that she hadn't applied. She kept meaning to, and her SAT scores were decent enough, but no one pushed her, no one insisted, and then suddenly it was too late and everyone began to talk glowingly about the community college as if it was a real institute of higher learning instead of a dumping ground for students with bad grades, out-of-date hairstyles and lousy attitudes.

Anyway, that's the reason I figured Mom didn't want Deirdre at the meeting with Chuck that afternoon—her attitude. It was lousy. She also wouldn't stop ragging everyone about Mr. Buddy being a possible suspect in the case of Leonard's disappearance, and we had been down that road plenty. As it turned out, Chuck had interviewed both Mr. Buddy and Ms. D., and afterward he announced that they were both in the clear as far as he could tell. But Deirdre wasn't convinced.

"Just you wait," she kept saying.

Chuck stopped by at exactly two thirty, and by two forty the three of us were sitting in the living room sipping iced lemonade. Mom and I sat side by side on the couch. Chuck plopped down on the green chair opposite us. Because Chuck had placed his blue binder on the coffee table in front of us, I had a feeling that we were about to enter Phase Two of the investigation, and I was curious to find out what had brought us to that point on that particular afternoon.

He began by reporting that there had been no real news regarding Leonard's whereabouts. And this, he told us, could be considered either good news or bad news depending on how we chose to look at it. For example, it was good news because a lack of evidence often meant the victim (in this case, Leonard) could still be alive and hanging out somewhere beneath the radar. The bad news was that the longer it took to locate a victim, the less likely it was that that person would ever be found.

Chuck pulled out a pile of papers from his black binder; and as he held them lightly in his big, rough hands, he made a short speech about Megan Nicole Kanka.

Megan Kanka grew up in Hamilton Township, New Jersey. She was only seven years old when a two-time sex offender with a history of child molestation invited her into his house to present her with a puppy. There was no puppy waiting for Megan. There was only rape. And death. Eighty-nine days after Megan disappeared, the state legislature of New Jersey passed a law in her honor. Megan's Law still stands. It requires that community workers, teachers, parents and neighbors be notified whenever a known sex offender decides to settle in a New Jersey neighborhood. There are now similar laws throughout the nation, though none are as strict as the one in my home state. Everywhere else, the sex offender has to register but no one is notified.

In the county where we live, there were sixty-three sex offenders listed on the New Jersey Sex Offender Internet Registry at that time. All of them were men. Twenty-four had tattoos. Forty-five had prior offenses against women or girls; eighteen had been caught with boys younger than sixteen years of age.

A thin puddle of sweat had accumulated on the curl of Chuck's upper lip, and his forehead was also pretty moist by the time he had finished his explanation. He took a swig of lemonade and then directed his gaze at me. He asked me if I understood.

I was like, "Hello? This is the twenty-first century. I watch TV."

Chuck seemed satisfied with my response, and so he continued.

"I'm going to show you some pictures of men in Monmouth County who have prior convictions for assaulting young boys. I want you to look at them and tell me if you've ever seen any of them. Arright?"

Mom and I nodded.

Chuck laid them out on the table one by one. They had the faces of carpenters, repairmen, delivery guys, the kind of men we saw every day of our lives all over the place but never really noticed. Each one of them was particular, with his own hairstyle and his own face. These were mug shots, so the subjects weren't smiling at all and every one of them seemed to have the same deeply sad and utterly lost look in his eyes. You could almost feel sorry for them, the way you might feel sorry for a favorite uncle or cousin who had lost his shoes.

They looked sorry for themselves. Each one had his own computer-generated page on which details were listed—age, weight, height, race, hair and eye color. Information about the make and license plate number of the guy's car was also included, along with his identifying body marks and finally what he was accused of doing.

The crimes were described in a style curiously lacking in detail, as if someone had drawn a veil over the actual events.

After flipping through the pages one by one, my first thought was, Well, none of these guys ever actually *killed* a kid. Leonard could be alive somewhere. Violated, but still alive. Odd as that sounds, I found the thought encouraging.

Then another thought occurred to me. These were just the obvious few, the men who'd been caught. There must be hundreds of men driving around Monmouth County every day in their Sunbirds, Corollas, Blazers, Cherokees, Spectrums, Prizms, Luminas, looking for a victim. Hundreds of men who hadn't yet been found out, photographed and registered were probably still at large doing what they do. Where were *their* faces? How many pages of them would appear in Chuck's database but only after being caught, accused, turned in?

Once, a few years ago, Deirdre and I passed a parked blue Chevy Malibu over on Oakland Street. A guy with a face like a fist was sitting low in the driver's seat. His window was rolled down, and he looked as though he was struggling to open a bottle of something that he was holding in his lap. He called us over to help him. Deirdre got there first, and that's when she realized it probably wasn't a bottle of ketchup or whatever that he was struggling with. It was something more personal. Deirdre grabbed my arm and quickly pulled me away from the car. She made me promise not to tell Mom no matter what. At the time I was very disappointed, because I was on the lookout for the opportunity to see an actual penis. Just out of curiosity. Deirdre told me that if that had been my first experience of seeing a penis, I would have been scarred for life.

"Have you talked to Mr. Buddy?" I asked. "I

mean, Buddy Howard. He was the majordomo of the Drama camp."

"I know. I did already." Chuck wasn't giving anything away; his face had gone into freeze mode. "You keep mentioning him. Is there something you think we should know about him?"

"No. It's just he spent a lot of time around Leonard, and well . . . I don't know . . . He was kind of . . ."

"Phoebe?" my mother said, as she rose from the couch and smoothed the front of her skirt, "Go outside and play. I want a word with Sergeant DeSantis. In private."

Telling me to "go outside and play" was as odd a suggestion as telling me to be "present." I haven't gone outside to play since I was about nine years old. But I did it anyway, because I know for a fact that when Mom starts using phony speech like that, something real is about to happen.

I said good-bye to Officer Chuck, and though I don't think he was quite ready to see me go, he waved me off with a cheery "Be good." Whatever that meant. I then stepped into the front yard. The whole neighborhood seemed like it was trapped in a bottle; there wasn't a breeze stirring. There was only one way to be able to hear what Mom had to say to Chuck: Take a deep breath, creep behind the azalea bushes close to the house, crouch down in the dusty earth below the open living-room window and listen. Which is exactly what I did.

We hadn't recognized any of the guys in the pictures. Mom just sat through the whole thing, holding her hand over her mouth as if she couldn't allow herself to speak even if she'd wanted to. Now she said, "How about I top off that lemonade for you, Chuck?"

He said, "No, thanks. 'S good though."

She said, "I guess you have a list of men in your computer who have, well, assaulted girls, huh?"

He said, "We do. Why do you ask?"

She said, "Do any of the men go for girls *and* boys?"

He said, "It's rare. One guy I showed you has two prior arrests. One for each. But like I said, it's rare."

She said, "I was just wondering."

(There was a silence. I heard some ice rattle in

a glass, which I figured was the last of Chuck's lemonade.)

He said, "Well . . . I oughtta—"

She said, "There is one more thing. Ordinarily I wouldn't bring it up, and I'd appreciate it if we could keep it between ourselves. But . . . well . . . um . . . it may have some bearing on Leonard's case."

(More silence. No ice.)

She said, "It's about my husband."

He said, "Uh-huh. What about him?"

She said, "Well, it was never reported. We . . . I didn't . . . it involved one of my girls. My oldest."

He said, "Deirdre."

She said, "Deirdre. Yes. That's right. Um. This is so hard. I . . ."

He said, "It's okay."

She said, "No. It's not okay. I never did anything about it, report it, I mean. To the police or anything. I couldn't. For Deirdre's sake I couldn't. It only happened that one time, but . . . well, that was it. We . . . I . . . he doesn't live with us anymore. Not after that. I never told anyone."

She blew her nose, and from the sound of her

voice, I figured she was crying.

He said, "Why are you telling me now?"

She said, "I know that Leonard was in touch with Jim. A few times. Jim is my . . . my . . ."

He said, "Husband."

She said, "Yes. Was. *Was* my husband. Leonard set up this surprise meeting between the two of us. He was trying to bring us back together. The family."

He said, "He didn't know about—"

She said, "Of course he didn't know. I told you, I never told anyone. But then I started thinking just now, looking at those pictures. Well, you know how the mind works. I just thought . . ."

He said, "I understand. I'll check it out."

She said, "You won't have to report it, will you? I'd rather not dig it all up. It was three years ago, and Deirdre is just getting on with her life and all. It's behind us now."

He said, "Sure. No problem. It'll be between us. I'll look into it."

She said, "I mean, I don't think Jim would ever . . . but you live with a person and you find out they're capable of something . . . it makes you wonder what else you don't know about them."

He said, "I appreciate your . . . honesty, Mrs. Hertle."

She said, "Please, call me Ellen."

He said, "I should get going."

She said, "Right. Yes. Well, thanks. Thank you so much."

And that was that.

As Chuck made his way out the front door and down the pavement to his car, I had to lie down in the dirt close to the house in order not to be seen. After his car pulled away, I heard Mom lock the front door from inside. I was alone, and the whole neighborhood was humming because every AC unit was cranked up full blast except ours, which was broken. An occasional car whooshed by our house. The passengers were sealed up and strapped inside their sports utility vehicles; and they probably didn't notice anything unusual as they passed by. All they saw was a row of dreary houses on some suburban street. Ours was no different from the rest except that the attached garage had been transformed and then extended to the very edge of the property line so that it accommodated the salon. Big deal. Passersby might wonder who in the world would get their hair done in a place like that. They might challenge the artistic merits of Mom's neon HAIR TODAY sign. They might even notice the CLOSED MONDAYS sign, which was displayed in the front window, and then remember that it was indeed a Monday. But no way in the world would a random person suspect that anything out of the ordinary had happened inside our house.

My head was buzzing and my mouth tasted sweet and sour at the same time. I thought I might throw up right there behind the exhausted azaleas, but then I would have to get up and go somewhere else, and I didn't know where else I could go. So I grabbed a handful of dirt with each fist and squeezed it tighter and tighter. I squeezed it so tight that soon the pain in my hands was greater than the sick feeling in the pit of my stomach.

How could she? How could she have made up a story like that just to get Dad in trouble? Even after Dad set Chuck straight, explaining that sometimes ex-wives can be pretty brutal, Chuck would have

Dad's name in his blue binder. Jim Hertle would become a part of Phase Two whether we liked it or not. *What a performance,* I thought. Tears were a nice touch. I knew Mom hated Dad, but I had no idea that she was capable of this. No wonder she didn't want Deirdre "present." Deirdre would have flatly denied everything and exposed Mom for the vindictive and spiteful person that she had revealed herself to be. But like she said, you live with a person, you find out they're capable of something and you can't help wondering what else you don't know about them.

ELEVEN

"That you?" said Chrissie Bettinger's voice through the sad little copper grating of the intercom in Dad's apartment building.

"It's me," I said. "Phoebe."

"Your Dad's not here."

"'S okay. Can I come up and maybe wait for him?"

I guess she was busy weighing the pros and cons of my presence inside her apartment or maybe she was checking out her surroundings to see if the place was presentable for an unannounced visitor. In any case, there was a longish pause before she buzzed me in.

Dad and Chrissie lived in a third-floor studio

apartment. It was the kind of place where all you could do was look out the window and wish you were someplace else. The view of the parking lot was not at all impressive. Once I was inside the room, Chrissie offered me a seat and asked if I wanted a Diet Coke. What could I say?

"Sure," I replied as I pushed aside a stack of outdated style magazines featuring B celebrities with unflattering hairstyles and failed relationships. I took a seat at the table with the turquoise top and the chrome legs. It used to be *our* kitchen table. Years ago when I was just a kid, before Mom had redecorated and relegated the thing to our basement, I'd eaten all my meals off that shiny tabletop. I'd spilled drinks there, banged fists, shed tears.

Chrissie kept her eye on me all the way to the refrigerator and never stopped talking. She'd probably heard all about how I had gotten into the habit of stealing stuff right after my dad ran off, and she was afraid I'd lift one of her semivaluable knick-knacks when her back was turned. But her kind of stuff was the kind I didn't steal, which is to say that I never stole people's personal stuff.

The mall was where I went to pocket makeup and underwear and the occasional food item. It was all just crap and I could've bought it all three times over. I had the money. It's not like I was poor. I don't know why I did it, really. Maybe it was the thrill, the feeling that I was getting away with something that I knew was wrong. Maybe Leonard was right; maybe I was just hoping to get caught. In any case, when I finally did get caught stealing a pair of earrings from the Dress Barn, they called Mom. She was pissed that she had to come pick me up, sit in an airless office and discuss her children with people she didn't know from Adam. I pretended like it was my first time and explained to everyone that I'd stolen the earrings to make up for the loss of my father. Mom didn't buy it, but she recognized that my excuse was going over big with the gal in the polyester skirt who was presiding over the whole affair, so she shook her head thoughtfully and said, "It's been a year of a lotta loss for us." We drove home in silence, but when we got home, Mom gave me a good talking to about how I could jeopardize my future and the family reputation. It didn't stop me from stealing, but still, never in a million years would I have taken one of Chrissie's knickknacks.

Chrissie had a thing for porcelain dolls, china horses, multicolored blown glass clowns, small statuettes of Indian gods and goddesses, plaster angels, paperweights and perfume bottles in the shape of antique cars—all of it basically junk. But the way she had arranged the stuff on a series of shelves almost tricked you into believing there was something there worth admiring.

The same could not be said for Chrissie herself; she obviously put all her effort into her knick-knacking. I knew for a fact that Chrissie considered herself a dead ringer for Julia Roberts. But even if Julia had been contracted to play a piece of Jersey trash who had stolen someone else's husband, she would've never smoked Newports or kept Cheez Whiz in her fridge, and she certainly wouldn't have answered the door wearing a tie-dyed halter top, cutoff jeans and no shoes.

Chrissie had been one of Mom's "helpers" at the salon. She started out as a part-time shampooer, worked her way up to doing combouts and then made a name for herself as an ace blow-dryer. For a while there was talk about her applying for her license and taking over the spare chair in the salon. But then Dad started fooling around with Chrissie, and that changed everything for everyone.

For a while, Mom was about the only person in Neptune who was unaffected by the change; she kept insisting that there was a big misunderstanding about exactly which Chrissie everyone was talking about.

"Not *my* Chrissie," she would say. "That could never happen. No. Remember, I gave Chrissie her first job."

Also, as it turned out, her first serious relationship.

Especially in the early stages, Mom maintained a level of denial that was truly impressive. When someone said that they had spotted the two of them together walking out of the multiplex on a Friday night, Mom considered it a coincidence. When someone saw Dad pumping gas into Chrissie's Honda Civic down at the Mobil station on Division Street,

Mom held to the idea that her husband was just being a Good Samaritan. Her behavior was the stuff that keeps daytime talk shows on the air.

Deirdre and I knew better. Chrissie had once confessed to us that she thought our Dad was "hot." After that, I kept an eye on Chrissie. And Dad. Every time he entered the salon, I couldn't help noticing how Chrissie perked up, fluffed out her dyed-red hair, expanded her bustline and bared her teeth in an effort to attract. It was like watching one of those nature programs on public television where the bizarre mating habits of some forest-dwelling female primate seem perfectly understand-able to her male counterpart, while to us they just seem gross.

Dad was acting pretty weird as well. He signed up at a gym and actually went. Who knows what tortures he submitted himself to there, but when he came home, looking exhausted and invigorated at the same time, he went on and on about the virtues of a good workout and how it was just the thing he'd been missing in his life.

Mom couldn't see what was going on; she didn't

want to. I was only eleven at the time, and even then I knew that forcing her to face the truth wasn't a good idea. It was June, and she was up to her eyeballs in other people's French twists, baby's breath and mother-of-the-bride anxiety. June is traditionally the biggest month for weddings, and weddings are the most compelling reason for a new hairdo. There was a lot of traffic in and out of Hair Today around that time, so it wasn't surprising that Mom didn't have five minutes to sit down and talk sensibly with us. Even so, we knew that she was still months away from revising her opinion of Dad. She needed him to be his old self in order for her to complete her idea of herself, in the same way she needed us to shut up about what was happening so she could get on with the business at hand. Her eyes were closed to anything that didn't support her public point of view about our family life and her business; and her point of view was that everything was just fine.

At the time, Deirdre and I made the fatal mistake of letting things run their own course. But if there's one thing I've learned during my years on this planet, it is this: If things are allowed to run their own course, they will definitely go in a downhill direction.

And sure enough, that's what happened. One hot night in August, there was a big fight that involved tears, slammed doors and a broken floor lamp. Dad left the house. Mom packed his stuff in boxes, and the next day she left it all sitting on the front lawn to be picked up at his earliest convenience. This was major. I tried to understand what was happening, but at the time, adults seemed directed by passions and logic that couldn't exactly be explained by my then-favorite authors. I felt like I was in over my head. Only the melodramatic goings-on of *Wuthering Heights* by Emily Brontë came close; but without the nineteenth-century setting and consumption and wild dogs baying at the moon on the untamed moors, Mom and Dad seemed like amateurs who couldn't hold a candle to Cathy and Heathcliff. They were just Jim and Ellen, another unhappy New Jersey couple headed for divorce court.

Deirdre did nothing to help me get a grip on the

situation. She removed herself from the scene, sulked in her room and told me to stay out of it. Mom cried, got angry and by mid-September had fallen into a major depression. For the first time in my life, I could sit in the living room and read a book for hours without being disturbed. Rather than making me happy, however, this only made me sad and caused me to wonder what the hell had happened to my family. I wanted the old life back. I wanted Dad.

A month later, Mom got out of bed and made up her mind to go on. If anyone dared to mention Dad's name in her presence, she simply smiled. If that didn't work, she increased her wattage and blinded them with her positive attitude about her new life. This had the desired effect of dissuading people from ever bringing up his name and convincing them that maybe it was a good thing, after all, that she was rid of the guy.

Chrissie went on to become famous in certain circles. She was branded "a home wrecker," and though it marked the end of her career as a hair stylist, she landed a well-paying job as a cocktail waitress at a dive called Jeepers that was situated right off the Parkway.

Because Dad had set everyone's unhappiness in motion, he couldn't offer much in the way of comfort; and since he wasn't around, he was no help in sorting things out. He stayed away and was very slow at returning my calls. Once when I ran into him by accident at the 7-Eleven, he jotted down his new address on a paper napkin and slipped it to me just in case I should ever need it. Each time I considered traveling the fourteen blocks to his new apartment building, however, I felt like a total traitor and scrapped the idea. What would I have said to him anyway? Begged him to come home? Told him to leave Chrissie? None of it made sense, and so in time I learned to keep him out of my mind and just go about my business. But that day my business led me straight to him. I thought that if I could just see his face, I would be able to tell what was what and if Mom had been telling the truth.

"How's school?" Chrissie asked, handing me a Diet Coke in a can.

"Over," I said.

"Oh. Right," she replied. "I'd ask how things are at home, but I better not 'cause that's prob'ly why you're here. 'M I right?"

I stared at her painted toenails, a deep shade of purple and definitely do-it-yourself.

"When's my dad coming home?" I asked her.

"He should be home any minute."

The TV news was reporting on some fourteen-year-old boy over in Oaklyn who had just been caught with an arsenal of weapons under his bed and a plan to kill a lot of people. Some gal with a blond pixie cut and puffed bangs was arching her eyebrows at us and saying how the boy had been plotting for six months and was discovered "in the nick of time." The subtitle read PLOT FOILED. The father of the boy was up next.

After the commercial, the father's big face appeared on the screen, and he began telling us that his son was a nice, normal kid who hung out in his room playing with the computer most of the time. Then they showed the arsenal of weapons hidden under the boy's bed—pistols, rifles, knives, hunting gear and two thousand rounds of ammo.

"Isn't he usually home by now?" I asked Chrissie.

"He'll be here."

She jumped up and went into the other room (the bathroom), but I could still hear her loud and clear.

"Wanna paint your nails? What's your favorite color? I'm crazy about this purple. Deadly Nightshade, it's called."

I could tell she wanted to chitchat and possibly even bond with me over girl stuff like nothing ever happened between us, as though we weren't enemies at all. But I couldn't let that happen. Not for a minute.

As she placed her tragic little plastic carryall of nail supplies between us on the table, I said, "What's the story with your hair?"

She looked at herself in the full-length mirror that was propped up against the wall.

"Why? What's wrong with it?"

I told her all about Leonard's hair theory, about how a woman just keeps repeating the same hairstyle from a time in her life when she was at her peak in order to make herself appear younger than she really is. I also explained to her that because I hadn't yet reached my heyday, I was still totally at liberty to experiment, try out different looks. But judging from *her* hair, I told her, I figured that maybe 1990 or '91 had been her really good year.

"You don't like me, do you?" she remarked.

Just then Dad's key turned in the lock. For once he got the timing right. Up until that moment I hadn't realized how much I missed the sound of his bag dropping in the hallway or the casual kicking off of his shoes. I wanted to run to him and throw my arms and legs around his body, burrow my head into his all-day work smell and feel the scratch and tickle of his beard against my neck.

"Phoebe!" he said when he saw me just sitting there at the table, sipping my Coke. "Wow! This is a surprise. What's the occasion?"

"The Pope shit in the woods," I said to him, which was the punch line of a totally lame joke that Dad used to tell years ago when he wanted to make me laugh.

He laughed out loud. Chrissie didn't.

"I'm gonna get ready for work." She went into the bathroom and closed the door behind her.

"So what's up?" Dad asked me.

I thought I would understand everything just by looking at him, I thought I would be able to tell him what Mom said and he would deny it and shrug it off like it was all to be expected, but that's not what happened. I found that I couldn't say anything about it. I was suddenly terrified that it could be true. And then what? All I really could be sure of as I stood facing him was that he was him and I was me and we were standing in the middle of a room, trying to figure out what was going on by looking at each other's faces.

"Nothing," I told him. "Just stopped by. That's all."

"Does your mother know you're here?"

"It's a spur-of-the-moment kinda thing. I'll call her. We got cell phones. Leonard's still missing. He was always trying to get us to call him Leo. I never did, though. I refused. I don't know why. I'm going to call him Leo from now on. I mean it. When he comes back, I really am. What do you think?"

He stood up quickly and said, "I'm going to call your mother."

"Really?" I replied. And then just for good measure, I added, "Actually, I don't think she'd want to know I'm here."

He spun around and squinted at me like I had suddenly gone all blurry on him. But he didn't put down the phone.

"Why not?"

"She thinks I'm sleeping over at Electra's house. We had a fight."

"What about?"

He was asking a lot of questions. *Wait*, I thought. *This is backward. I should be the one asking questions. Not him.*

"Oh," I said, making myself sound bored with the whole business, "she's stressed. Leonard and all. It's getting to her, I guess. All the not knowing." And then in an attempt to sound sarcastic and grown-up, I added, "She's on Zoloft now too. That's fun."

"Still," he said, offering me the receiver of the

phone, "I think she'd want to know where you are."

Chrissie came out of the bathroom transformed. She was wearing a short black skirt, black Reeboks and a red, off-the-shoulder top with south-of-the-border frill. I couldn't help noticing that she had rearranged her hair. It was all bunched up on the top of her head, spilling over like a fountain and held together with a bright red scrunchie.

"I'm going," she said to us. "There's cold cuts in the fridge, bean salad, some cole slaw. And if you feel like boiling water, I got corn on the cob. There's enough for you too, Phoebe. If you want some."

She leaned over and kissed Dad on the lips and arranged his hair as if he was one of her knick-knacks that she was putting back into place. She probably did this every day—kissed him, touched his hair, said good-bye—but somehow I felt that she was doing it for my benefit, to prove her point; and her point was that she had a power over Dad that I didn't. I hated her. Then she was gone.

So much of what I remember about my dad is accidental, just stuff that happened on the fly, but when it was happening I never stopped to think,

"This. This I'm going to remember." Memory isn't like that; it isn't that selective. Anyone who has anything worth remembering will tell you that memory has a mind of its own; things we tend to remember are often not even real memories, but rather the memory of memories that just happen to stick in the mind.

Like this one memory—I was about seven or eight, and I went along with Dad on one of his after-dinner runs to Avon-by-the-Sea. Even though Dad was the big cheese in charge of the entire parts department for a Ford dealership in Asbury Park, he sometimes made after-hours deliveries to garages and auto-body joints all over the county. If one of his customers needed a carburetor or a tail pipe or a fuel line pump, Dad pulled the thing from his inventory and drove it home, and then as soon as dinner was finished, he was back in his car and on his way to deliver it. Once he even drove as far as Newark. The fact that he was willing to literally go the extra mile for his customers made him a hero up and down the Jersey coast. I sometimes went along to keep him company. I told myself that I just wanted to get out of the house for a while, but looking back on it, I see now that there was more than just a desire to move *away* from something. At the time, I was hoping to move *toward* something as well—him.

Dad never said much as we drove the back streets and highways from here to wherever, but that wasn't so unusual. He had always been a guy of few words. Mostly we just listened to news on 1010 WINS or some rock station that played oldies from the seventies and eighties. Sometimes he sang along as if he knew the words. Me too. But this one night the news was on and the reporter was quoting something that someone said, and he actually used the words "quote" and "unquote" before and after the thing that was said.

"What's that mean?" I asked Dad. "Quote, unquote."

"It's those two little marks they make in a book when someone says something," he explained. "Y'know, the actual words."

Then he mimed the quote sign with two of his fingers.

Why should this be something I remember? All those nights sitting together in the front seat of his Country Squire station wagon, all those places we stopped, all those grease monkeys and trucker types I got introduced to ("This is my youngest— Phoebe") and yet my most outstanding memory is "quote, unquote." Makes no sense.

And now years later, sitting with him, this time in the little apartment he shared with his girlfriend, all I could think of was "quote, unquote." Perhaps what I always wanted from Dad was for him to fill the quotation marks with some truth about himself or about life or about how two people who have lived their whole lives together could end up sitting oppo-site each other at a turquoise table on a Monday evening with nothing to say. Had it always been that way? I wondered. I couldn't tell. But this, I thought as I sat there with him, this I will remember.

He made a bed for me out of old quilts and extra pillows and then placed the whole arrangement as far from his own bed as he could manage in a space so small. He insisted that I call Mom and tell her where I was, so I pretended to call her on my cell and got all chatty with no one on the other end about how totally cute the place was and how Chrissie had made us a delicious dinner and how cozy my little made-up bed was. I pretended that Mom was pleased with the idea of my staying over. Dad was suspicious, but he didn't push it. He just said, "Jesus. The Pope really *did* shit in the woods."

Because there was nothing to hold our interest on TV, we flipped channels between an animated feature about dinosaurs and a retrospective of Cher's entire career. After a while, I got so sleepy I couldn't tell the difference between the two.

It was after midnight when a terrible noise woke me up. Someone was leaning hard on the downstairs buzzer. Dad bolted out of bed like a shot and said, "Who is it?" into the intercom.

"Is she there?" I heard Deirdre say. "Is Phoebe there?"

Dad didn't even bother to answer. He just buzzed her in. I'm guessing that she skipped the elevator and sprinted up the stairs two at a time, because she was pounding on the door before Dad could even get his pants on. He fumbled with the locks as quickly as he could, but it wasn't fast enough for Deirdre. When the door swung open, she just came striding in, sailed passed him, no hello. She only stopped short when she saw me lying there, a cocoon in my covers. Her eyes were wildly looking around the room. Her face had gone pale, and her features were indistinct as though her whole self had been stretched thin to the point of dissolving.

"Get up," she said to me. "Come on. You're going home."

"But . . ."

"*Now!*" she shouted, sounding more like my mother than my mother ever did. And then, as if to make her point, she gathered up my clothes. My hand was reaching up toward her in protest, but she simply grabbed hold of my arm and yanked me to my feet. I was not even standing properly when I realized I was headed toward the front door.

"Deirdre," Dad pleaded as he stepped forward to block our way. "Now hold on. Let's just wait a second here and . . ."

But she didn't wait a second. She sidestepped him and kept moving without looking at him. Not a word either. Nothing. She was all forward motion, taking me along with her until we were out the door, down the stairs and out into the cool, soft air of the parking lot.

I was seriously out of breath by the time we got to Mom's car. I couldn't speak. But who cared? Deirdre was in a white-hot rage, and that said it all. Whatever else needed to be expressed was taken care of by the sound of screeching tires hitting the night-slicked streets as Deirdre and I took off toward home.

Somewhere in my brain a timeline began to shift and click into focus. Once in their proper place, events and episodes that had no particular chronology or explanation took on new meaning. Suddenly it all lined up, and everything made sense. Mom and Dad hadn't split because of Chrissie; they had split because of what had happened between Dad and Deirdre. Chrissie came after. Deirdre had changed not because Dad left home; she'd changed because . . . I couldn't even finish the thought.

Deirdre pulled into our driveway and cut the motor. She grabbed the rearview mirror, examining her reflection to make sure that her tears weren't streaking her cheeks.

"Not a word about this," she said. "Not to Mom. Not to anyone. Got it?"

I nodded.

"I went to pick you up at Electra's house. End of story," she said, dabbing her eyelids with a crumpled tissue she had found crammed into the front-seat cushions. "If anyone asks, you were at Electra's. You understand?"

I nodded again. I understood all too well. But the part I didn't understand was why she had never told me. Why hadn't she confided in me about what happened between her and Dad?

I started to cry a little.

"Don't," she barked back at me. "Just don't. Okay?"

"Why didn't you ever tell me?"

"What was I supposed to say? You were way too young to understand. Jeez, I was too young. Just . . . let's not . . . I picked you up at Electra's house. Got it?"

I nodded for the umpteenth time. Deirdre

squeezed my shoulder and said, "Fix your face."

Then she bolted. She was already striding across the lawn toward the house when I got out of the car. All the house lights were on, inside and out. If I hadn't known better, I would've thought that a party was going on in there. But once inside, I saw that it was just Mom and Chuck sitting in the living room, staring at one of Leonard's platform sneakers. It had been placed in the center of the coffee table, and it just sat there like a trophy commemorating some kind of humiliating defeat by the home team. Mom had been crying; her eyes were rimmed with red and her skin had gone papery thin. Chuck just looked worried and kind of blank. I stared at the sneaker, then at Mom, then at Chuck, then at Deirdre. When nobody spoke, I did the drill again—sneaker, Mom, Chuck, Deirdre. Mom tried to open her mouth to speak, but she could only manage a little breath without sound. Unable to offer anything else to the room, she slowly lowered her head onto her knees and let it rest there.

TWELVE

When the reporter from the *Asbury Park Press* telephoned to discuss the case of the missing Leonard, I had an opportunity to speak with her. She asked me a lot of questions, but I kept interrupting her to say, "I feel I ought to mention the platform sneakers again. Okay?" I then offered to draw a picture and send it to her so that she could publish it in the paper. I heard her smile through the receiver as she assured me that just a mention would do the trick.

"Fine," I said into the phone, "just don't forget. It's very important."

As it turned out, I was right. Without the

mention of the sneakers in the local paper, it would never have been found, been fished out of the lake and then ended up sitting on our coffee table.

The good news was that we finally had a clue. The bad news, as Chuck put it, "looks not so good." He had already arranged for a crew, and had gone to the trouble of hiring two professional divers from Atlantic City to explore the murky depths of the lake where the sneaker had been found.

Once upon a time Shark River was the reason people settled in this area. Its beauty was a big draw not only to day-trippers and summer renters, but also, starting in the 1940s and 50s, to folks who were looking for a place to settle down and make a home. People came from all over to see what Neptune had to offer, and many of them discovered all-season houses at affordable prices sprouting up all over the place. For a while, Neptune actually became known as the "Crossroads of the Jersey Shore," and I suppose back then the fact that Routes 18, 33, 35, 66 and the Garden State Parkway all converged here convinced people that this might turn into a real hot spot someday.

No one has ever been able to tell me exactly why the lake was named after a shark. Some people thought maybe an actual shark found its way from the ocean into the freshwater lake. Others said that it used to be called Shirk River, because years ago everyone in the area was pretty lazy and shirked their jobs on a regular basis. Either way, it sounded fishy to me, no pun intended.

I had been out to the area a couple of times as a kid, once with my Brownie troop to collect pinecones to decorate with glitter; and another time with Mom, Dad and Deirdre to watch a pretty dull fireworks display on a drizzly Fourth of July. Though it is technically called Shark River, it looks more like a lake with homes along its wooded shores and sandy inlets where folks can sunbathe. I sort of knew the way to Shark River, but I had no idea where to find the woman who had rescued the sneaker.

I told Chuck that I wanted to meet Peggy Brinkerhoff and thank her personally. He said that wouldn't be necessary.

"Why not?" I asked him.

"Because," he said, "she really doesn't need to

be thanked. The thing washed up at her house. It was just dumb luck."

I didn't push it, because obviously Chuck didn't understand how Peggy had become my only living link to Leonard and it was important that the connection be strengthened if we were ever going to find him. If Chuck had actually known Leonard, he might have understood that the whole world was a pulsing, glowing web of invisible fiber optics that connect one person to another. Leonard would have told him this; Leonard would've explained why it is that the more strands there are, the brighter the overall glow. And then Chuck would've been sympathetic to my idea of contacting Peggy Brinkerhoff; he would've known that what I really wanted was to make a connection with her as a way of creating more light by which we might, just maybe, see Leonard if we really looked.

Mom had just finished making a big pot of coffee, and Chuck was chitchatting and adding milk and sugar the way he liked it. Deirdre had already gone upstairs to bed, so I was sitting alone in the living room, staring at Chuck's big blue binder lying flat on the coffee table next to Leonard's sneaker. This was such a no-brainer. All I had to do was:

1. Open the binder.
2. Find Peggy Brinkerhoff's name and address, which would be written as plain as day in Chuck's perfectly legible handwriting on the first page, right below Dad's name and address.
3. Copy the information on the inside cover of my copy of *Lady Chatterly's Lover* by D. H. Lawrence.
4. Close the binder.
5. Yell good night to Chuck and Mom.
6. Get the hell out of there.

And that's exactly what I did—steps 1 though 6.

The next morning, I set about trying to find a ride out to Shark Lake. I don't usually "set about" doing anything. If I decide to do something, usually I just do it. But these were unusual times, and suddenly not everything I wanted to do made sense to everybody else. Mom definitely would not have agreed to drive me to meet Peggy; she was already hard at work in the salon, and even if I had gone to the trouble of asking her permission, she would have told me that not in a million years was it going to happen because Chuck had told me to forget about it. Deirdre wasn't a possibility either; she was locked in her room, unavailable for comment and, as I've pointed out, without a car.

So who else?

There was my father, but of course after what I'd discovered about him, he was definitely out of the running—not only as a possible ride, but also as a father. As far as I was concerned, I wanted nothing more to do with him for as long as I lived.

Electra was also out. In the old days I might have called her and convinced her to convince her brother to become our designated driver. But ever since the incident at the Fourth of July picnic, we hadn't spoken on the telephone and I saw her only in passing. And that was weird, because I really thought she and I would be best friends for life. I just assumed that we would graduate high school and go to college together. Afterward we would move to the same city (probably New York), live in the same apartment building; we would meet our boyfriends at the same art opening and refuse to marry them. With the success of her artwork and my novels there would be plenty of money; we would buy some land. We would take up with wilder boyfriends who rode motorcycles and weren't afraid to cook. We would bake bread, and our children would be homeschooled. It was a good story.

But the moment Electra began championing the war in Iraq, every time she explained how we had to support our troops even if we thought the whole thing was wrong, the fantasy of our combined future chipped a bit and lost its shine, our present grew thin and our shared past seemed to dwindle and disappear. If I saw her coming toward me on the street, I looked right through her. Once I even turned away. Eventually we settled into a routine that involved ignoring each other, not exactly enemies, but not exactly friends anymore either. When I mentioned this to Mom, she sighed and repeated her latest mantra: "Honey, things change."

And then there was Travis Lembeck. He lived on the far side of Route 33, and because he owned a car and things had certainly changed between us in the past few weeks, I figured he was worth a try. The houses in that part of town were different from ours; they were smaller, less colorful, and many were surrounded not by shrubs and flowers but by stuff that you wouldn't find on the front lawns of any of my neighbors. Broken toys, rusted car parts, damaged furniture, discarded exercise bicycles, abandoned refrigerators and busted-up televisions were a few of the items that doubled as lawn orna-ments up and down Travis's street. Over there, it was as if the boundaries between the insides and the outsides of the houses were not so fixed, and life seemed to spill out of them and into the yards in an alarming and violent manner.

The house where Travis lived was in a state of severe neglect; it had been painted so long ago that the pale minty green was more a memory of the original color than an actual color. The front steps were crumbling, and the pavement leading up to the door was cracked as badly as the devil's back. One of the slabs was missing, like a tooth that had been yanked out just for spite. The gutters at the edges of the roof had long since given up. The mailbox was a milk crate nailed to a wooden post. A single sheet of plywood, which had been nailed up at a haphazard angle over one of the living-room windows, gave the impression that the house itself was half blind.

When I pressed my finger to the doorbell, there was no indication that it worked. I knocked hard on the screen door and waited. Nothing. Just dead morning air.

After a few minutes, Travis appeared at the door, looking all sleepy eyed. He had obviously just woken up.

"Hey," he said.

"Hey," I replied.

Neither of us knew what to say, so I decided to get to the point.

"Look," I began, "I'm not here for a make-out session or anything like that. That's not why I came. So don't . . . I just need a ride and I didn't know who else to ask. If you can't do it, if this isn't a good time, it's totally fine."

He looked out the door, squinting into the daylight, and then said, "I can do it. Hold on a minute."

After he disappeared into the darkness of the house, I leaned in and pressed my face against the screen. All I could see was the hulking presence of a big plaid sofa pushed against the far wall and some stacked boxes. The place didn't look very neat, and the lingering smell of cigarette smoke, beer and burned popcorn was a total turnoff. I went and waited in his car.

"Where to?" he asked as he slid into the driver's seat and started up the engine.

"Shark Lake."

He gave me a look.

"Shark Lake?"

"Yeah." And I said it again, "Shark Lake."

"What's goin' on there?"

As we drove, I told him what I knew about the sneaker, about Peggy Brinkerhoff; and because I thought he could handle it, I told him about the web of brightness that needed to be strengthened. He lit a cigarette and got quiet for about a mile. Then he said, "You're a good person, Phoebe." This, I figured, was his way of telling me that I had a nice personality and he wasn't going to kiss me anymore. He exhaled a big cloud of smoke, and when he was finished he said, "People probably think I'm shit, huh?"

"People?" I said, stalling for time. Then added, "Well, yeah. But me too. I mean, they think that of me too."

Meanwhile, strip malls, car lots, fast-food joints and office complexes whizzed by us in a blur of uninterrupted dullness. All of a sudden Travis suggested that we skip Shark Lake and go to the beach instead.

"Ocean's better any day of the week. Wanna?"

"Can't," I told him without looking at him. "I've got to do this thing. We can go after maybe."

We didn't have any trouble finding Peggy's house. It was a real fixer-upper that had been fixed way up in a cutesy, cottage-by-the-sea sort of way. The shutters had little sailboats cut out of them, and there was a lot of nautical-inspired filigree around the edges of the house. Six sock ducks were planted on the lawn, but because there wasn't a hint of a breeze, they just hung there looking like dishrags on sticks. The same with the American flag, which drooped unpatriotically from a pole. Above the door there was a wooden sign with THE BRINKERHOFFS spelled out cursively in rope.

"Yup," I said to Travis. "This is the place."

I could see the lake out beyond the house, but so much light was skittering across its surface and the glare was so strong, I had to shield my eyes and then finally turn away. I was just about to hop out of the car when something happened to me. My stomach dropped and I felt that something wasn't right. Maybe the reality of Leonard being gone for good was suddenly impossible to ignore. Of course, no one had said it, not yet, but Leonard had drowned in that lake. It was what everyone had been thinking ever since the sneaker washed up. I knew it. Chuck knew it. Everyone knew it. But what if that Peggy woman didn't understand the rules? What if she didn't know that I am a Hertle, and Hertles have always been the kind of people who aren't ready to discuss the obvious until it's staring them straight in the face? I didn't know a thing about Peggy Brinkerhoff other than her name, her address and the fact that she'd found

Leonard's sneaker. She could've been the murderer for all I knew. But then I took another quick look at the sock ducks and the sailboat cutouts and I realized that she was probably not the type of person who was capable of talking about anything too real right off the bat. About her being a cold-blooded killer I was less certain.

"Will you come in with me?" I asked Travis. From the way he turned his head to face forward, I could tell he wasn't expecting to do anything other than just drive me.

"Um," he muttered.

"You don't have to." It *was* a bold request, but I couldn't think of any other way to get myself out of the car and up to the front door. A full five minutes had gone by, and I was still sitting in the front seat unable to move any part of my body. I needed help.

"I dunno. What would I do?" he asked, turning his face even farther from me and looking out toward the brightness of the lake.

"Basic hand-holding," I said, and then I quickly added, "not literally. I mean . . . you know, like support or whatever."

He flicked his cigarette into the street, and we both watched it sit there until the cherry went dead. Then he reached over and took my hand. Literally.

"Sure," he said. "C'mon."

Peggy Brinkerhoff was a sweet-faced woman with a gray perm and piercing pale-blue eyes. She wasn't the type to wear high heels, but she was a convincing argument for their invention. In her stocking feet she was barely five feet tall. If it hadn't been for her voice—a voice that seemed to crack and whine and cut through glass—people might not have paid much attention to her. Now retired, Peggy used to work at Hackensack Hospital in Bergen County as an electroencephalogram technician, recording the brain waves of patients who had suffered blows to the head, migraines, dizzy spells and grand mal epileptic seizures. She wasn't trained to read the wavy lines and sharp peaks that appeared on the computer screen and then spurted from her printer. That was the business of the doctors who were her superiors. But she did get to wear hospital whites and a nametag and was allowed to use the staff cafeteria on Wednesdays and Thursdays. She liked the work. It was easy, steady, and she was promised a good pension. All she had to do was to fix the electrodes to the patients' heads, tell them to relax, turn on the machine and then sit there for the thirty minutes it took to make a record of their cerebral activity. Sometimes, while the machine was busy recording, she read crime novels. Reading crime novels was Peggy's hobby. When she retired from the hospital, reading crime novels became her full-time job. She couldn't get enough of them. Not only did she read the trashy whodunits in paperback form, she was also a big fan of the better writers who wrote the hardbacks, like Patricia Highsmith, P. D. James and Ruth Rendell.

Unlike the reluctant spies, granny detectives and hard-boiled sleuths of novels, Peggy had never come in contact with evil: She herself was a no-crime zone. She had never been mugged or raped or shot at. No one had ever stolen anything from her, hijacked her car, hit her on the head with a lead pipe or left her for dead. In fact, she'd never been a victim of any kind, and neither had anyone in her family. She found this amazing, and she often thought that her husband, Dick, her two grown sons, Frank and Ted, and she herself would seem like very dull characters if they ever showed up in one of her books.

Then one afternoon in the summer of 2001 when Dick was standing next to a boiler (he had a business repairing them), the thing exploded. Technically it was an accident, but because Dick was dead, Peggy felt that finally she had been touched by something bad.

"These things happen," her friends told her.

But Peggy wasn't satisfied with that kind of talk. And so she began questioning Dick's coworkers, going through his files, combing the evidence for clues and getting on everyone's nerves. People rolled their eyes behind her back and said, "Grief," as if that one word could explain all that Peggy was up to. But despite her best efforts, she never found out anything to prove that Dick's death was more than a plain old accident, just one of those things that happen.

Without Dick around, the little house on the edge of Shark Lake suddenly seemed enormous. Briefly, Peggy considered moving; but really, where would she go? Her sons lived nearby. The lake was a kind of comfort. And she was already familiar with the names of all the streets and neighboring townships. Every morning when she sat down with the local newspaper, she scanned it page by page for headlines of crimes and misdeeds. Usually in the first paragraph the location of the crime was mentioned, and usually Peggy was able to picture the scene exactly. Incidents involving drunk driving, petty thievery, carjackings, hit-and-runs, B and Es (breaking and enterings) and muggings became her new hobby. She also followed stories about corporate embezzlement, child molestation, drug busts, domestic violence, stolen cars and her favorite, missing children.

Peggy knew that identifying criminals was not such an easy business. Even if one were able to examine pages and pages of a person's brain waves, there was nothing there to indicate that that person was evil or capable of performing deeds that would later show up in the newspaper under headlines like "Car Thief Drags Victim 1 Mile." Dr. Seligman, the man who had trained Peggy in her job, had explained all this to her during one of her training sessions. He pointed out the various lines on the printout and explained to the class that an EEG was a snapshot of the brain's activities, not a blueprint of its content or hidden intent. Aha, she thought at the time, so that's it—evil could be riding those waves and no one would ever be the wiser. She decided that it was the same in everyday life—you just couldn't spot the criminals in the crowd until they actually *did* something to identify themselves. What was needed was a clue. A clue, Peggy felt, was like a spiky peak of agitation on the computer printout of human behavior, an indication that there might be trouble up ahead. When Peggy mentioned her theory to Dr. Seligman after class, he looked at her blankly, blinked and said, "Well, perhaps. I really don't know." And then he disappeared down the hallway.

Naturally, when the article featuring Leonard appeared in the *Asbury Park Press*, Peggy paid close attention, imagined the locale of the incident and made notes. She memorized all the details or, as she liked to call them, "clues." The fact that Leonard was a townie heightened her excitement and allowed her to feel more involved than if Leonard had hailed from, say, Wildwood, New Jersey. So imagine her thrill when she spotted the platform sneaker bobbing on the inky blackness of Shark Lake right outside her cottage. She fished it out with a long pole and then sat with it for several hours before dialing 911, savoring her good fortune.

Peggy was totally stoked to have company. She served us doughnuts and soda, and when she found out that Travis hadn't had a proper breakfast, she made him sit down to a meal of eggs and bacon and toast and juice. While she cooked, she told us her whole life story, a story that included the bit about brain waves and evil. Travis didn't say a word throughout; he ate whatever was put in front of him and watched Peggy like she was a TV show. I asked questions just to be polite. As Peggy zipped around the kitchen riding what looked like a pretty impressive caffeine buzz, I couldn't help but notice that she would have made a fine candidate for one of Leonard's makeovers, because the woman defi-

nitely needed something. Her floral smocklike top
and pink polyester slacks were hopelessly last century. Her dust-colored hair was permed within an
inch of its natural life. And the heavy glasses that
kept slipping down her nose, so far down that her
nostrils were often completely closed, were a disaster.
After about an hour, I began to wonder how she
could muster so much talking breath while her
brain received so little oxygen.

When she started to discuss the big search
party that was scheduled for the following day and
then yabber on about how experienced the divers
were and what they might discover, Travis said that
it was getting late and we ought to get going. Peggy
insisted that I take some of her homemade blueberry
cheesecake to Mom and Deirdre. She didn't even
wait for me to say yes or no, just wrapped it up for
me. Travis went outside to wait by the car.

"Nice boy," Peggy said. "Quiet, though. Known
him long?"

"Kinda," I told her, which was true. I had
known him all through grammar school. He had
been in Deirdre's grade, so I got to watch him grow

up alongside her and graduate with her. And, of course, I'd kissed him. But I didn't feel like getting into the particulars, so I left it at that.

By the time I made my escape, Travis wasn't in the car or anywhere near it. I called his name, but there was no answer. I walked around to the side of the house, swinging my little to-go bag and trying to remember why I'd thought visiting Peggy was a good idea.

Travis was standing at the edge of the lake, gazing out, his balled-up hands pushed deep into his back pockets, his elbows jutting out to either side of him.

"You all right?"

"Yeah," he answered without turning around. "Just thinking, that's all."

"'Bout?"

"I dunno. Getting out, leaving town."

"For good?"

"And maybe about my mom. I was thinking how she woulda been 'bout Peggy's age. It'd all be different if my mom was still around to make breakfast, cakes and shit like that. Maybe."

Everyone in this town had heard the story of how Travis's first house burned to the ground with his mother trapped inside it. They never found out what caused it. There were rumors about how the boy liked to play with matches, about how he used to light them and throw them against the house; but nothing could be proven. Most people pitied him, especially when he and his dad became homeless. Afterward, he went to live with a neighbor because there was nowhere else for him to go. There were like a million bake sales that year for his family, which now consisted of just him and his father. Eventually his father scraped enough money together to buy the house over on Stanhope.

"How old were you when she . . . she died?" I asked him.

"Eight."

I wanted to say something that I had learned since Leonard had gone missing. I wanted to explain to Travis how sometimes it's only when a person leaves that you begin to feel just how much space they occupied in your life. But I was afraid that it would come out sounding wrong, especially to someone who was busy missing his dead mother. Instead, I just moved in close beside him and took his hand in mine, and we stood there looking out at the lake together for a good long while.

As he drove me back home, I sat so close to him, I could feel the heat of his body moving into mine. The fact that I could feel my body at all was a big improvement over the day-to-day numbness that I had come to expect as normal. I was alive at that moment, and full of wonder because I'd suddenly become the kind of girl who sat up close to a boy in the front seat of his Nissan while he was feeling sad about his mother. When he took his right hand off the steering wheel and reached over to take my hand in his, I experienced the same giddy surge of happy hormones that overtook me at the mall when I stole something. Everything in the world around me, and Travis in particular, became instantly transformed by this gesture. The very atoms of the air were seemingly turned inside out, revealing possibilities that had been lying dormant and just waiting for their cue to appear.

But more than anything, it was me who seemed

most affected, most visibly turned inside out. My hair just seemed to fall right. My legs, rather than being the two twin pegs holding up this huddled bundle of self, looked to me like the means a beautiful girl might use to get where she wanted to go. Every one of my fingers, entwined in his, looked like it could handle a ring. And though I did my best to hide the exquisite pain of this awakening, I'm sure that something different was showing in my eyes when I looked over at him. How strange, I said to myself, that it was Leonard who brought Travis and me together. So typical of him. He had found a way to give me a makeover after all, working from the inside out.

THIRTEEN

Mom didn't intend to close up the shop. Her original plan was to wake up early, get busy with appointments and hopefully forget that people were searching the lake for Leonard's body. But when her first customer of the day, Mrs. Artman, jokingly accused Mom of rolling her curlers too tight as a way of giving her a natural face-lift, Mom threw down the tools of her trade and stomped upstairs to her room.

I finished up Mrs. Artman and then called the rest of Mom's customers to reschedule. Everyone was very understanding. I spent the rest of the day trying to distract myself by reading *Lady Chatterly's Lover*. Every time the phone rang, I held my breath; even Lady Chatterly's orgasm, which is described by D. H. Lawrence as a kind of rippling brilliance with flapping feathers, couldn't hold my attention. I listened with all my senses until I heard Mom's voice reassuring the person on the other end of the line that nothing had happened—nothing yet. No word. And then I went back to the shuddering convulsions of Lady Chatterly's molten insides.

At about five o'clock, Chuck's car pulled up in front of our house. Through the living-room window, I watched him get out and walk toward the house looking like bad news in shorts and hiking boots.

Of course he would come by in person. Chuck wasn't the type to make you cry over the phone, then hang up and leave you so that you could wander around the room, trying to figure out what to do next.

"Mom!" I called upstairs, trying to sound as normal as any kid in a TV sitcom. I opened the front door for Chuck before he even had a chance to ring the bell. He just stood there looking at me. That's when I knew. His blue eyes were brimming

with the lake and everything that he'd seen down there. The corners of his mouth were turned down in what I would call an expression of grim determination. He didn't need to say a word.

Mom came down the stairs slowly, carefully, like a blind person feeling her way along the banister. When she reached the bottom step, she looked up at Chuck and her legs just gave way and folded underneath her. She fell onto the first step and sat there, looking horribly helpless and small. When she finally let out a loud, unruly wail, the hairs on my neck and arms stood up like the tiny antennae of a bug trying to figure out the best direction forward.

Chuck tried to speak, but every time he opened his mouth, Mom said, "No." She said it a lot. She said it so many times that Chuck finally gave up trying to offer his condolences or to explain anything.

Deirdre, who had rushed downstairs when she heard Mom's first anguished cry, tried to take control of the situation.

"Pheebs! Get Mom some water. Hurry!"

By the time I came back from the kitchen,

sloshing the water over the rim of the glass and onto the carpet, Deirdre was already helping Mom up the stairs and back into her bedroom.

"No," she kept saying. "No."

Chuck and I stood there at the bottom of the stairs, watching until they were out of sight. I had no idea what to do next. Nothing like this had ever happened to me before. Not even close. When Nana Hertle had died, we had been expecting it for months. After her cancer progressed and she slipped into a month-long coma, death was the logical next step. Barring a miracle, we knew what was coming. But this was different.

I stared at Chuck, but to be perfectly honest, he looked about as clueless as I felt, so I adopted the tone and gestures more appropriate to a daytime TV drama than to my usual self. I was on automatic, using remote control.

"Shall we sit down?"

As Chuck described the scene down by the lake—the divers, the boats, the netting, the walkie-talkies—I began to imagine that he was just someone on TV and any minute they would break for a commercial so I would be able to leave the room and get a snack. But the commercial never came. And when he finally got to the part I'd been dreading, the part where they found Leonard, I was stuck in my seat.

"One of the divers came up," Chuck said, wiping his brow with the back of his hand and then continuing with the story. "They'd been up and down all afternoon. Good guys. Really good guys from over in Atlantic City. Total pros. But they didn't find anything. Not till this one time when he comes up. Brian's his name. Brian came up and shouted over to us. All the boats headed to where he was. I was in one of the boats. We gave a signal to cut the motors. It was quiet. Both divers, Brian and this Russian guy, Vlad, went down again. After a while we lowered a towline with a gurney type thing from one of the boats. The boat had a winch, and once we got a signal from below, we brought it up . . . brought *him* up . . . Leonard."

Chuck paused here. He spotted the water glass that had been sitting on the coffee table; he picked it up and took a long gulp. This is what people do in movies or novels, I thought, when they want a dramatic pause.

"You sure you want to hear all this?" he asked me.

"Yes."

Chuck had come all the way to our house, and I figured he needed to tell *someone*. Besides, this was just a TV show I was watching. None of it was real. Dad didn't live with Chrissie Bettinger; he still lived with us and was due home from work any minute. Deirdre was upstairs, her old self, listening to music on her computer, talking on the phone, combing her long, luxurious chestnut-colored hair. Mom was in the kitchen making microwave meat loaf and julienne vegetables. Leonard was downstairs wrapped in tulle and covered in glitter, inventing a look that would quietly appall us when he finally made an entrance at dinner. Meanwhile, I was watching public television in the living room, no commercials.

"We're considering it a homicide," Chuck said. "We still have to do an autopsy, but there's enough evidence to suggest foul play."

Homicide. Autopsy. Evidence. Foul play. This, I said to myself, was not your usual Wednesday. Peggy Brinkerhoff must be having a field day.

In an effort to keep my voice from trembling out of control, I pretended that I was Sam Waterston in an episode of *Law & Order*.

"What kind of evidence?" I asked Chuck. I thought I sounded pretty convincing.

"The body was tied up," he said. "Tied up with rope and weighted down with an anchor."

This was the first time anyone had referred to "the body"—as though Leonard himself had been separated from it, as if they had become two separate things.

We sat there together letting the news sink in. Leonard was gone. Someone had killed him. And though the question remained unspoken, it was enormous. Why would anyone do such a thing to Leonard? I've watched enough TV in my life to know that sometimes a motive can lead you to the person responsible for the crime. But, as Chuck explained it to me, "We're up the river without a clue." In other words, we didn't have a motive or a suspect.

"Is my dad in the running?" I asked him. "As a suspect, I mean."

Chuck grabbed the hefty knobs of his knees tight, gave them a hard squeeze and then looked around the room. He was either making sure no one was listening to our conversation or he was hoping to get a second opinion about how to proceed.

"We're not ruling anything out," he finally replied. "We need more information. But I had a talk with him yesterday, and it seems unlikely."

Deirdre came down the stairs and made apologies, told us Mom was resting and asked if Chuck needed anything.

"Well, actually," Chuck said, "there is something."

Then he lifted the water glass and took another dainty sip. A fly was buzzing around the living room; it was a mad thing, colliding with lampshades, ponging off the window screens and desperate for an exit.

Chuck put the glass down, took a deep breath and said: "We're going to need someone to come down and identify the body."

Since Deirdre didn't know the full story, I was afraid she might volunteer without understanding exactly what was involved. Mom couldn't do it—not until she had moved beyond the "No" stage, and I figured that wouldn't be happening any time soon.

"When?" I asked.

As soon as I opened my mouth, I realized that I had signed up for the job without meaning to.

"Tomorrow morning. About ten o'clock. I'll give you the address."

Then Deirdre, who was still standing in the middle of the room, asked, "Are you sure, Pheebs?"

I was not sure. I was not sure of anything. And wasn't she the older sibling? Wasn't she supposed to take care of these difficult, dreadful things when they came up? Wasn't it her job to protect me? But the world was spinning way too fast, and I was scared that any minute gravity would stop working and we would all be flung off the face of the planet into an outer space of danger and uncertainty. Somehow the simple movement of my head bobbing up and down kept us all in place. It was the least I could do.

Chuck wrote down the address of the morgue on a piece of paper that he had torn from his blue binder. And as he did, he said, "It'll have to be your mother who identifies the body. Or your father. Someone over eighteen." He then left the information on the coffee table, as if handing it to me would have been too much of a dare. Deirdre and I walked him to the door. He turned and looked at both of us, as if he wanted to say one last thing.

"What?" I asked.

"Nothing," he said wearily. And then, focusing his big baby blues on me, he added, "Be good, okay?"

"Sure."

Later, when I was lying in my bed, I could almost feel the piece of paper still sitting on the coffee table; it was vibrating down there, throbbing, keeping me awake. Minutes went by. Hours. But at some point I must have fallen asleep, because I had a dream.

In the dream I was sitting up to see Leonard standing at the foot of my bed. He was soaking wet, his face and clothes dripping lake water onto the yellow carpet in my room. I worried that the water would stain the carpet even though it's old and worn and faded around the edges. Leonard was smiling at me as if there was nothing in the world worth getting upset about. I opened my mouth to speak, but before I could say a word, he reached out and offered me his closed fist. Then slowly, very slowly, he opened his hand to reveal the gold Yves St. Laurent money clip.

"Thank you," he said.

When I woke up (this time for real), it was morning and my eyes were wet with tears. I had been crying in my sleep, and Leonard was still dead.

By nine o'clock Mom had pulled herself together just enough to get herself down to the county morgue at the appointed time. She said I could come along for the ride, but really I could tell she needed me there more than she was willing to express. Without her makeup or breakfast or her trusty smile, she looked like a temporary version of herself, a stand-in sent to do the job.

We sat in a large wide corridor with high ceilings. The floors were highly polished and there wasn't a single picture on the wall, no plants, no people, and no sign of life. The place smelled of antiseptic and formaldehyde. The stillness bothered me, because every sound was amplified and seemed more important than it actually was—a door opening, a cough, a pen hitting the hard floor. These noises were proof that even in a place where life had stopped for some, life was going on for the rest of us.

There were swinging double doors, and just beyond them, I knew, bodies were laid out in cool compartments, oblivious of the ongoingness of everything. And perhaps out of respect for those bodies, we the living tried to keep the ongoingness to a minimum.

Chuck arrived right on time, and the minute I saw him, I realized what a sorry sight Mom and I were, the two of us sitting there on the bench, leaning against the wall, dressed in whatever, no makeup, waiting. Chuck tried to prepare Mom for what she was about to see. As he spoke, I focused on his mouth, his teeth, his big tongue, and wondered if he liked his dentist, if he flossed regularly, and if he had a girlfriend.

"Is it all right if Phoebe comes in too?" Mom

asked as she slipped her hand into mine. She was shaking.

Chuck looked me straight in the eyes and then gave a quick glance down the empty corridor.

"Sure," he said. "Come on."

We followed him through the swinging doors. Immediately I was aware of a deep hum in the room. I tried to pretend that the high-pitched buzz was the baseline of some angelic chorus keeping a vigil over the corpses as they began the long, unsteady journey away from their corporeal selves, but it didn't work because I knew it was really the sound of the refrigerated units that lined the wall.

We were introduced to a guy wearing wire-rimmed glasses and a knee-length lab coat. His job couldn't be less fun, I thought to myself. I mean, opening and closing drawers with cadavers in them, arranging bodies for viewing and dealing with the undisguised grief and horror of family members is nobody's idea of how to spend a summer day. And though for the life of me I couldn't tell you the guy's name, I found myself wondering about his home life and what his wife thinks about when he kisses her. I noticed that the guy's hands were delicate and waxy looking, like fake fruit; he used both of them to grab hold of the bright chrome handle on one of the refrigerated drawers and give it a good, solid yank.

I had never seen a dead body before. Nana Hertle had been cremated, so when we went out in Mr. Federman's boat to dump her into the high sea on a stunningly hot day in the middle of October, she had already been reduced to a box of ashes. We poured her remains over the side of the boat, and though some of the dust of her blew back onto our life jackets, most of her disappeared into the ocean without a sound. My dad said a few words, and that was that. Other people I've known about who died were famous, so their bodies live on in celluloid form, untouched by decay or rot or the effects of having spent a month at the bottom of a lake. Leonard's death was something entirely new for me.

His whole body was covered with a white sheet made of a very coarse material, like linen or sailcloth. I forced myself to look at the lump of him under the sheet, lying on a shining, cold slab of chrome. He came out headfirst. I told myself to pay attention, pay attention, pay attention, because really, when would you ever have this kind of experience again? But the moment I saw that shocking bit of flesh sticking out of the bottom of the cloth, too swollen and bluish to be the big toe of the Leonard I remembered, I felt all interest drain from me. The toenail seemed like just an old piece of plastic that had been stuck on like an afterthought with Elmer's glue. Then the hum in the room got louder and seemed to be coming from inside my head. I heard the high notes of other angels coming in as if on cue. And then there was nothing.

They say that fainting is the body's response to a sudden lack of blood flowing to the brain. The central nervous system is designed in such a way that in moments of extreme distress, the brain has a plan; it knows just how and when to knock you out and send you down for the count. Then, whether the cause is physical or psychological, the idea is to get your head down closer to the ground, where the blood can once again begin to circulate in your brain. It's an ingenious safety mechanism.

But when it happens to you and your body is sprawled out on the cold tile floor, time stops and the movie of your life is, for a moment, interrupted. You are gone. When your eyes finally flutter open and you grope your way toward consciousness, the picture has been changed completely. You are horizontally arranged at shoe level, staring up at the concerned faces that are hovering above you. And there is a gap of time you can't account for.

"What happened?" I asked.

"You fainted," said Chuck. His eyes were as big as teacup saucers, and he was offering me water from a paper cup that was shaped like a little upside-down dunce cap. "Here. Drink this."

Chuck and the guy in the lab coat got me onto my feet. They helped me out through the double doors and then into the hallway, where they propped me up on the bench. Mom kept saying, "I knew this wasn't a good idea."

Once everyone was convinced that I was fine, considering that I'd just fainted and fallen on my face, they all went back inside to finish what they'd come to do.

As I sat there in the chilled and narrow corridor of the county morgue waiting for my mother, I tried not to think about the horror of Leonard's toe. I forced myself to focus instead on the details of last night's dream, the image of Leonard standing wet and happy at the foot of my bed, thanking me for finding his clip. I tried to reconstruct the living Leonard to counteract the image of that toe—him ridiculously dancing like Britney Spears in front of a full-length mirror; him standing beside the before-and-after photo booth and waiting for his first victim; him with his toenails glued and glittered and leaving tracks across the living-room carpet; him tearstained and mortified when we had to wake him from a nightmare; him walking like wrecked royalty down the corridors of our high school while everyone made fun. And as I played these memories over in my mind, I suddenly realized how difficult it must have been for Leonard, and how much he had had to overcome in order to appear that happy. Despite his circumstances, he'd always put on a good face and rarely let on that he was struggling. He was so determined to make the best of everything, to fit in, to triumph over his tragedy.

I sat there on my bench, breathing in the antiseptic air, aware of the ongoingness of the world and thinking of everything that Leonard would miss. And then, because I couldn't stand it another minute, I crowded my mind with memories of the living Leonard and flooded them in a light so absolutely bright, tragedy didn't stand a chance.

FOURTEEN

Leonard would have wanted flowers, a few tears, and of course plenty of style. Afterward he would have expected a party, music, a light lunch and perhaps cocktails. But he would have been the first to remind us to keep the service brief and to the point. Everybody, he would have told us, has things to do and places to be. It was, after all, a Saturday. In the end, we chose the basic cremation package from Fallucci's Funeral Home; they picked up Leonard's body from the morgue, reduced him to ashes and bits of bone and teeth, and then handed over his remains in an attractive bronze urn, which they had named "The Standard." All for $550.

The Urn of Leonard was then transported by car to Monmouth Memorial Park, a modern overly designed cemetery where the gently dipping, rising hills extend into a kind of infinity, making it look like someone's idea of suburban Heaven. The word "cemetery" is rarely used when referring to Monmouth Memorial Park. For as long as I can remember, people have called it "The Park," as if it served some recreational purpose.

The first thing you notice when you come into The Park is that there are no headstones; only thousands of discreet bronze markers embedded into a square mile of earth like little metal door-mats. Occasionally the grass is interrupted by a potted geranium or a memorial wreath—stuff left behind by families who make a habit of checking in with their dead members and decorating their places of eternal rest.

Almost every one of my mother's customers showed up at the funeral. And more astonishing was the fact that they were all wearing that one smart black dress that Leonard had insisted they add to their wardrobes.

"You have to, have to, *have to* . . . ," Leonard told each one of them. "You *have to* own a black dress. At least one. It's de rigueur. Y'know, for when you get invited to cocktail parties and the like."

That these women had lived in Neptune, New Jersey, almost their entire lives; that they had husbands who were either retired or dead; that they lived on fixed incomes and had last been invited to a cocktail party when Ford was president—none of this discouraged Leonard in the least. The women had tried explaining to him that a black dress just wasn't as essential as, say, groceries, and maybe Leonard didn't exactly understand their lifestyle.

"Nobody invites me nowheres," Mrs. Geleski pointed out to him, as she counted out her singles to pay for her perm at the reception desk.

Leonard closed his eyes, shook his head and held up his hand as if to stop the flow of yet another unwanted thought. "Mrs. G., let me tell you something. This has nothing to do with lifestyle. This has to do with the fact that if you *had* a smart black cocktail dress, people would start inviting you places."

Eventually they gave in to his suggestion.

But who knew that they would all end up at his gravesite, parading their black dresses in his honor. In some sense it was a real fashion coup. Leonard had done more for the women of Neptune than the combined talents of Calvin Klein and Donna Karan. The only sadness was that Leonard himself wasn't around to enjoy his success. His was one of the classiest funerals Neptune had seen since 1989, when basketball's world free-throw champion, Bunny Levitt, was buried, and Bunny's funeral wasn't nearly so well attended as Leonard's.

"Who *are* all these people?" Deirdre groaned as she tossed her lit cigarette behind a mausoleum and pulled a stick of gum from her slim black purse. She was wearing a simple black sheath and a pair of black patent leather flats. Her hair had long since grown in, but she continued to keep it short, which made her look like an obscure French movie star who refused to conform to the modes of conventional beauty. She knew as well as I did who everybody was, because like me, she'd known almost every single one of them since before she was born. I think she meant to ask, Why are so many people showing up at Leonard's funeral?

Deirdre didn't have much interest in the effect Leonard had on the women of Neptune, on Mom, on me and, until her hair debacle, even on herself. She never spoke about the fact that he had somehow managed to transform her or how he had talked her into it. But staring at her as she stood there in the cemetery grass looking tall and elegant, refined and slightly detached, I could see that the end result wasn't such a bad thing after all. Leonard had lifted the burden from her of always being Neptune's golden girl, and with one decisive action, which included a barbershop, he had inched Deirdre toward a new life as an independent woman.

"Look," Deirdre said, pointing with her chin to a bunch of young people who were gathered near the grave. "Sheesh. Talk about nerve. Who invited them?"

Ms. D. and Mr. Buddy were standing head and shoulders above a group of kids from Drama Camp who buzzed around the gravesite like the extra townspeople from a production of *Spoon River*, except they weren't dead. And though Ms. D. and

Mr. Buddy were trying to get certain factions to stop practicing leg extensions in public and explaining to others why expressing grief with jazz hands was out of the question, it was a losing battle. For many of the Drama Camp kids, death was something that either happened onstage with a sword, stage blood and plenty of choreography, or was discussed by the principal players after the fact in rhyming couplets. In both cases, the actor who played the part of the deceased could be seen later that day at the local Wendy's ordering fries and a frosty. Actual death was something else; its finality was a new experience. And like many new experiences for the people of the theater, it became a fresh opportunity to act.

"We're so sorry for your loss," Mr. Buddy said to Deirdre and me. He had walked over when he noticed us staring in his direction.

"Thanks," said Deirdre. She lit another cigarette and narrowed her eyes at him.

"You've probably heard," he continued, unfazed by Deirdre's chill and smoke, "but we're going ahead with *The Tempest*. You know. For the kids. But we're dedicating the entire production to the memory of Leonard. I hope that's okay."

"Are you kidding?" I said. "That's so nice of you, Mr. Buddy. Really. We'll tell our mom. And maybe we'll come see it."

Mr. Buddy looked down at his shoes. They were ecru canvas lace-ups with leather soles, and already soaked by the wet grass. They were probably ruined, but Mr. Buddy didn't seem to mind. He tapped the blades of wet grass with the tip of his soaked toe.

"Leonard was a very special boy."

Deirdre and I couldn't say a word.

"Very talented," he added.

Mr. Buddy glanced back behind him to see Ms. D. struggling with the kids. She shot a pleading look at him.

"Without Leonard, I don't think Sal and I would've realized our love for each other."

"Sal?" Deirdre wanted to know.

"Oh. Sorry. Ms. Deitmueller."

Before we could catch ourselves, Deirdre and I let out a simultaneous burst of laughter. Deirdre and I had both had it in mind that Sal was a short, stocky Italian guy with a handlebar mustache and bushy eyebrows who had fallen madly in love with Mr. Buddy. The idea that Ms. D. was Sal knocked us for a loop. But Mr. Buddy, trouper that he was, plowed on.

"I realize that this isn't exactly an ideal situation for an announcement of this kind, but I wanted you two to know. Ms. Deitmueller and I have decided to get married during Christmas break. And well, if it hadn't been for Leonard . . . You see, he made us realize . . . I guess he saw it before we did. He was like that, wasn't he?"

Deirdre dropped her cigarette in the grass. By the time she'd lit another, Mr. Buddy had returned to Ms. D. We just stood there, trying to see this unlikely couple, as Leonard did, in a whole new light.

At that moment, Uncle Mike, Mom's brother and Leonard's legal guardian, arrived. He got out of a rental car and took in the scene before him. He had just flown in from Mexico, and he was leathery tan and wearing a peasant shirt and sandals. He had strong, dark features, the kind a child could draw from memory—thick, dark, wavy hair, a single line of eyebrow that sat heavily above his deep-set glinting eyes, and a strong Roman nose that sailed above his prominent chin. Mike was a man who met the world face first, but his expression of perpetual surprise was proof that he was unprepared for almost anything that the world could dish out. Certainly he was unprepared for Leonard's funeral. It was as if he had been raised by bears and stumbled out of the wilderness to attend a civilized rite, the particulars of which he could only dimly recall. He was too large, too clumsy at the gravesite, and by the time he found us, he was already sobbing.

"Oh, Phoebe," he sighed, burying his big head in my sky-blue tank top and hugging me hard around the waist. Even the scent of his cheap cologne couldn't disguise the smell of cattle and late-night Mexican campfires that had seeped into him over the past year.

"I know," I said. Though, in fact, I didn't. Not quite.

Uncle Mike had dumped Leonard on our doorstep. He'd been foolish enough to assume that Leonard had enough spunk to get him through no matter where he was plunked down. I couldn't decide whether to feel sorry for Uncle Mike or be furious with him. In any case, everyone's sorrow at the gravesite seemed muted next to his.

My mother, who was usually so adept at consoling the grieving women at her salon whenever one of them lost a husband or a child or a beloved pet, had suddenly misplaced the knack. She left Mike to his tears and stood beside him, just staring out into the daylight as if she was waiting for a bus. Occasionally she moistened her lips with her applicator (a touch of Glossimer with high-beam gleam by Chanel), and sometimes she snuck a wad of tissue under the lens of her large round sunglasses. At one point in the ceremony, she leaned over and whispered in my ear, "Are you holding up okay?" Other than that, she showed no signs of life. She had clearly lost the ability, or desire, to connect with others.

After much discussion about what to wear to the funeral, Mom chose a bright-pink Ann Taylor A-line sleeveless dress and black patent leather pumps. Deirdre declared that it was a little upbeat, even for a daytime funeral. Mom didn't care what anybody thought and announced that she was going to wear it anyway. This, as it happened, was the ensemble that had been chosen for her by Leonard himself just days before he disappeared. He chose it, he told her at the time, to coincide with her new, younger, more "with it" look. Deirdre and I didn't say a word after that. We just looked at each other in the hallway as Mom finished dressing. We knew what was happening. Wearing that particular ensemble to Leonard's funeral was Mom's way of signaling to the crowd that she placed the good opinion of a ghost above that of any Earthbound well-wisher standing by the grave. And Mom was no fool; she knew that she'd be a standout next to all that basic black.

And that is exactly what happened. When I saw her, a bright spot of hot pink in the cemetery, I thought, *This. This I will remember.*

"Thank you so much," she said to people who paused to offer her their heartfelt sympathies.

"Yes, we are getting through it."

"No, you've done so much already."

Her affect, flat and semidetached, had a lot to

do, I guessed, with the Zoloft, which had finally kicked in; but to strangers it must have appeared an act of sheer will on her part, a strategy devised by a grieving guardian to get through a tragic event, a brilliant performance.

My mother took the loss of Leonard pretty hard. From the very beginning, his presence in our household seemed to enlarge her own. He had a knack for making her into more of the woman she had always wanted to be. Leonard never rolled his eyes or talked back to her, he didn't turn away from her bad taste or make demands and give ultimatums the way Deirdre and I always did. Leonard had taken my mother seriously, he had appreciated her beauty business, he had laughed at her jokes and encouraged her emerging sense of purpose. Without Leonard, Mom was without her biggest cheerleader, and so she reverted to her old accustomed self, the self that simply smiled in the face of adversity, the self that didn't want to change.

But it wasn't only Leonard's death that had hit my mother so hard and broken her heart; it was as if all her other losses over the past few years had been suddenly stirred up by this single incident and she was feeling all the hurt at once. Her divorce from Dad, Deirdre's depression and withdrawal, all the failed hopes and disappointments she had somehow endured and survived. Leonard's death tore into everything, until she was now a person who, despite her best efforts, had been irrevocably changed by events beyond her control.

A hard, heavy rain had fallen during the night, and the air was clear and clean, the sky unbearably blue. The grass up and down the sloping hills of The Park was soggy, and the ground shimmered in the bright morning sunlight like green Christmas foil. As we stood there, the soles of many shoes got soaked straight through; my flip-flops squished beneath me, some pumps were ruined. But no one mentioned the wet ground or complained of its effect. This was just one of the inconveniences that the living had to endure, and under the circumstances, we simply stood our ground and faced forward.

Father Jimbo had agreed to officiate at the grave. A few days before, he'd told us in his confessional voice that until recently the Catholic Church considered cremation an unsanctified form of burial but then assured us that he didn't expect much of a problem. And maybe we would like to make a "donation" to the church in Leonard's name. Mom forked over a hundred bucks, and sure enough on the day of the funeral Father Jimbo showed up in his black Lexus with all the appropriate prayers, paraphernalia and expressions for bereavement and burial.

Father Jimbo was Ethiopian. He had smooth dark skin that shone like an espresso bean. His features were narrow and elegant, and his limbs were thin and long. Because he jogged ten miles every morning, he moved with the grace of a professional athlete. Father Jimbo's real name was Ngimo, but he soon discovered that Ngimo was a name as difficult for Neptunians to pronounce as it was for them to remember. So he finally settled on Jimbo.

Right away Father Jimbo distinguished himself in Neptune by doing the kind of outreach that is more customary for missionaries and Episcopalians. He also had a way of including personal details of his own life into his homilies, a practice that endeared him to the community while annoying his superiors.

For example, he once told us from his pulpit that tending a flock of predominantly white parishioners in a place called Neptune, New Jersey, was not exactly what he would have chosen for himself. But after a serious shortage of Americans willing to join the priesthood and fill the U.S. parishes, the higher-ups decided to go looking elsewhere for priests. He paused to smile and then admitted to us that as a boy growing up in Africa, he never would have dreamed of such a thing. Not in a million years. "Beyond the beyond," he called Neptune. And then in the next breath he told us that if ever there was proof of God's wicked sense of humor, his fate was surely it.

"Over one hundred years ago the church was literally beating the Ethiopian bushes to find converts," he informed us with half his mouth turned up into a smile. "And now they have their pick of them, turning them into proper priests like me, sending us to places like New Jersey."

"Are we all here?" he asked the crowd in his singsong African cadence. When there were no objections, he began reading some prayers from his book and making elaborate hand motions over the grave, all of which added an air of solemnity and occasion to the gathering.

Hanging back at the edge of the crowd, my father and Chrissie Bettinger stood like life-sized cardboard cutouts of their better selves. No longer a part of the family, my father had assumed the role of bystander. He made no attempt to offer us his personal condolences. His face was slightly twisted and full of grief. Once, when I dared to look directly into his eyes, silently challenging him to exist, he turned away. But in that split second before he did, I think I saw in his eyes a yearning to be nearer to the grave, closer to us, one of the grieving principals. Sorry, pal. No go. You're dead. Chrissie, on the other hand, just looked intense and nervous and perhaps slightly dazed due to the heat.

I looked over the tops of all the heads and hairdos hoping to catch a glimpse of Travis. I half expected him to be loitering out beyond the gathering, smoking a cigarette and leaning against a gravestone like some punk. It was only when I didn't see him that I realized that my expectation had been more than merely half.

I did see my ex–best friend, Electra, though. I recognized her gnarly dreadlocks, which were peeking up above a few of the more traditional hairdos. I shifted position and lifted myself on my toes. She was looking solemn and standing with her parents. Her brother, Larry, was there too. When Electra spotted me, she lifted her tiny round hand and gave me one of our old secret hand waves. That was when it hit me: We weren't friends anymore. Not really. She was my past. How had that happened? And how had she and her whole family ended up on the periphery of the moment?

Only a month before, the Wheelers had been at the center of all the fuss and attention this town could muster. Aunts, uncles, cousins and Electra herself were busy revolving around Larry like tiny, inconsequential moons, held in the thrall of his gravity and reflecting his light. He had been the hometown hero returning wounded from the war. But then Larry and the whole Wheeler clan began to be eclipsed by current events. They stood (or in

Larry's case, sat) toward the back of the crowd, aware that my dead cousin, Leonard, had once again taken center stage, Neptune's latest hero.

Of course, Leonard wasn't the kind of hero who saved lives; he had never walked into a burning building or battled terrorists on their native soil; and notwithstanding the restyling of Mrs. Barchevski's wig after she lost her hair to chemo, he hadn't created a particular moment of glory that would survive in anyone's memory long after he was gone. Nothing like that. He had simply been courageous enough to be himself in the face of everything that had tried to persuade him to be something else. Despite the fact that I was unwilling to recognize it when he was alive, Leonard's determination to live his life was a desperate act of daring worthy of note, if not deserving of actual medals and a VFW picnic.

The ceremony was almost over. The little Urn of Leonard had been lowered into a hole in the ground, and Father Jimbo was wrapping things up by reading a selection from the Bible about shepherds and green fields. Uncle Mike had stopped crying—finally—and the women were stuffing their tissues back into their purses.

Father Jimbo raised a little baton from a silver bucket, and when he whacked the baton a few times over the open grave, drops of holy water sprinkled into it. That's when I realized not a single word had been said about Leonard. The whole affair seemed too generic for someone so original and so flamboyant. Soon the mourners would disperse down the hill into their cars and return to their lives, their schedules. A handful of them would come back to the salon, where they would stand around with us talking, eating sandwiches and feeling Leonard's absence like so many tongues feeling around for a lost tooth. Someone had to say something before it was too late.

"*Excuse me,*" I practically shouted, and caused quite a few people to jump in their wet shoes. "I just wanted to say something . . . a few words. Y'know, about Leonard."

It wasn't as if I had written a speech that I could pull from my skirt pocket and read exactly the way I'd rehearsed it at home in front of my bedroom mirror. I hadn't prepared anything. So naturally there was a bit of a delay as I organized my thoughts and gathered my courage to speak. Someone over to my left let out a wild soprano sneeze. There were a few nervous coughs from the crowd. Then the whispering and shushes began.

"Is she going to say something?"

"What's happening?"

"Can we go?"

If I wanted to keep their attention, I was going to have to speak, and quickly. My mouth began to move, but just like in a dream, no sound came out. Father Jimbo stepped toward me in what appeared to be an effort to help me out.

"No!" I said, finding my voice all of a sudden and with alarming force. Father Jimbo jumped back, adjusted his clerical collar and decided to encourage me by simply nodding vigorously in my direction and offering me what was either a look of terror or a smile. I cleared my throat and began again.

"I used to steal."

"We can't hear you!" someone piped up from the rear.

My heart was pounding so loudly that I could barely hear my own voice. I took a deep breath and started over.

"I said I used to steal. Not from people. From stores. Just junk, really. Makeup, clothes. Once I stole a radio. That was the biggest thing I got away with."

The sunlight was blazing down on us, and the crowd was getting restless. They must have been wondering why I was bringing all this up. Why now? But I noticed Mom looking over at me from behind her dark glasses; she gave a quick nod, which I interpreted as a signal to continue.

"The other thing I did was write to people who never wrote back. Movie stars. One movie star, actually. Winona Ryder. I don't suppose she's with us here today. Winona? You here?"

I paused and looked out at the crowd as though I was really hoping to spot Winona in the mix. This was my idea of a joke. I had read in one of Nana Hertle's books on public speaking that it's a good idea to throw in a little humor, both verbal and visual, as a way of keeping the audience alert and involved. And it worked too, because someone laughed out loud. But it was followed by a quick shush and then silence.

Why was I saying this? Why wasn't I talking about Leonard? I could practically see the cartoon bubbles of thought hovering over the heads of the people gathered around the grave: *What's with her? What's she saying? Why isn't she talking about Leonard?*

"Leonard made me see something else, I don't know, some other way. I don't steal anymore. I gave up writing to people who don't write back. Leonard did that. He did. The thing about Leonard was that he didn't get all hung up on the wrong things. You know what I mean? Like, I never met anyone who actually liked people as much as he did. People mattered to him, we all did, and he wasn't making it up. I always thought this was weird, because if anyone ever had a life that could turn you against your fellow human beings, it was Leonard. We all know his story. But God knows he was having more fun on a regular basis than most of us. I mean, until the end.

"Look, I'm not saying Leonard was some kind of saint, because ask any of us who lived with him, he could be a total pain in the ass. Sorry, Father Jimbo. But I don't know, I just wanted to say that Leonard's life mattered. To me. I think it mattered to us all. A lot. He was here with all of us. He was one hundred percent present. And now he's gone."

Everything was quiet after that. There was only the distant whoosh and thrum of the highway drifting in from over the hill, reminding us that life might be happening elsewhere. But we were there, a group gathered together on a hot July morning to mourn the passing of a friend. And for a moment we were all there, one hundred percent. No one was straining toward the next thing about to happen, no one was hoping for more. For everyone gathered at Leonard's grave there was this, only this.

Just when I thought the crowd wouldn't be able to stand the heat and the stillness another second, something extraordinary happened. Five of the biggest monarch butterflies I've ever seen appeared in our midst. It was as if they'd materialized out of the still, blue morning air. They fluttered just above our heads, flashing black, orange and gold and playing the air in patterns that seemed to spell out some

secret code of pure delight. It was a dazzling display, and everyone noticed. There were sponta-
neous oohs and aahs of appreciation. Mrs. Pissaro
let out a high-pitched trill of laughter when one of
the butterflies veered too close to her and threatened to tangle in her teased-up hairdo. And though
some others in the crowd would later stand at the
buffet table with a ham sandwich in one hand and
a drink in the other, dismissing the coincidence as
just that—an accident of timing to which we, in our
hour of need, gave more meaning than was due—I
wanted desperately to believe that it was a sign
from Leonard that he hadn't left us for good.

After the butterfly incident, we all made our
way down the hill toward the parking lot. A few of
the mourners stopped to ask if they could bring
anything to the party; some complimented me on
my speech, or my midnight-blue wraparound skirt,
or my hair (I had dyed it midnight blue to match the
skirt). But mostly we were all silent as we shuffled
back to our lives, observing some rule of cemetery
etiquette that the dead don't really require of us.

"Pssst!" she said when she caught up with me in

the parking lot. "Remember me?" I turned to see the tiny out-of-breath figure of Peggy Brinkerhoff, her puffy face topped off by a visor. When she tipped up the front of the overly wide brim and smiled, I acted as though I had only just then recognized her.

"Oh. Yeah. Peggy, right?"

She smiled weakly at me, stopped in her tracks and then looked around as if someone might be spying on us. She lifted her finger and crooked it at me, daring me to approach.

"You dyed your hair," she whispered, as though we were already the co-conspirators that we would later become.

"Yeah," I replied, fussing with the blue-black straw that was now my hair. "Magenta is so before. This is after."

"Looks good," she said.

"Want to come back to the house with us? It's not much, but, well, you're welcome."

"No," she said. "But thanks. Listen, I've got to talk to you. It's important."

I wasn't used to having dark hair; with the sun beating down on the top of my head, I was burning up. I was a human heat magnet. I started to walk, trying to get to the car before I melted into a puddle on the blacktop. Peggy followed alongside me; she kept talking, but this time with added urgency and less volume.

"They used my dock as a kind of staging area for the crime scene. That's where they brought Leonard's body. I only got to see it for a minute or two. Ghastly. Even though it was in my backyard, they didn't want me butting in like some old Miss Marple, so I kept out of it and let them do their thing. I'm pretty sure of what I saw, though."

She paused, waiting for me to give her some kind of encouragement. "Really?" I was supposed to say. Or "And what did you see?" But I didn't play it her way. Instead, I just kept quiet and continued to walk without looking at her. There was a knot in my stomach. I didn't want to hear the gruesome details. I stopped and turned toward her. I stared at the little dome of hair that was pressing out the top of her visor, gray and smooth as settled dust.

"Maybe this isn't a good time," I said.

My mother and Deirdre were already waiting

at the car, and my mother was calling out to me across the lot.

"Phoebe! You coming?"

I waved and then offered Peggy a helpless shrug.

"I gotta go."

"Come by my house tomorrow," Peggy said, grabbing hold of my arm and pressing her point. "Tell me you will."

I nodded, though at that moment all I knew was that I wanted to be free of her grip. It was a beautiful day. I wanted to be back with the butterflies.

When I slid into the backseat of the car, our neighbor old Mrs. Kurtz was sitting there beside me. Unlike most of Mom's customers, Mrs. K. wasn't wearing a smart black dress. Instead, she wore a black and blue floral housecoat gathered at the waist with a wide, white patent leather belt. She had on a pair of white tennis shoes with holes cut out of them to accommodate her aching corns. Instead of the rag she usually carried to mop herself with, she held a man-size handkerchief in her right hand. She looked tiny and frail and utterly exhausted from the heat. Obviously we were giving her a ride back to the salon, where she would chow down on sandwiches and then stuff her pockets full of macaroons. Later she would feed small bits of the soft cookies to her mean, toothless Chihuahua named Joey while she described to him what he had missed.

"It was a lovely speech," she said, touching me gently. It seemed as if everyone was reaching out to touch someone. Hugs, kisses, small pats on the back or on the forearm, faces touched with an open palm, hands squeezed, wordless gestures that allowed us to reaffirm the warmth and reality of what was once Leonard.

Mrs. K. seemed to guess what I was thinking, because suddenly she grasped my hand tightly. I could feel the steely strength of her thin fingers as they interlocked with mine. There it was—more powerful than speech, more pressing than even touch—her need.

I couldn't look over at her. Not yet. I stared out the window at the passing minimalls and fast-food joints. I was sure that if I saw her dyed-black hair that was sticking flat to the side of her head, or the little rivulets of perspiration running from her temples, or her dim, tiny eyes straining to see me through her thick lenses, I would change my mind. I would not offer to go over to her house the following Friday and sit in her musty, airless front room while Joey panted and growled at my feet. I would not have the heart to read aloud to her, as Leonard had, from a book about a boy who is orphaned and alone and ends up happy at last.

"So," I asked her, careful to keep my gaze fixed on the passing landscape, "what chapter were you and Leonard up to in *Great Expectations*?"

"I can't remember," Mrs. Kurtz said with a plaintive edge to her voice. "But I know we were just getting to the good part."

FIFTEEN

Uncle Mike was fast asleep on our living-room couch, looking like a dead person, and I was standing over him. I gathered my SAVE THE WHALES T-shirt tight around my thighs so that he wouldn't wake up to a view of my panties. He was family, but he was still a guy.

"Uncle Mike?" I whispered urgently.

There was no response. I tried again, and this time I tugged at the flowered sheet that was tangled around his legs. When that failed, I gave him the old one-two—a quick jab in his side and a hard cough in his right ear. That did it. He probably thought I was a hired ranch hand trying to make off with his wallet in the middle of the Mexican night, because he jumped clear off the living-room couch, yelling, *"Paco! I'm tellin' ya! Clear out!"*

Naturally, I screamed.

The next thing I knew, Mom was in the room with us. She had rushed out of the salon and stood there with a teasing comb in one hand and a can of Volume Plus hair spray in the other. What she saw probably didn't look good to her. Uncle Mike was standing there in nothing but a pair of Joe Boxer shorts, his fingers were digging into the soft, fleshy part of my upper arm, and his eyes were spinning in their sockets.

"What the hell's going on here?"

"I woke him up," I said, trying to explain the situation. "I scared him. It's not what you think."

Mom stood for about thirty seconds looking at the two of us as if we were a complicated equation and she was determined to do the math and get it right this time. She had gotten the answer wrong once before, and I guess she didn't want to take any more chances. When she was satisfied that it all added up to nothing, she told me to go upstairs and make myself decent, but she said it in a tone of voice that implied that the whole thing had been my fault.

"He should be up already," I added as a way of presenting my defense. "It's late."

Afterward, I fixed Uncle Mike a hot breakfast. It was just a frozen waffle and a cup of coffee that I'd reheated in the microwave, but still, he seemed to enjoy it.

"Said I was sorry," I reminded him as I handed over a paper napkin and pointed to the thin dribble of maple syrup on his chin.

Finally he gave in and smiled.

"Yeah, well, it was a rude awakening."

"Ha ha," I replied, because I recognized this as one of Uncle Mike's lame attempts at being witty. I offered him more waffles.

"Nah," he said, "I'm good."

On our way out to Shark Lake in his rented blue Malibu, I explained to him the purpose of my mission. I told him that I had to give some woman a perm. Her name was Peggy Brinkerhoff, I explained, and because she was a pathetic, bedridden invalid for whom trips to the salon were too painful to be considered, I was required to visit her home on a semiregular basis and fix her hair. But at the moment we pulled up in front of the house, Peggy was scrambling around in her garden looking about as healthy as a person can look for a woman of her age. How was I going to explain her sudden recovery? Before I could figure it out, she had spotted us and was practically sprinting toward the Malibu.

"Hey, you came," she said to me. Then she leaned into the car so she could get a better look at Uncle Mike.

"Hi," she said, this time directing herself to him. "I'm Peggy Brinkerhoff. I'd shake, but you can see my hands are filthy."

And then she let out a girlish laugh.

"This is my uncle," I told her. "Just give me a minute, will ya?"

And that's about how long it took for me to make up a story about how Peggy had a mother who was also named Peggy, and Peggy Senior was the one who needed the perm; not Peggy Junior, who was the Peggy we had just met. I went on to assure Uncle Mike that witnessing a perm would be just about as exciting as watching someone rake a lawn, but in miniature. I told him that he might want to drive around the block a few hundred times or maybe wait down by the lake.

"This is the place, isn't it? This is where Leonard was . . . where he died."

"Yeah," I told him. "Will you be okay?"

We both stared out at the still, blue lake; it looked like a big chunk of sky that had plummeted to Earth on a hot day in August and landed flat in the middle of nowhere. The trees around the lake were leaning in toward the water; their branches, full of summer, hung down until they just touched the surface.

"Yeah, no, sure. I mean, I'm working on a new song so . . . yeah, I'm good."

My mother considered Uncle Mike a lost cause. For years she *tsk-tsk*ed over his hair, his clothes, his choice of girlfriends, and especially his liberal use of marijuana. She commiserated with anyone who would listen because she was sure that without the pot, everything would have turned out perfectly for Mike and he would have made something of his life.

In high school he had been the star quarterback, he was offered several scholarships to name-brand colleges, he had girlfriends calling the house at all hours. But after graduation, Mike decided to blow it all by taking a series of menial jobs in cut-rate department stores so he could pursue his dream of becoming Bruce Springsteen. He taught himself to play the guitar, he sometimes talked about getting a band together, and even after he moved to Phoenix, got a job, and met Leonard's mom, he continued to get high and write songs that no one ever heard.

"It's just not finished," he would say whenever any of us asked to hear his latest.

As he ambled down toward the lake, humming a half-baked tune, I thought that the same thing could have been said of Uncle Mike—he was just not quite finished. But as he was always reminding us, he was good.

"I really didn't think you'd come," Peggy said, showing me into her cozy little dining area.

I don't think I had any intention of visiting Peggy when I woke up that morning. But lying alone in my bed, I suddenly knew that despite all my best defenses and regardless of the many excuses I was making to myself, I was going to be with Peggy before the day was out simply because I needed to know.

Her home was just as clean and tidy as I remembered. There were the studio portraits of her family members lined up just so along the mantel of the fireplace, the porcelain figurines of melancholy shepherdesses arranged around the room, the furniture looking catalog appropriate. I had grown up in a house where we were always fighting back a rising tide of mess and dust, bobby pins, hairnets, curlers and misplaced homework. A place like Peggy's set my teeth on edge. I just wasn't used to such order. It seemed to me that in a home like Peggy's where everything had a place and everything was in its place, anything could go wrong at any moment.

Sunlight was bouncing up from the lake and into the house; it filled the dining area with a silvery sheen and shot through the fake Tiffany lampshade that hung over the table. Patterns of tiny colored squares were reflected onto the wall, and if I stood in the right position, I could make them play across my hands and face.

"I told you I'd come."

"Yuh," she said, adjusting her glasses so that she could read the message on my T-shirt. "Whales. Nice. How's your friend? Travis, is it? He didn't come with you."

"No. He's . . . um, he's busy. I mean, I guess he's busy. I haven't seen him much since, y'know."

"Must be a lot going on. I mean, for you. This past week. How're ya handling it all?"

I didn't want her to think that I was the kind of girl who gets dumped by cute boys with cars and then forgets to get properly dressed when she goes to visit strangers, so I told her that I was fine. And then added that I'd been keeping myself pretty busy.

"Really?" she said, scrunching her face at me. "How?"

"Oh, y'know. Stuff."

This didn't seem to satisfy her, because she just stood there staring at me.

"Actually," I finally said, "I'm thinking about writing about it all. Y'know, about Leonard. But . . ."

"Good good good. You do that! Wish I could write. But I can't. Not for beans."

And with that she was off to the kitchen to root around in what sounded like a large junk drawer.

"Is this a crime novel you're gonna write?" she asked me from the kitchen, clearly hoping that I would say yes.

"No."

"Detective story?"

"No."

"Murder mystery?"

"No.

"Then what?"

"I dunno. I don't really like those kinds of novels," I explained to her. "I think they're totally bogus."

When she came back to the dining area, she was carrying some rope and a metal ring about six inches in diameter.

"Bogus?"

The table was covered in one of those easy-wipe tablecloths, the kind that have pastel pictures of old-fashioned kitchen items printed on one side and a fuzzy felt underlining on the other. She pushed a neat pile of newspaper clippings to one side and placed the rope and the metal ring on the table.

"Yeah," I told her. "I think it's a cheap way to get people to care about reading a book when really they should just be reading because they care about the words, the ideas. Maybe it's just me. I mean, does everything have to always be a problem or something that's got to get solved?"

"I don't know," she said. "I just like 'em. Here. Sit."

She used a pair of gardening shears to cut the rope into lengths of about a yard each. I felt as though she was preparing to perform a magic act—or a murder.

"What's this all about?" I asked, nervously picking up the metal ring. She took the ring from me and gently placed it back on the table, but this time closer to her. Then she continued until she had cut three pieces of rope. She arranged them in front of her, laying each one alongside the other. She counted them just to make sure she had the right number for her demonstration.

"One. Two. Three. Okay," she said as she splayed her hands out flat over the setup. "I'm ready. So this is what I wanted to talk to you about. It's kinda complicated and it's gonna take some follow-up. But we might as well start somewhere."

With her forefinger, she pushed her glasses onto the bridge of her tiny nose and then picked up the ring and a single piece of rope. She slipped the end of the rope through the ring and then brought it around a second time to create a loop. She repeated this two more times, making three loops of about the same size. Holding the three loops against each other with her left hand, she began to wrap the end of the rope three times around the loops with her right hand. Finally she pulled on both ends of the rope, causing the tangle to magically organize itself into a neat, tight knot. It was quite a trick, made all the more amazing by the fact that she continued to talk as she performed it.

"My husband was big on fishing. He was. All he wanted to do was fish. Out on the lake a lot. But he loved ocean fishing best. I wasn't much interested, really. I took it up, though, 'cause it was a way the two of us got to spend time together. Anyway, I learned what I had to. Tying knots was top of the list."

As she presented me with the first of what I assumed would be a series of rope tricks, the doorbell chimed.

"I'll get it!" I said, practically knocking back my chair as I jumped up and ran for the door. "It's probably my uncle checking on me."

When I opened the door, Chuck was standing there, wearing one of his everyday off-duty outfits— a blue short-sleeved shirt, tan slacks and work boots. But because he was carrying his blue binder under his arm, I knew that today was not like every day; he was there on business. We were definitely into Phase Two.

"Phoebe?" he said tentatively, not sure it was really me. Maybe he thought I was some girl living on the other side of town who amazingly looked just like Phoebe Hertle except for the hair, which was now midnight blue. In any case, he seemed genuinely surprised, and confused.

"Wait. What're you doing here?"

"I got a call," he said, peering past me and into the coolness of the house. "I got a call from the woman who lives here. Mrs. Brinkerhoff. What're *you* doing here?"

By this time Peggy had found her way to the door and was already pulling Chuck inside. After she thanked him for coming, told him to call her Peggy, offered him coffee (he declined), she was ready to resume her lecture demonstration.

"I saw something out there on the dock the day . . . y'know. That day. I'm pretty sure I'm right and all. It was the rope. It was tied to the anchor in such a way that . . . let's just say I know a thing or two about fishing. Only a fisherman would do it like this."

She held up the neat, tight knot that she had just made for me and handed it to Chuck. He looked at it closely and turned it over and over. It was a pretty thing, and Peggy obviously knew what she was doing.

"They call it a Jansik special. It's slip-proof. It's a good way to fix your hook good to a line. And lemme just say you'd have to be a darn good fisherman to do a knot like this in the dark. And there's another thing. I'm not positive, and that's why I asked you to bring the pictures, Chuck. Can I call you Chuck? Whoever made the knot I think was a leftie."

Chuck opened his blue binder and pulled out a manila envelope. He undid the clasp as we watched, and then he slipped out a few black-and-white eight-by-ten photographs. They were closeups of either the knots that had been used to tie up Leonard's body or the one used to secure the rope to the anchor. He laid the photographs out on the table alongside Peggy's rope trick. Peggy pushed her glasses in place and leaned in close over them.

"Yuh," she said, nodding and pointing to one particular picture, the knot that was tied to the anchor. Even I could see that the design of the knot was reversed.

Then she picked up one of the other photos lying on the table to have a closer look.

"Okay. That's strange."

"What?" Chuck asked. By now he was hooked,

leaning in, and good old Peggy had proved her worth as a reliable expert in the case.

"Look," she said as she held the photo out so we could all see it. "This knot is where the two ends of the rope are tied together around the boy's middle. It's just a plain overhand knot. Sloppy work. The kind of knot that just about anyone in the world would make. And it's not even that good."

She picked up the remaining two pieces of rope from the table and tied them together. Though her knot was cleaner than the one in the picture, she'd made her point. This was clearly the work of someone who didn't know knots, someone *other* than the person who had tied the Jansik special.

We all looked up and waited for someone to say it.

"So there was more than just one person." Chuck finally said it.

Peggy looked at him over the rim of her glasses and nodded. "Yuh. Looks that way."

Just then we heard a splash out in the water. When we looked up and squinted out the picture window, we saw someone swimming away.

"It's my uncle Mike," I told them. "I'd better go see what's up."

I left them and walked out the back door and into the yard. The lawn sloped gently down to the water's edge, and it had been clipped and maintained by a gardener who obviously believed in the military style. The orderliness and uniformity was almost spooky. A large sycamore tree grew in the middle of the yard and provided plenty of shade. Planted off to the side where the light was strong and unobstructed, a couple of young fruit trees were struggling to grow. But what really caught my attention were the clothes piled neatly by the sandy shoreline—a blue T-shirt, a pair of khaki shorts, two white socks, a scuffed-up pair of gray Nike running shoes and a pair of Joe Boxers.

"Holy shit," I said aloud. "He's naked.

"*Uncle Mike!*" I yelled, but he just kept swimming farther away. Only the high-pitched whirring of the cicadas answered back. Either Uncle Mike was too far out to hear me or he had decided to swim without letting anything stop him.

"What's up?"

It was Chuck; he was standing behind me and looking out at the sunstruck lake.

"He's such a total nutcase," I said, letting out a sigh of exasperation. "I mean, what's he think he's doing?"

"He'll come back," Chuck said, and then he laughed. "Maybe he's just cooling off."

We watched my uncle skim the shimmering surface of the lake, his big arms going in an easy rhythm and taking him farther and farther away from us.

"I heard he was in Mexico when it happened."

I turned and looked at Chuck with one eyebrow raised and said, "He's not a suspect returning to the scene of the crime, if that's what you think. Jesus, I can't believe I'm using words like 'suspect' and 'scene of the crime.' It's so Nancy Drew. What's happened to my life?"

Chuck just stood there with his hands in his pockets, squinting against the glare and breathing. Finally he said, "I don't know. Maybe your life's just got complicated. The world's a complicated place."

"Thanks," I said as I turned back toward the

water. And then I shouted, *"Uncle Mike!"*

"Don't worry," Chuck mumbled as if he was talking to himself, "we'll find whoever did it."

"Why do you care?"

"Um. It's my job," he replied.

"That doesn't really answer my question. I'm just asking 'cause it seems weird to me. A job chasing down evil."

"Like I said, it's a complicated world."

I shot him another raised eyebrow.

He looked up into the cool center of the tree towering above us as if he might find the answer hanging there. Then he took a deep breath and said, "I don't know. I used to think people were basically good and sometimes they just behaved bad. Then something happened to me. I was about your age. It's a long story. Let's just say I realized there's a little evil in all of us. It just takes the right conditions for it to come out full force and do damage."

"Wait. Are you saying that deep down any one of us could've killed Leonard? I mean, given the *right conditions*?"

"No. Not exactly. I'm just saying that without

restraints, any one of us could end up on either end of evil. It's out there. But it's also in here."

He pointed to himself, just so there was no confusion.

"Restraints?"

"Yeah. Like society, like laws, the church, whatever. For a while, I thought about becoming a priest, y'know, as a way of encouraging the good in people. But it just wasn't for me. So I thought the next best thing I could do was become a cop. I thought maybe I might discourage one or two people from being bad. "

"How you doing?"

"I dunno," he shot back at me. "You tell me."

And we left it at that.

By this time, Uncle Mike was out in the middle of the lake. He had stopped swimming, and only his head was bobbing above the water line.

"*Uncle Mike!*" I shouted. This time his head whipped around and he raised an arm to signal that he'd heard me.

"*We have to go!*" I added, just so there was no mistaking my meaning.

He gave me another quick wave and began the swim back toward us.

"I'm going to wait in the car," I told Chuck. "The last thing in the world I need today is to see my uncle's naked ass in broad daylight. Tell him to hurry it up, will ya? And don't mention the rope thing to him. My mother doesn't know I came out here."

"Sure," he said.

I walked up the grassy slope toward the house, and just as I made it to the back door, I heard Chuck's voice calling out to me.

"Hey, Phoebe!"

I turned around and saw him standing alone in the middle of the yard where I had left him. He was smiling with one half of his face, and I knew what he was going to say before he said it. Then he said it.

"Be good, okay?"

SIXTEEN

When I was about nine years old, Nana Hertle told me that she'd chosen me.

"For what?" I asked, thinking that all my efforts to be good had finally paid off and I was about to be rewarded with a load of candy or toys or money. But no. She told me that she had other plans for me. She said that after she "crossed over," she would make every effort to come back from the dead and tell me what it was like in the spirit world.

Nana Hertle had read plenty of books on "the afterlife" and even went so far as to attend a few séances while she was still alive. Despite her best efforts, however, she was never completely satisfied that contact had been made with the other side. She said she never could be sure whether it was in fact her childhood friend Agnes Hrabel spelling out a lazy request for remembrance on a Ouija board or if it was a manifestation of her own wishful thinking. But rather than conclude that the whole enterprise was crackpot, she decided that the dead people she had targeted for communication didn't have the right attitude or know-how to make it a complete success.

"Conditions on both sides have to be just right," she once explained to me. "It's sort of like waterskiing."

It was a warm afternoon in June, and we were strolling down the boardwalk in Asbury Park. Dark clouds hung heavy over the horizon; they were rolling in toward the shore, bringing with them a curtain of rain. No one seemed to care very much. Not yet.

"Now, if you've ever been waterskiing, you know . . ."

She paused here, turned toward me, and focused her dark-gray eyes on me with birdlike intensity. "*Have* you ever been waterskiing?" she asked.

"No," I told her. "Have you?"

"Oh, yeah. A zillion times," she replied. Then, looking straight ahead and ignoring the first few raindrops that were beginning to dot the rotting boardwalk at our feet, she continued. "Waterskiing takes real effort. Both mental and physical. But once you get the hang of it, you wonder why more people don't put sticks on their feet and let themselves be pulled across the surface of the water at sixty miles an hour. It's a thrill and a half."

She looked out at the ocean and squinted into the distance as though she might actually see a waterskiing version of her former self go whizzing by. Nana Hertle was a good-looking woman in her day. As an older woman she tended to dress in comfortable clothes, slacks and tops with a bright sweater that was, like her, faded some from use. Her skin was clear and powdery smooth. She had a thin knowing smile, and her nose was as sharp as her wits. Sometimes when I tried to look at her objectively, to see her as someone I didn't know and love, I saw an old woman who didn't take crap from anyone.

"It's not for everyone," she added wistfully,

"but then again, neither is life. You up for it?"

"Waterskiing?" I asked.

"No," she scoffed. "Being my contact once I cross over. Would you be up for it?"

Earlier that same month, Mom had sat Deirdre and me down in her bedroom and explained to us that Nana had been diagnosed with cancer. It was in her colon and had already spread to her liver, an indication that there was only a slim chance of recovery. Mom told us that after a lot of fact-finding and soul searching and several second opinions, Nana had decided to skip medical treatment of any kind. She said it wasn't her thing and claimed that the radiation followed by aggressive chemotherapy did something like poke holes in your aura. Since she didn't want her spiritual body to end up looking like an overbleached undergarment, Swiss cheesed beyond recognition, she was opting out of the process altogether. She would trust the deeper knowledge of her own physical body, treat herself with herbs and affirmations and book herself into a hospice when the time came. She was ready, we were told.

Deirdre and I cried and cried until we had each soaked a wide circle of tears into Mom's bedspread. When I had finally cried myself dry, I got up from the bed and life continued pretty much as before. But then one day out of the blue, I dialed Nana's number. She answered, cheerful and chipper as ever, and I heard myself insist that she come over right away and take me for ice cream.

"Now?" she had asked me.

"Yes," I replied a little too sarcastically. "I'm ready."

That was the day she and I walked the board-walk together, and typical of me, I forgot every-thing I wanted to say to her. I just kept trying to memorize her smell, the sound of her voice. I had even forgotten about the ice cream; I was too busy defending myself against the thought of her no longer being with us. She looked fine to me. A little pale, a little thin, but fine. I didn't want her to die. Ever. But if she *did* die (a situation that she said she figured would happen before the end of the year), I would most likely want to hold on to her even if it meant teaching myself to do something as ridiculous as learning how to water-ski.

"Sure," I told her. "What do I have to do?"

She gave me a crash course in what it takes to contact the dead. She taught me how to light a candle, manipulate a Ouija board and write automatically. She handed me a hot-pink business card with Madame Sandy's address and phone number. Madame Sandy had been appointed as the medium best suited to connect me with Nana after her *transition*.

"She's totally one of us," Nana had explained. "Only don't let her charge you for the sessions. I paid in advance, and she knows it. If she gives you any guff, tell her I'll come back and scare the bejesus out of her and I'll make sure she gets no psychic traffic for as long as she lives."

After Nana made her transition, I gave everything a try. I even became a frequent visitor to Madame Sandy's storefront parlor in Bradley Beach, where I sat for hours in a dimly lit room supposedly speaking to dead people through a spirit guide named Morris. It was very entertaining and Sandy was a hoot. She taught me to play pinochle,

served me sardine sandwiches and let me smoke cig-
arettes in her house, but I'm sorry to report that I
never received even so much as a hint of Nana
Hertle from the other side. I can report, however,
that after about a year, the experience of missing
my grandmother became almost as real to me as her
actual presence. In fact, I began to believe that this
was her way of coming through to me—through
the force of my own desire to lay eyes on her.

It was down in the basement sitting so close to
her stuff that I could really feel her presence. Even
after Leonard moved down there, I sometimes
waited for him to leave the house so I could sit
beside her boxes, smell the traces of her perfume
and lean against the weight of her old life. And
that's what I did after my meeting with Peggy and
Chuck—I went home, dropped my bag in the
kitchen, tiptoed down to the basement and sat
beside my grandmother's boxes. But this time
instead of just sitting there and communing with
her spirit, I began to tear into the boxes in search of
I-don't-know-what.

If I were writing a novel that involved the

supernatural, this would be the perfect moment for my grandmother's ghost to appear. She would look pretty much the way I remembered her— wearing jeans, sneakers, a crocheted vest and a shell top. Her hair would be less gray, but as always disastrously permed. She would look happier, less burdened by the concerns of the living, and she would tell me something about how it is over there on the other side. She might quote Jesus or Dr. Phil or Neil Diamond. Then, with a bit of trumped-up fanfare, she would present Leonard. She would push him forward like a prize pupil while saying something about how even death can be conquered if we put our minds and hearts to work. And finally Leonard would offer me a clue that would lead me to his killers.

Imagine me sitting on a blue metal stool down in the basement on a late Sunday afternoon in August speed-reading one of my grandmother's books, a little red paperback entitled *The Magic of Believing* by Claude M. Bristol, in an effort to forget the gruesome photos of Leonard's bound and swollen ankles and his twisted blue wrists.

If you were going to judge *The Magic of Believing* by its cover, you would come to the conclusion (as my grandmother must have done) that powerful forces are locked in your mind and those forces can turn desires into reality. And if you happened to open to page 68, you would discover (as I did) that one of Claude M. Bristol's handy suggestions about this business of unlocking your mind can be easily proven even if you are not a big believer in such things.

Here's a simple experiment that will demonstrate to you this strange power of attraction through visualizing or making the mental picture actually work. Find a few small stones or pebbles which you can easily throw and locate a tree or a post of six to ten inches in diameter. Stand away from it twenty-five or thirty feet or any convenient greater distance and start throwing the pebbles in an endeavor to hit it. If you are an average person, most of the stones will go wide of their mark. Now stop and tell yourself that you can hit the objective. Get a mental picture of the tree figuratively stepping forward to meet the missile or the stone actually colliding with the tree in the spot where you want it to strike, and you'll soon find yourself making a perfect score. Don't say it's impossible. Try it and you'll prove that it can be done—if you will only believe it.

Later that night while I was lying in my bed, unable to sleep, I reviewed this particular passage in my mind: *Try it and you'll prove that it can be done.*

I got up, threw on a pair of cherry-colored shorts and a black tank top and tied my white Windbreaker around my waist. I tiptoed in my flip-flops down the carpeted staircase and then quietly slipped out the back door and into the night.

As I made my way through the darkened neighborhood, everything looked unfamiliar to me. Without people or pets or the familiar brightness of day, without the many small distractions of my neighborhood that I had come to think of as my right-of-way, every house up and down the street seemed suddenly insubstantial and empty.

Even my own house appeared flat and dark, without substance, a stranger to the daylight version of itself.

Only the damp of the dew on the late-night lawns and on my toes as I made my way across the lawns felt real and true. And the only stories I could believe in were the ones shimmering in the black above me in the form of stars. Eventually I arrived at the Turnpike overpass. That too seemed real. The highway beneath me was busy with rattling sixteen-wheelers, buses filled with Atlantic City gamblers, and solitary, all-night, No-Doz drivers. I paused, grabbed hold of the chain-link fence and felt the pulse of good and evil blazing through the night, on its way to somewhere.

If you are an average person, most of the stones will go wide of their mark.

It was already very late, so I continued to walk. I had, after all, come out with a purpose in mind. I had miles to go.

I made my way around to the back of Travis's

house and into his derelict yard. It wasn't much of anywhere really, just a scrap of scrubby earth with thin patches of wild grass jutting up here and there. There were a few rusted and disabled bicycles leaning up against a wrecked chain-link fence. I stood in the tall grass near the house and looked up at what I hoped was Travis's bedroom window. I held a smooth pebble in my hand and repeated Claude M. Bristol's mantra to myself: *Try it and you'll prove it can be done.*

Since Travis had been acting as remote and unresponsive as a fence post for almost a week, I considered him a perfect target for my experiment. I threw the pebble and missed. Clearly I didn't believe. Not enough. After seven failed attempts, I realized that I believed in the wrong thing. I hadn't been focused on hitting the window, as I should have; I was concentrating too hard on my belief that Travis and I were meant for each other.

On the eighth try I heard the sharp crack of the stone splitting glass. A light went on inside the room, and Travis's silhouette was at the window. He popped out the screen and stuck his head into the dark.

"Down here," I said, waving my arms like a crazy person.

"What the hell're you doing?" he yelled back at me. "You broke the window!"

Obviously, he wasn't that happy to see me.

"Forget it," I said, dropping my arms to my side and walking quickly toward the front of the house. I heard him shout *"Wait!"* but I was already gone.

When I was out by the sidewalk, he came bounding out of his house in his bare feet. He was struggling to get his T-shirt over his head.

"Wait up," he said.

Now stop and tell yourself that you can hit the objective.

I stopped, but that was as far as my belief could take me. I could go no further. I didn't turn around, and since I had nothing to say, I just stood there waiting for the next thing to happen.

"You scared the shit out of me," he said to my back. "What're you doing here? What time is it?"

When I didn't respond, he touched my shoulder

very gently as though he was touching the top of a just-baked cake to see if it was fully done.

"Phoebe?" he whispered.

I swung around and glared at him as hard as I could manage. His face looked crumpled like a pillow, soft and creased with sleep. And judging from his startled expression, he was clueless as to why I thought it was a good idea to show up at his house in the middle of the night. This could easily have been a dream he was having where people do and say extraordinary things for no apparent reason.

"This was a bad idea," I said, stating the obvious. "It's just that . . . I thought after what happened last week . . . I thought there was something between us, something going on. I was wrong. Obviously."

Don't say it's impossible. Try it and you'll prove that it can be done—if you will only believe it.

A police car happened to be cruising down the street; it slowed and came to a dead stop beside us.

"Everything all right here?" asked the cop. He

looked like a younger slimmer version of Chuck, another cop doing his duty, riding around the neighborhood, discouraging people from being bad.

"Fine," I replied, trying to relax so I didn't look like a victim.

His sidekick was a lady cop with blondish hair that had been slicked back and pulled into a ponytail. She leaned over so we could see her, and more important so that she could get a good look at Travis. I smiled brightly at her and said, "Hello there."

"Okay, then," the first cop said, and the car moved along.

Travis and I stood there without saying anything for the longest time. Finally he said, "You weren't wrong. I mean about coming here."

SEVENTEEN

Travis and I hung out on his front steps for about an hour while he smoked one cigarette after another. His toes gripped the edge of the step like a bird on a perch, and I couldn't help noticing how surprisingly elegant his feet looked. My own feet have never been anything to write home about, although my toenails were especially good that night due to the fact that I had had them professionally polished for Leonard's funeral.

"So?" Travis asked me, after a lot of chitchat about nothing in particular. "What's goin' on with you?"

I responded by burying my head between my knees. For the next four or five minutes I managed to spot the concrete with my dripped tears. It was a ridiculous outburst of emotion, totally unexpected. Travis placed his hand gently on the nape of my neck and held it there as if he was trying to steady an appliance that had gone out of control. Between my sobs and the apologies for my sobbing, I forgot all about my toenails, I forgot about Travis's feet, I forgot Claude M. Bristol. I forgot just about everything, except for one thing.

"Leonard," I said, choking back a sob. "What was the deal with him? He was so deeply weird. And he wasn't even with us that long. Why do I even care? And what am I doing with my life? I've lived here ten thousand times longer than Leonard did. I know everyone. My grandmother had a big funeral. Well, a memorial service or whatever. Everybody came. People from her childhood came. But how many people will come to *my* funeral? Electra? We used to be best friends, but now she just seems like a character out of a stupid book I read a long time ago."

Travis just squinted and looked at a spill of streetlight that was falling on the grass.

"Oh sure," I said, wiping the drip from my nose

with the back of my hand. "My stupid family would be there, but only because they *have* to. Old Mrs. Kurtz will show up. For the macaroons. But then they'll go on just like before. I won't be missed. Not really. Nothing will change."

"I'd come," Travis said quietly.

"Yeah, but you didn't come yesterday. Where *were* you?"

"I was away."

"Right. Away. Whatever."

He tossed the last of his cigarette onto a scabby patch of dirt and dead grass. Then he took hold of my hand. With one big yank, he lifted me onto my feet. The screen door screamed for oil when it was opened, and before I knew what was happening, we were inside his darkened house.

The air was still, cool, and it smelled of metal mixed with the fetid odor of the old carpet and the sour smell of beer.

"I shouldn't be here."

"Shh," he told me. "My dad's away. It's just us."

I let him lead me up a steep staircase. Each footstep echoed throughout the house as we went up and up. As we reached the bedroom at the top of the stairs, Travis switched on an overhead light, but then he thought better of it and we were plunged back into darkness that was as stunning as it was sudden. My heart began pounding against my rib cage; it pounded so violently, I was afraid that it might actually break loose, make a getaway and be lost to me forever. Travis still had hold of my hand, but I placed my other hand over my heart in an effort to calm myself and contain the panic. Was I having a stroke, I wondered? Was I dying?

As soon my eyes adjusted to the dark, I could see the outline of a mattress lying flat on the floor, flush against the far wall.

"Lie down now," he told me.

I was grateful just to let my legs buckle under me, since they were headed in that direction anyway. The lumpy mattress took the weight of me without a sound. Travis removed my flip-flops, and each one fell to the floor with a thump. Then I felt his weight beside me. He moved in close, and I could smell the sharp tang of tobacco on his breath mingling with the all-day smell of his body. I could feel the heat of his skin as he pressed up against me, but mostly I was feeling something else, something like desire rising in me, rising, and then, as D. H. Lawrence had described it, I began to feel the rippling brilliance with flapping feathers deep down inside me. This could be it, I thought. It could happen. Get ready.

Suddenly I remembered Bethany and the stupid certificate that I had signed in the auditorium back when school was still in session. Of course, at the time no one had taken the thing seriously; it was just one of those things you did because you had to. Peer pressure and all. But the fact that I was thinking about it while lying beside a boy who was working his hand into my pants proved that it was more than just a meaningless piece of paper. Somehow by signing my name, I had agreed to install a little Bethany inside my brain, and now her singsong voice was chiming in my ear, *"Just 'cause no one catches you doing something wrong, well, that doesn't mean you won't suffer consequences."* But *was* it wrong? Or was it exactly what I'd wanted from Travis ever since I first saw him at the mall and kissed him in the parking lot? I needed a minute to breathe and figure it out, but—

"Don't you want to?" Travis whispered into my hair. He was on top of me now. I could feel his ribs pressing against mine, his hipbone digging into my pelvis, pressing up against my thigh; he was moving with a jerky rhythm that wanted my attention, burrowing down as though I was lost ground that he was desperately trying to claim for himself.

And even though I'd never done it before, I knew enough to know that all his heaving and pushing was not what I, personally, was after. Clearly he wasn't so good at this. He was trying too hard.

"Wait," I murmured, though admittedly I wasn't as forceful as Bethany had instructed us to be if it ever came to this. I said it again, this time louder, and I added a thrust of my forearm for emphasis. My elbow knocked him in the jaw. He leaned back and looked me in the eye.

"What?"

"Nothing, I just think—"

He didn't wait for me to finish. Instead, he sprang up from the bed and let out a wild hiss of a sigh that quickly turned into a mournful cry. For a second I thought he might jump out the bedroom window, but he stopped short, pressed his hands against the sill and stuck his torso out into the night.

"Look," he said, as though he was talking to someone floating right outside his bedroom window. "You might as well know instead of hearing it from someone else. I'm gonna enlist."

"Enlist? What? Like in the army?"

"Yeah. Maybe even the marines."

What was he saying? And why was he saying it? Why now? This is very sudden, I thought. Was he trying to get me to pity him, to admire his manhood, to just lie back and let him have his way because this was his last chance to score as a civilian before they shipped him out? I couldn't tell. All I could think of were his feet, his lovely feet, so elegant and almost ladylike gripping the stoop on a hot summer night. What would become of those feet? Where would they take him? Iraq? Like Larry Wheeler, would he come back without one of them? It could happen. He might lose them both. He might not come back at all.

"The world's so messed up," Travis said as he

pulled himself back into the room. "Someone's got to fight the Axis of Evil and all. Might as well be me. And what's happening here? Same old shit."

He lit a cigarette and then heedlessly tossed the match out into the backyard. He could've started a major fire in the weeds down below. We could've been blown to pieces by some kind of explosion from a gas leak or something. I waited, but nothing happened, just the distant whir of cicadas and the deep hum of someone's central air. Same old shit.

"Are you sure?" I asked him. "I mean is that really what you want to do with your life?"

"It's not my whole life. Four years. I come out and what's the worst thing that could happen? I get a party at the VFW like that loser, Larry Wheeler, and everyone treats me like a hero. Not so bad."

"You could get killed."

He shrugged one shoulder and blew a slow, steady stream of cigarette smoke out the window.

"Maybe you should talk to Larry," I said as I propped myself up on my elbows. "He could tell you what it's really like and all."

"I know what it's like."

He leaned over so that he could reach a key on his computer and give it a tap. The screen came to life and illuminated the room with an eerie blueness that seemed equal parts light and shadow.

"See this? It's called Full Spectrum Warrior. But it's way harder than trying to make a fat plumber rescue Princess Toadstool."

"Y'mean like with Super Mario Brothers?" I said.

I wanted him to know that I wasn't a total technopeasant. I understood his reference to one of the vintage video games made by Atari, back when video games were still fringe and designed mainly for kids and not for killing. I'd never been an expert, but I had spent some time playing these games on Electra's home computer, and though I found them entertaining and even challenging at first, they didn't take hold in me the way they had in, say, Electra's brother or in Travis. I was more the *Jane Eyre* type. I read books.

After some careful clicking, Travis got his cursor to find its way into an electronic game the likes of which the Super Mario Brothers could never have imagined.

"This game was made by the army to train troops. You buy it in stores and it's way more violent. There're more fractal explosions, shit like that. You run out of ammunition, you can just get more illegally from the back of an ambulance or whatever, which you definitely can't do in real war. So it's not like actual life. And the people who die are . . . well, it says right here."

Travis leaned over the computer, his face glowing as he squinted into the light. He read the type written on the left-hand side of the Full Spectrum Warrior home page.

> *The object of war is not to die for*
> *your country, but to make the*
> *other bastard die for his.*

"Cool, huh? Watch."

Even from the bed I could see the tiny figures of American soldiers on the screen; they were wearing desert fatigues and hiding their faces behind guns aimed at an imaginary enemy. None of them were moving, not yet; but any minute they would come to life and perhaps die if Travis didn't click his thumb on the mouse fast enough.

The game began, and instantly his attention was sucked into the screen. Muted sounds of explosions, gunfire and general mayhem filled the room. It was impossible to believe that this was the same boy who, only moments ago, was tenderly slipping his arm under my neck, feeling for my breast and whispering "'S all right" into my ear. His face had now taken on the ghostly pallor of the dead. His jaw was clenched, his mouth was pursed and his eyes had gone glassy. Only the twitch of his fingers as he manipulated the mouse, and the occasional wince or involuntary groan when he lost an American soldier, reminded me he was human. A tank blew up and he seemed to take the hit physically; he jumped away from the screen for a moment, got his footing and his nerve and then returned, ready for more.

But out of the corner of his eye he caught me staring at him, and perhaps because he was being watched, he felt the pang of losing more strongly. In any case, he let the game go and quickly moved back to the window ledge.

"I'm really good at this," he told me. "I'm not going to get killed, if that's what you're worried about. I know what I'm doing. "

Just then I remembered Leonard telling me the same thing.

"Look, Pheebs," Leonard had said to me once upon a time while sitting on a garbage can and dangling his legs, "I know what I'm doing." And if anyone was proof that he didn't know jack about what he was doing despite the fact that he said he did, it was Leonard. Look where he ended up.

But do any of us know what we're doing? I mean, really? Isn't this rightness, this I-know-what-I'm-doing attitude in each one of us, isn't it just something figured into our DNA so that we won't always be looking over our shoulders, second guessing and generally freaking ourselves out, because we don't know *anything*? Could it be that survival, on some level, depends on the belief that we *think* we know what we're doing? And whether some unseen, all-knowing and omnipresent God has installed this trait into our hard drive or it's the result of a long and drawn-out process of Darwinian natural selection, well, it hardly matters. Chances are that anyone will tell you that they know exactly what they're up to. But do they? Do they *ever*?

I could feel myself on the verge of crying. There was a load of tears gathering in my head and they were about to fall—big, fat, weepy girl tears, like the ones that had spotted the front stoop while Travis touched the nape of my neck. I couldn't do this. Not again. Not in front of Travis. Crying once was understandable; but crying twice made me a head case. I had to get out of there before it was too late. I began groping around the floor at the foot of the mattress for my flip-flops.

"Wha'smatter?" Travis asked.

"Nothin'," I said as I stood up. "I'm tired. I should go home."

My eyes had fully adjusted to the darkness, and I could see that the place was a major mess of discarded clothes, soda cans, crumpled-up papers, candy wrappers, old sneakers. It was a room that hadn't heard many bedtime stories, seen many playdates or enjoyed even the occasional sleepover. It certainly wasn't the kind of room a girl would want to remember years later when she recalled the night she lost her virginity.

But the décor was not the reason I wanted to run. And really, it wasn't the threat of tears either. The reason I had to get away was the same reason I was about to cry. I had suddenly realized that I didn't have the slightest idea who Travis was. For the past month, I'd been making up a picture of Travis in my head, and in the process I had refused any information about him that came to me from the real world. If it didn't fit with the picture of Travis that I already had in mind, I had no use for it. Travis Lembeck was my creation, my Frankenstein. Even the very real business of kissing him, smelling him, being pressed up against him in the dark couldn't disturb my fine-tuned, half-baked fantasy. Now with the revelation that he was going to join the service, that he blew up cyberpeople and destroyed cybervillages just for fun, the Travis

I'd been cherishing in my heart suddenly seemed trumped-up. Like those life-size, cardboard cutouts of presidents and movie stars that you can stand beside and have your picture taken with so you can give everyone the impression that you hobnobbed with the genuine article. I was sure that if I stayed there in his room another minute, the real Travis would reveal himself to me, and I wasn't sure I could handle that.

"I have to go," I repeated, like a robot programmed for flight. My left flip-flop wasn't really on my foot, so I grabbed hold of a wooden dresser just to the left of the door to steady myself. And as I was scootching the flip-flop onto my foot, I saw it. It was peeking out from under a pile of random junk, just sitting there in plain sight on top of the dresser like anybody's business—Leonard's money clip.

Travis was standing behind me saying something about how I couldn't just leave, and what was going on with me? But I couldn't really hear the exact words, because I was focused on that glint of fake gold.

"Where'd you get this?" I said after I had swung around to face him. I was holding the clip between my fingers, holding it out for him to see.

"What?"

"Where'd you get *this*?"

"He gave it to me," Travis said without skipping a beat. His expression was difficult to read, because the light from the computer was directly behind him, his face in full shadow. But judging from his voice, he hadn't flinched and there was hardly a breath between my question and his answer. He took a small step toward me, which caused me to clutch the clip and press it against my tank top.

"Who?" I asked. "Who gave it to you?"

"You know. Your cousin."

"This is crazy. Why would he give it to you?"

"I don't want to talk about it. Could we maybe just change the subject?"

"*No!* His mother gave this to him," I said, my voice shaking. "This was all he had left of her and—"

"I told you," Travis said, cutting me off. He sounded bored, as though the whole subject had been discussed and the case was closed. "He *gave* it to me."

He popped the top of a Mountain Dew. After slurping the fizz that rose up over the lip of the can, he parked himself on the window ledge and casually offered me a sip. I gave my head a little shake. I had no intention of putting my lips to anything that had touched his. He just shrugged, downed another slurp and then turned away from me like he couldn't care less. Something moved through me, a chill, something that was the exact opposite of the rippling and flapping and overlapping of soft flames that I had been in the thrall of a short time ago. Somewhere deep down inside me, the Travis I'd constructed took its last gasp and died. I was standing in the upstairs bedroom of an empty house with a total stranger, and I was suddenly afraid.

"He told me you were a good friend to him," Travis said, with such calm in his voice that it sent a shiver down my spine. He wasn't looking at me. "He told me you were lucky for him."

There was that old story again. Me and

Leonard, buddies for life. Total fiction. Why was everyone so intent on this idea of me being best friends with Leonard?

"I wasn't so great."

"I saw you two together once. Remember? At the mall? You stood up for him."

"Whatever."

"No. Not whatever. You did."

"When did he give it to you?" I asked. "When?"

I was almost pleading with him now. I needed him to tell me, because the seams of my known world were ripping, and the universe was pulling apart and splitting into a million particles. If Leonard and Travis had had the kind of relationship that included gifts, heart-to-hearts or even a single casual conversation in which I was the subject, then everything needed to be refigured. For example, why hadn't Leonard, a person who really never understood the value of keeping anything to himself, ever told me about his friendship with Travis?

"He gave it to me a while back." And then he added, "I'm not gay, if that's what you're thinking."

Maybe it was the unexpectedness of this declaration, but I just laughed out loud.

"What's funny?" he wanted to know. "You think it's funny?"

Travis placed the soda can on the window ledge and he leaned in to me, dead serious. Was he threatening me? Was he about to hit me? The darkness seemed to veil his face, obscuring his intentions. But his voice was sharp and menacing.

"You're not going," he said, and before I could disagree, he had gotten hold of my upper arms and was pulling me toward him. He tried to kiss me, but I kept pulling away, inching my face out of his range. He shook me with a sudden violence, as if he was trying to force loose change out of me. He stopped and then he did it again. I relaxed into it. There was no use fighting him; he was definitely stronger than me. He forced himself on me, pressed against me like he was trying to prove something. I loosened my arm from his grip, and with one swift jab I elbowed him hard in the gut. He sprang back like a wild animal.

He switched on a tiny lamp next to his computer.

A light intensely bright and white filled the room, and my eyes smarted. I was forced to turn away, but as I inched my head back in his direction, my eyes blinking to accommodate the unexpected brightness, I caught sight of something leaning up against the wall. It was a sleek and modern fishing rod with a fancy, complicated reel of taut nylon that seemed to glisten, like a single strand of a spider's web wound up tight.

"I really have to go." I turned and bolted.

"You'd have to be a darn good fisherman to do a knot like this in the dark."

Peggy Brinkerhoff's words were booming in my head like in cheesy movies when the heroine suddenly remembers the essential clue with the killer standing behind her, literally breathing down her neck. How could I have been so stupid? How could I have let him touch me?

I took the stairs two at a time until I was down and out the door. The sky was brightening at the edges, and the birds were twittering in the treetops. I wanted to scream, but I couldn't afford to waste my breath. All I knew was that I had to get away. A block later I was sweating bullets, my lungs were strained to the point of popping and I had developed a sharp pain in my side. As I crossed over the Parkway, my heart was working hard. Don't think, don't think, I told myself. Don't stop. Just run. And keep running. Run, and whatever you do, don't stop to look over your shoulder.

EIGHTEEN

Seven months later I was sitting in my first real-life courtroom. It was the first day of Travis's trial for the first-degree murder of Leonard Pelkey, and all I could think about was how an actual courtroom looks nothing like the ones I've seen depicted on TV. And why was that? After twenty minutes or so, I had the answer: It's the lighting. On TV, people get sworn in, tell the whole truth and nothing but the truth, lie, argue a case, present evidence and give closing remarks while standing beneath fixtures designed to make them look like movie stars. What you get when the cameras aren't rolling in a place like, say, Trenton, New Jersey, is lighting more cost-effective than flattering.

The face of an accuser looks just as desperate as that of the accused; the color of even the brightest correctional jumpsuit seems to have been dulled down so as not to distract from the proceedings at hand; and the highlights in everyone's hair (even those that have been chemically enhanced) lose their brilliance under the fluorescents; in short, the lighting is far from TV quality.

This may have been my first trial, but I quickly learned that the key players in these not-made-for-TV courtroom dramas are also not quite up to snuff. Actual lawyers, judges, members of the jury and assorted bystanders don't get selected because of their sharp profiles, shapely figures or outstanding ability to cry on cue. And it's not just that they are less attractive than the actors who appear nightly on any of the three hundred or so episodes of *Law & Order*; it's also a matter of costuming. In real life, people tend to wear a lot of bargain-basement outfits, clothes that are not so well fitted to their various body types, ensembles that are knockoff and off-the-rack. I sat there in that courtroom day after day flooded with emotion, but what kept coming up for me again and again was the wish that people would make more of an effort with their appearance. Maybe this was Leonard's legacy to me—maybe he would always be sitting beside me shaking his head in disbelief, discouraged by the bad outfits and unfortunate hairdos, determined to give everyone a brand-new look.

Travis, of course, was excused from looking good. Since he was required to wear one of those ghastly one-piece orange jumpsuits during the day and sleep in a courthouse prison cell at night, there was only so much effort he could make on his own behalf. At least his hair was clean.

When I first saw him entering the courtroom wearing handcuffs and leg shackles, I remember thinking how much smaller he looked. But that could have been because the two guards at his side towered over him. I also thought that I might have been comparing him with the other Travis, the one I had invented, the one I had kissed once upon a time.

He shuffled across the room, his eyes cast down and focused on the linoleum. Once, he shyly scanned the place like a girl at a dance looking for a willing partner. There were no takers. Maybe he was just counting heads, estimating his importance based on the size of the crowd gathered together all because of him. Who knows? I wondered if he might be looking for me, or for anyone who might have known him before all the trouble began.

I pretended to drop my purse, and then once I was down there, I fussed with my sports sock.

There were people in town who were sure I was going to be called as a witness for the prosecution, and therefore I was cautioned to steer clear of the boy and have nothing to do with his lawyer. They were afraid I might inadvertently let loose some bit of information and tip the case in favor of his defense. Now that this fiend, this monster, this cold-blooded murderer had been apprehended and put behind bars, they didn't want anything to go wrong. The hope of ending Travis's life by lethal injection was like a giddy little secret everyone in Neptune shared—everyone, it seemed, except for Father Jimbo and me.

Don't get me wrong. People didn't go around

town saying that they wanted Travis to die. They were never that obvious about it. But they did find ways to express these darker sentiments in surprising ways just in the course of their normal, everyday conversation. For example, people would run into one another in the supermarket, discuss the case and quietly discourage the expression of any tender feeling toward the accused. As far as they were concerned, Travis was the devil incarnate, and any contact with him might lead a person straight to Hell. A few of my mother's regulars had already begun to evoke Travis's name as a warning to their naughty grandchildren. "You don't want to end up like that Lembeck boy, do you? You know what's going to happen to him, don't you?" It seemed as if everyone had already decided that the Lembeck boy was guilty. It was just a matter of time. Just wait, they said: You'll see.

Travis's defense attorney, a short woman with dark, cropped hair, was not in agreement with the general public. She thought her client was innocent. Sort of. Her name was Ms. Fassett-Holt. She had no discernible waist and wore an outfit that seemed to have been designed specifically to accentuate this fact. All wrong, I thought when I first saw her sitting beside Travis. A boxy suit in a shocking shade of royal blue looked like a birdcage cover with buttons. I later discovered that she had five of them, one for each day of the week. In her hair she wore punishing amounts of goop.

In the beginning Ms. Fassett-Holt presented the idea that Travis was just a boy who had survived a few too many hard knocks, eventually leading him to a life that was beyond his control. She argued that Leonard's death wasn't exactly Travis's fault because it hadn't been premeditated. Sure, Travis may have killed, but he wasn't responsible. Not really. Ms. Fassett-Holt claimed that because Travis's dad, Carl Lembeck, used to beat the boy on a regular basis, because Carl Lembeck locked the boy in the shed in the backyard on several occasions, because Carl Lembeck had pretty much failed the boy as a parent in every way, because the mother, Nancy Lembeck, had died early and tragically, because of all of this the boy had failed to learn the basics of right and wrong. It was a vicious cycle, Ms.

Fassett-Holt explained to the jury. Because the boy had been abused, he abused others. This was her opening argument, and though she went on to say that she intended to show just how damaged the boy was because of his background, I wasn't really listening. I was too busy counting the number of times she referred to Travis as "the boy" during her opening remarks (fifty-two). It wasn't difficult to see where she was headed.

To be honest, I don't think the jury bought Ms. Fassett-Holt's theory. Anyone with half a brain knows that tying up a fourteen-year-old kid with rope and then sinking him with an anchor in a lake is as far from right as wrong can get. But any hope of having the father share in the sins of the son was put to rest when Carl Lembeck took the stand. He said that though he loved Travis as much as any guy could love his only son, he wanted it made perfectly clear that he was just another struggling single parent without the time or money to handle a wild and willful child. In other words, he wasn't gonna take the rap for his kid. No way.

After that, Travis was pretty much on his own.

He became the star attraction, the psychopath. He was the monster with a mind of his own, and no one could hold a candle to him. It was just a matter of charting his every move, exposing his world, plumbing his life for the damning details to prove beyond a reasonable doubt that he did it.

The prosecution—in the person of Mr. Griswold—was assigned to this task. Mr. Griswold was tall and thin and wore double-breasted suits that had a silky sheen to them. His hair was an indeterminate color, not exactly gray, with a patch of scalp showing through at the top. From his plain masklike face, it was impossible to tell what he was thinking.

Watching Mr. G. present his case was like watching a high school biology teacher dissect a frog—gross, but also fascinating. Everything was laid bare. Even Travis's most private thoughts in the form of amusing or hateful or tender emails were pulled apart, examined and assessed by the courtroom. When the details got to be too much, we looked away, appraised our shoes, checked out everybody's hair and makeup, thought about lunch.

There was not much debate about whether Travis did it or did not do it. The evidence was overwhelming. First-degree murder, aggravated assault, kidnapping. Crimes like these had to be someone's fault, and someone had to be the evil behind them. Mr. G., along with his prosecution team, worked hard to expose Travis as the source. They created a portrait of a boy who had gone astray not because he lacked guidance and a firm hand, but rather because he was born with the cold heart of a criminal and a clear intent to kill.

Curtis Calzoni's confession in exchange for the lesser charge of accessory to murder and the promise to try him as a minor, followed by his teary-eyed appearance on the witness stand, didn't leave much doubt in anyone's mind. Travis had done it.

But even after several weeks of presenting and disputing the evidence, calling witnesses to the stand, asking experts to weigh in on matters related to the boat, the dead body, the scene of the crime, the rope, even after everyone had had enough of the whole case and all its players, one big question remained: Why did Travis do it? After sitting in the courtroom, listening to the endless drone of expert witnesses, the sobbing testimonies, the steely exchange of the cross-examination, I still didn't get it. Not really. And I doubt whether the jury understood it either. Whatever happened that night to make the violence seem inevitable and irreversible remained out of reach, unknown.

What we learned from the trial was this: Travis had been driving around with Curtis, looking for trouble. When they happened to spot Leonard walking west along Colter Road, Travis suggested that they give the kid a ride. Leonard was on his way home from Buddy Howard's house, where he had spent the evening proving to Mr. Buddy that he had, in fact, learned all his Act One lines in *The Tempest*. Usually Mr. Buddy drove Leonard home as arranged by my mother; but we learned from Mr. Buddy's own testimony that Leonard said he wanted to walk instead because he was meeting a friend. After Leonard had said good night, Mr. B. continued to read Act Two of *The Tempest* and then he answered some emails. All of this was corroborated by Mr. Buddy's computer records.

Travis pulled over, and after a brief exchange, Leonard got into the car and sat in the backseat. Had their meeting been arranged beforehand? Not according to Curtis; he claimed it had been purely accidental. Leonard leaned his head forward into the front seat so he could discuss with Travis and Curtis the details of his upcoming performance. He asked them if they wanted to be backstage crew. They laughed at the thought of themselves standing in the shadows while Leonard, dressed as a fairy, jumped around in the light. Leonard said they were Philistines.

"Whatever," Travis reportedly replied.

At some point, according to Curtis's testimony, Leonard suggested that they head out to Shark Lake. To cool off, Curtis had told the court. "Y'know, to swim." This was odd, because as I told Mr. G. earlier, Leonard didn't know how to swim and it seemed unlikely that Curtis would've come up with this idea himself. At the time Mr. G. grunted, scribbled something down on his legal pad and said that bit of info might come in handy.

Travis parked the car on a quiet side street and

all three boys got out. There was no indication of a struggle. Not yet. One of them (Curtis wasn't sure who) suggested the possibility of breaking into a nearby house and stealing stuff, but they decided against it. Leonard had to pee and he insisted that they find someplace private so he could do it. Together they worked their way farther down the street, where they couldn't be seen from any of the lakefront homes. When they reached a small natural cove, surrounded by a stand of birch trees, Travis said he wasn't going any farther. He quickly stripped naked and dove headfirst into the lake. When he had cleared the pontoon that was floating about twenty feet from the shore, he turned and called to the shore. He wanted Curtis and Leonard to join him.

"Now!" he shouted.

Curtis stripped down to his underpants, kicked off his sneakers, tore off his T-shirt and made a splash as he dove into the water. Leonard remained on the shore, watching. Curtis hooted a few times, a reaction to the cool temperature of the water and, as he reported it, the pure fun of it all.

What happened next isn't exactly clear. Curtis's testimony became sketchy at this point, and even Mr. G.'s no-nonsense examination technique couldn't clear things up. Why, for instance, did Travis swim back to the shore? Was he trying to get Leonard into the water, or did he already have darker motives? According to Curtis's calculations, there were about five or six minutes that he was unable to account for. What happened between Travis and Leonard during that time and what they said to each other remains a mystery, because Travis refused to elaborate.

What we do know is that by the time Curtis reached the shore, Leonard was still alive and lying unconscious on the grass. Travis stood over him with a large rock in his hand, and he was still naked. As a way of explaining what had happened, Travis allegedly muttered, "Fucking faggot."

Travis then handed his car keys to Curtis and told him to hurry up and get him the rope that was in the trunk. Curtis said he was probably in shock at this point. But when Mr. G. examined him further, he said he figured Leonard was already dead (he was not), and he was scared that he'd be Travis's next victim if he didn't do as he was told. In any case, Curtis did as he was told. He claimed that he wasn't an accomplice or an accessory or anything like that. The judge advised him to calm down and just continue answering Mr. G.'s questions.

After getting the rope from the trunk of the car, Curtis returned to the scene of the crime. By this time Travis had found a small rowboat that was moored nearby and had pulled it ashore near to the place where Leonard's body lay. Curtis watched as Travis leaned over Leonard.

"Help me," Travis said, and that was when Curtis stepped in and performed his lousy rope trick—the square knot, also known as "Exhibit F." Then quickly, efficiently, Travis and Curtis picked up Leonard's limp body and placed it in the hull of the boat.

"Did you at any point notice that Leonard was still breathing?" Mr. G. asked Curtis.

"Objection," Ms. Fassett-Holt offered.

"Overruled," said the judge, and then she slid her eyeballs over to where Ms. Fassett-Holt was standing. "We've already heard from the experts that the victim died from drowning. I think we can agree that if he was still alive when they put him in the boat, he had to be breathing. Or do I have my science wrong?"

Ms. Fassett-Holt sat down again to chew her pencil end, and the story continued.

Curtis did not in fact notice whether Leonard was still breathing, but he assumed that the kid was dead and they were getting rid of the corpse.

Curtis helped Travis lift Leonard's body into the boat. Together they paddled out to the center of the lake, cut the anchor loose from the boat and attached it to Leonard. Then they dumped the body overboard, slipping him into the water without a splash. Leonard sank to the bottom of the lake, where he remained until he was found by the divers Vlad and Brian.

"Were you aware that Leonard had two-pound weights attached to his ankles?" Mr. G. asked Curtis.

"Yeah," said Curtis, trying to suppress a smirk. "Everybody knew about that. It was for the play he was in. He never shut up about it."

"Since you are so familiar with the story," Mr. G. intoned, "would you be kind enough to explain it to the court for us."

"Okay," Curtis began. "Leonard was in a play at the high school. We didn't think he'd seriously flit around the stage in tights. Nobody did."

"And what was the play?"

"Shakespeare. Something by Shakespeare, and he was going to play a kind of fairy."

The courtroom erupted in titters and suppressed laughter. Judge Gamble whacked her gavel.

"Go on," Mr. G. said.

"Anyway, his character was trapped on this island. I don't know the play. And I didn't get what he was talking about. Something about how wearing the weights would help him to flit about like . . . well, like a fairy."

More titters. Another gavel whack.

And then, even though Mr. G. was addressing himself to Curtis, he did this thing where he turned to face the jury.

"You realize of course, Curtis, that if Leonard had suddenly become conscious in the water and managed to free himself from the weight of the anchor, his ankle weights would've taken him down. You saw that as a possibility?"

"Objection, your honor. Leading the witness."

"Sustained."

"I'll withdraw the question," Mr. G. said, knowing he had done the damage he'd set out to do. He didn't care about the court records; he only wanted the jury to understand the situation clearly. "No more questions, your honor."

NINETEEN

Judge Gamble instructed the jury that while it would be emotionally satisfying to have a clear motive in this case, it wasn't essential in establishing guilt beyond a reasonable doubt. But without a clear motive, all the evidence in the world is just stuff laid out on a table. Without a *why*, the story hangs there unresolved. Turns out it's the motive that connects the dots, makes a case and allows us to sleep at night. And really, there was no motive—nothing that could be said out loud and with certainty.

Once the trial began, all the reporters we had seen the previous year after Leonard died were back in our lives. They were free to speculate about what Travis's motive might have been, but for them it was a professional matter. Most of them camped out in front of the courthouse in Trenton and reported daily what was going on inside the building. A few of them with names and microphones that we recognized parked their vans on our street, determined to get a statement from one of us set against the charming backdrop of the salon. Usually we just stayed indoors when they were around. None of us appreciated being local color for the evening news. Not again.

When Deirdre, Mom and I weren't busy hurrying from the house to the car with a coat draped over our heads, we were peeking through curtains to watch on-the-scene reporters with TV hair stand in a shock of light and yak about us to their at-home audience. In their most professional tones and snazziest outfits, they speculated about how we felt, why Travis did it and what would be his fate when the whole thing was finished. Some of the more seasoned reporters, like my old pal Carol Silva-Hernandez, spoke directly into the camera and tried to convey the impression that she was feeling something for all of us, even for Travis. If she talked about the future at all, she made it clear that she had adopted a wait-and-see attitude.

Of course, once the gays and lesbians got wind of Leonard's fate, they all hopped on their bandwagon and headed in our direction. They claimed that Travis's motive was hate. They called it a hate crime. At first I was like, "Wait. Isn't all crime about hate?" But then Jodi, a lesbian from Weehawken, informed me that some people are targets of violence because of their "difference." Jodi had come to Trenton to "be a public face," talk to the press and demonstrate outside the courthouse. She frequently held forth on the steps of the courthouse and also on our front lawn when she came to visit us. Reporters either made the most of her, offering her airtime and egging her on with questions, or they ignored her completely and treated her like a nutcase. Jodi couldn't have cared less what people thought of her. She was an activist—also a poet. Her life, she told me, was her art. Take it or leave it.

Personally, I don't think art should ever be an excuse for bad hairstyling. Everybody should take pride in the way they look, especially if they happen to be appearing on TV. Jodi had a mullet. When she appeared on TV, her head looked as though it had been set in a box of flyaway and fuzz. Not a good look. Mom and I tried many times to break the news to her that she was in need of a makeover, but she was so busy explaining the proceedings at court to us whenever she had a chance that we rarely could get a word in edgewise. Clearly, beauty was not a priority for Jodi. If only Leonard had been around, I thought, Jodi would've been invited back to Neptune for an overnight, and she would've left our house the next morning a changed person.

This crime, she explained, wasn't motivated by greed or passion or jealousy or even rage; it wasn't that personal. She said that the perpetrator (Travis) saw the victim (Leonard) demonstrating certain traits of a particular type (gay), and though the perpetrator may not have had any feelings one way or the other for the victim, he certainly had strong feelings (hate) toward the type. In this particular case, she explained, it was pretty obvious from Curtis's confession that the real reason Travis singled

Leonard out was because he couldn't tolerate the fact that Leonard might be gay.

I think if you had asked Leonard point-blank if he was gay, he would have totally sidestepped the question. He would have told you (as he told me) that he was just being himself—obviously. But I think everyone who knew Leonard would agree that "being himself" involved giving off homo signals like fireworks off a lit barge. If he wasn't already officially there, he was definitely on his way. It was just a matter of time.

A chorus of people took the stand, one after another, and each of them backed up the idea that even if Leonard wasn't exactly gay, he was at the very least "flamboyant." "Colorful" was also a word the witnesses used to describe Leonard. And "original" was tossed around too. Leonard's teachers, some of Mom's customers, Uncle Mike, and even a few of Leonard's classmates all said the same thing in so many words—Leonard was a big sissy. From there it was just a short leap for Mr. G. to propose that Leonard was what he called "pre-gay," and therefore subject to the same prejudices that gays and lesbians might suffer. The case wasn't being tried as a hate crime, not officially, but Mr. G. had made his point.

Every once in a while Travis moved his head, but he never fully turned toward the witness stand or toward the jury, and as far as I could tell nothing seemed to register with him. Even when Mr. G. pointed at him and referred to him as "the defendant" and accused him of doing something called "entrapment," Travis never moved in his chair. Jodi told us later that Mr. G. was playing the hate card. And Travis just watched him do it without budging. Jodi said it was either an impressive show of self-control on Travis's part or the guy was just plain dead inside.

When Mr. G. introduced Travis's emails as evidence and had Curtis read snippets of them aloud in court, Travis leaned over and whispered something into Ms. Fassett-Holt's ear. But at that point she didn't raise an objection. How could she? She seemed to realize right then that her boy was sunk. Though the words Travis had used to describe Leonard in those emails were shocking to the people in the courtroom, the content of them was pretty straightforward. Gays were dead meat.

What was still missing, however, was an indication that Leonard's murder had been premeditated. Sure the hate was there, but not the plan.

During our lunch break, Mr. G. told us that he hadn't been able to prove beyond a reasonable doubt that Travis had planned the whole thing, with or without Curtis. An important point, he said. Still, he explained to us as he delicately bit into his machine-vended KitKat bar, without an airtight alibi, without credible character witnesses and with so much of the evidence stacked against the defendant, Ms. Fassett-Holt didn't stand much of a chance. He said Travis would most certainly be found guilty and then only one question would be—how harsh would his sentence be?

"What about motive?" I asked him. "Is that over with?"

He raised his shoulders and then let them drop. It was anybody's guess. The jury would have to decide for themselves if there was enough to support a probable motive. But Mr. G. explained that unless something unexpected was introduced at the last minute, he felt the case was sown up. And then he chomped the last of his Kit Kat and licked his fingers as if to emphasize his point.

The next two days were spent listening to Ms. Fassett-Holt present her case. She called several people to the stand: experts and witnesses who testified about the extent and depths of Travis's miserable childhood; and together they shored up the argument that the boy deserved, at the very least, kindness. There were no big surprises or star witnesses, and as a result the proceedings were at times almost too painful to sit through. Nonetheless, Ms. Fassett-Holt persevered.

At the end of day two, I watched as they led Travis out of the courtroom. He was (as my nana Hertle used to say) "calm as damnit," floating above it all and showing not even a flicker of human emotion. He didn't seem to have any idea of the trouble he was in or of the consequences he was going to suffer if found guilty. It was as though he didn't care if he won the case or not, and that afternoon, instead of looking back at the courtroom as he usually did when he was led away, he just went with the guards. As they hustled him through the doorway and out of sight, I remember thinking, *That's it—he's gone.* Travis Lembeck was already living in another world, another dimension. The Past had ceased to exist for him. The Future was too painful to consider. He was already serving time.

But then suddenly, on the third day, something happened. Ms. Fassett-Holt asked if she could approach the bench. Mr. G. joined her, and together they stood before Judge Gamble with their backs to the courtroom. We waited. Shortly after that there was a recess. I knew something was up because when Mr. G. sidled up to us, he didn't look good— his face had gone ashen and his eyes seemed sunk into his head. Then, after a lot of hemming and hawing, some discussion about the introduction of new evidence, and a fair amount of complaining about the inadvisability of calling a witness to the stand without first doing an interview, he explained to us that Ms. Fassett-Holt was simply making a very desperate, last-ditch attempt to save her client's life by calling me to the stand.

Just then a weaselly-looking guy in a gray suit elbowed his way through the crowd, came up to me and asked if I was Phoebe Hertle. I was still reeling from Mr. G.'s announcement, so I barely nodded, but it was enough to make the guy hand me an official-looking piece of paper, which Mom swiped out of my hand before I could get a good look at it. It was a document that said I was to appear as a witness.

The next hour or so was pretty much a blur for me. I do remember that Deirdre tried to improve my overall presentation by restyling my hair and makeup.

"Basically, you want your eyes to pop, up there on the stand," she told me. This was one of the handy catchphrases that Deirdre had picked up since enrolling in Roberson's Beauty Academy in Asbury Park. I just sat there thinking about Leonard and wishing that he'd lived long enough to witness Deirdre's change of attitude and her dexterity with a mascara wand.

"Don't make her look too much like a tramp," Mom said, which I believe was her way of getting Deirdre to tone down the eye shadow and make me look more like a model citizen.

I said nothing. I was still getting used to the fact that I was about to become a player in an actual court trial.

Of course, if I known that I was going to be called to take the stand, I would have worn an entirely different outfit and I certainly would have fixed my hair in a style more fitting for a witness. The worst part, however, was how they used me, or how Travis *let* them use me, in order to make it seem like maybe the case was not as airtight as it was. Ms. Fassett-Holt did just what she had to do in order to cast a reasonable doubt over the proceedings. That was her job, but clearly Travis had had a hand in it. Was it his idea, I wondered, or did Ms. Fassett-Holt just happen to have a sudden brainstorm at the eleventh hour, a brainstorm that involved me?

Travis didn't look up from the table when I took the stand and put my hand on the Bible. And he never looked over at me while Ms. Fassett-Holt was grilling me about my whereabouts on the evening in question. Nor did he look up when I explained that yes, I knew the defendant. But no, it would not be accurate to categorize our relationship as romantic. Definitely not.

Did Travis see his lawyer smirk at that? I wouldn't know. I was too busy sweating under my oversized cable-knit and side glancing at the jury box. Did he notice how Ms. Fassett-Holt turned toward the jury and shared her bemused expression with them, like they were her private little army of confidants? She had their attention. Finally. How happy she must have been. And who told her, I wonder, that Travis and I had kissed? Who besides Travis and I knew that he had once discovered me standing in his backyard trying to get his attention after midnight by throwing stones at his bedroom window?

"I didn't mean to break the window. That was an accident."

Travis had definitely told her about that.

But still he didn't look up to see my expression when Ms. Fassett-Holt asked me point-blank if I had ever been inside the shed, which was situated in the Lembeck backyard.

"No," I told her. "I didn't even know there was a shed."

I saw where she was going with this. She was suggesting that I could very easily have planted the rope in the shed, the rope they later found linking Travis to the murder.

"I told you, I didn't even know there was a shed."

Travis also didn't look up when Ms. Fassett-Holt asked me to explain to the court what I was doing in the Lembeck backyard in the first place. She didn't seem that satisfied with my answer. But then maybe she never had a cousin who was murdered, maybe she never had to go down to the morgue with her mother to identify a body and then return home feeling bad because she hadn't been a good enough friend to that body when it was alive. Maybe she didn't understand that sometimes a person needs to reach out to someone who won't ask a lot of stupid questions, but instead will just place his hand gently on her breast and tell her it's all right. Ms. Fassett-Holt wanted it to seem like a romantic thing between Travis and me, like a sex thing. She wanted details about our "prior date," as she called it, on the Fourth of July.

"It wasn't a date," I told her. "It wasn't, like, planned or anything. It just happened."

"Yes, but you kissed on that occasion. Isn't that right?"

If Travis had been looking up at this point, he might have seen a lot. He might have seen me blush, for instance, and if he'd turned around in his seat, he might have seen my mother take a deep breath and turn her head toward the ceiling, which is her way of appealing to a higher power and at the same time registering her exasperation with what's going on here on earth. She didn't like where this was going any more than I did. But what could we do? Of course, though I was trying desperately not to look over at Travis, I couldn't keep myself from looking at him. How could I not? Ms. Fassett-Holt couldn't have known about the kissing unless he had told her.

"But you kissed."

She said it again. And how was I supposed to respond? I mean, there are laws about perjury.

"Yes, we kissed."

I hated her and I hated her cheap royal blue Anne Taylor knockoff double-breasted suit with its black plastic buttons and sewn-up pockets. She was like a bad actress on an episode of *CSI*.

"Is that all you did? Kiss?"

"Yes, that's all we did."

"And yet wasn't there another date?"

"It wasn't a date. He gave me a ride."

"Did you kiss then as well?"

"Yes."

She then asked me if perhaps I felt "spurned" by the defendant when there hadn't been a follow-up to our first date. Spurned? Who says spurned? Spurned isn't a word people use anymore. Someone should have told her. When I sarcastically repeated the word "spurned" back at her, I instantly sensed the jury beginning to shy away from my version of the story. I was a hostile witness who was actually turning hostile. But really—spurned? Characters in novels by Bronte feel spurned. Edith Wharton heroines actually get spurned. Those of us in the twenty-first century get dumped. Maybe we feel bad about it and sit at home reading trash novels, eating too many peanut butter snack packs while cursing the guy in question; but we don't usually plant phony evidence in a backyard shed or try to frame anyone for crimes they didn't commit.

"And the money clip?" she asked me. "It was you who found the money clip. Isn't that right? Tell me about that."

So I told her. I told her about that day at the mall when Leonard came running up to me all hysterical, because Travis and Curtis had stolen the money and the clip from Leonard. I explained how the clip was Leonard's most prized possession, and that he never would have parted with it. Ever. I told her how that day at the mall Curtis accused me of being a lesbian just because I was hanging out with Leonard, and how I kissed Travis on the mouth to prove there was no danger of my being anything like a lesbian. It was all bravado, I explained to the court. Ms. Fassett-Holt raised her eyebrows at the word.

It didn't matter that all Travis and I ever did was kiss. My life was suddenly and inexplicably linked to his. We had become part of the same story, and thanks to Ms. Fassett-Holt, it was the kind of story that everyone on the jury could relate to—girl meets boy, girl kisses boy, boy spurns girl, girl tracks down boy and makes him pay. And no matter what I said up there on that witness stand, Ms. Fassett-Holt made it seem as though I had planted the evidence out of spite, as an act of revenge.

"I'm not asking you if you did it, Phoebe. I'm asking you if it was possible that you *could* have done it. After all, you had the opportunity."

"Objection."

"Overruled. The witness will answer the question."

But I just sat there unable to speak, seething in my own truth and probably looking like someone's picture of a spurned girl.

I was wearing a skirt, and the wood under my bare thighs was literally heating up. Every person who'd ever sat there had agreed to tell the whole truth and nothing but the truth. Maybe some of them had lied outright to save their skins. Maybe some of them had told the truth like they were sworn to do. Maybe some of them had lied so often to themselves, they couldn't tell the difference. It didn't matter. It didn't matter because as I sat there on the witness stand, the truth suddenly became as slippery as that seat under my bare thighs. Under the circumstances, a person can be made to say things that are technically true, but at the same time are not the God's honest truth.

"Yes, it's possible." And then I quickly added, "But I didn't plant the rope. And I told you, I found the money clip on the dresser."

Travis was definitely not looking up at this point. He missed how Ms. Fassett-Holt turned to the jury and, with a half smile on her face, said, "Yes, as you were on your way out of the defendant's bedroom. And what time would you say that occurred, Miss Hertle?"

Why didn't she just call me a slut and get it over with?

Then came the part of Ms. Fassett-Holt's performance that was truly remarkable. She had saved the best for last. She pretended that she had one more question for the witness, and if the court would indulge her, she would keep it short. Judge Gamble gave her the go ahead, and Ms. Fassett-Holt straightened her jacket. There was a pencil in her right hand, which she kept twirling between her fingers like a tiny baton. She practically shouted the question at me from across the courtroom.

"Phoebe, I just want to get this straight. You testified that you were able to retrieve Leonard's money clip from Travis that day at the mall. Is that right?"

"Yes."

"Okay. Just so we understand, can you tell us exactly how you got the clip from Travis?"

The jury didn't know me, and they had no reason to believe a word I said. As far as they were concerned, I was just a girl—possibly spurned—who was involved with both the defendant and the victim. I had been the link between the two, the common thread. I was also, it should be remembered, the person who, after allegedly finding the money clip in Travis's bedroom, alerted Officer DeSantis that he could be a suspect in this case, a possible murderer. If the jury chose to believe me, it would be because of my character, because I seemed sincere, honest, trustworthy, a respectable citizen just doing her civic duty in apprehending and convicting a criminal. Ms. Fassett-Holt's brilliance was in knowing how to hold up a light to my actions so that it would cast a shadow on my character.

"Maybe you didn't hear the question."

"I stole it."

"I'm sorry. Could you speak up?"

"I said I stole it. I stole the money clip from Travis's pocket."

After that, it didn't matter what I said. I was definitely out of the running as a reliable witness or as a respectable citizen. As far as the jury was concerned, I was a girl who stole things, a girl who cried murder, a girl who kissed boys in the backseat of cars on the first date, a girl who vandalized homes in the middle of the night. Jersey Shore white trash. Standard issue.

She had another question for me, and the way she announced it, I just knew it was going to be a whopper. I'd watched enough episodes of *Law & Order* to know the telltale signs.

"Is it true that prior to Leonard's murder you actually had a plan to smother him with a pillow?"

"Objection!" called out Mr. G. from across the room.

Just 'cause no one catches you doing something wrong, well, that doesn't mean you won't suffer consequences, does it? It was Bethany again, her voice inside my head. Obviously, she was never going to leave me alone. It's true—that day in the auditorium I *had* announced my wish to kill my cousin. But as Nana Hertle used to say, "Wishes are horses without riders."

"I didn't mean it," I cried. "It was like a joke."

Honestly, I can't remember much about Mr. G.'s cross-examination except the first few questions, which were about my relationship with Leonard. After that, it's all a blank. Although I do know that I broke down crying. I cried hard. So hard I had to bury my face in my skirt. The pressure had been too much, and I cracked.

I was told later that Travis actually did look up from the table when I started sobbing. I was sorry to have missed the moment, because if I had seen his face, I would've been able to tell if it was the evil in his heart or the goodness that made him steal a glance at me. Deirdre said she couldn't tell which it was, because she was seated behind him in the courtroom, so she didn't have a clear view of his expression. But even if she had, she told me, she doubted whether she would've been able to tell what he was thinking.

"I don't know him as well as you do," she said, with the slightest trace of admiration in her voice. And then just so her point was made, she added, "Obviously."

As I made my way back to my seat, I heard Judge Gamble's remarks signaling the end of the morning's session and then the sharp crack of her gavel calling a recess until after lunch. That's when it happened—Travis looked over at me. Our eyes met. My heart stopped, but I could still hear the thudding of blood in my brain, so I knew I wasn't dead. He silently mouthed the words "Thank you" at me, and then he smiled and quickly turned away, back to whatever it was he was doing. I wanted to speak, but like in those nightmares when your whole life depends on your ability to scream and not a single word comes out of your mouth, I was speechless. I just stood there, paralyzed in the middle of the floor. Days went by, weeks, years, and there I was, still in that room, still wanting to say, Don't *thank me. Please, don't thank me. And don't you dare smile. I did nothing. Nothing for you to smile about. If I was helpful, it was not because I wanted to be. I was doing my duty, telling the truth, I was telling the whole truth and nothing but the truth. But the truth didn't come out. Not really. Something else was revealed, some shade of truth that may benefit you in the end, but I didn't make it happen. So don't thank me.*

But like I said, not a word came out.

My mother, realizing that I was stuck there in the middle of the floor, came to my rescue. She took my arm and gently led me away. It had been a rough day for me. I was like a shell of my former self, walking around with bad hair and the wrong clothes, unable to speak in full sentences.

The following day we were back in our usual courtroom seats waiting to hear closing remarks from both sides of the aisle. Judging from the expressions of the jury members, I'd say the lawyers each made worthy arguments and came to conclusions that supported their sides of the story. I tried to listen, but after my performance the previous day I couldn't help feeling as though everyone was looking at the back of my head in a whole new way. I began to imagine that everyone was sitting behind me, thinking that I was Travis's girlfriend. *That's her!* they were saying to themselves. The girl who kissed a killer. Surely my picture would appear in tomorrow's newspaper with a caption identifying me as "Phoebe Hertle, girlfriend of the accused." My hair would be an honest wreck, because the photographers would have caught me as I hurried down the steps of the courthouse at the end of the trial. They wouldn't have cared that I looked like someone ducking flying debris. And with that kind of publicity, I would naturally come to the conclusion that I'd better stay at home for the rest of my life rather than subject myself to more questions, misidentifications and photographs in broad daylight. Eventually, everyone would forget about the trial, but by that time I would be a very old woman, famous for never having left her house.

When they were finished, Judge Gamble gave instructions to the jury and then made a speech about the seriousness of their decision and the importance of justice in the world.

The jury didn't even need twenty-four hours to come to an agreement on the verdict, and the very next day we were back in the court, ready to find out the fate of Travis Lembeck.

A blond woman with a serious puffed-out hair-do, a set jaw and expensive fingernails had been elected to speak on behalf of the jury. Judge Gamble reiterated the charge against the defendant (murder in the first degree) and then asked the blond woman how they had found the defendant. She stood there and responded in a quavering voice, "Guilty."

Judge Gamble said a few words and smacked her gavel down hard. The guards took Travis away, and that was that.

As we were making our way out of the court-room, the bailiff slipped us a note from Judge Gamble informing us that she wanted to have a word with us in her chambers. Mom, Deirdre, Uncle Mike and I hustled ourselves through the chamber door and into a wood-paneled office with high ceilings. There was a big desk plunked down in the middle of the room, and we stood before it in our coats and scarves like overheated students who had been unexpectedly called in to see the principal for who-knows-what.

Judge Gamble was a very small woman. Down from her legal perch and out of her judicial gown, she was not at all the imposing figure she projected in the courtroom. She had a surprisingly tiny head and very large feet. She had brown hair with gray streaks, and it was cut in a no-nonsense bob that fell just below her ears. Cute. She sat, or rather leaned, on a corner of her desk and offered us water or coffee. There were no takers. She reminded us of the date when the sentencing portion of the trial would take place and then took her glasses off to say that it was very possible that the jury could levy the harshest punishment on the defendant. No one else in my party knew what the hell she was talking about, so I acted as translator.

"She's saying Travis could get the death penalty," I informed my clueless family. They all gave a quick nod in my direction, like they knew what had been said in the first place.

Judge Gamble told us that though there were, currently, eleven people on death row in the state of New Jersey, no one had actually been executed since 1976. If Travis Lembeck received the death sentence, it would be more for show than anything else. To send a signal that Jersey is tough on crime. She added that the heinousness of Travis's offense, the cruelty inflicted on the victim and all the publicity surrounding the case could mean that the jury might feel justified in calling for stricter penalties. She also wanted us to know that, as Leonard's family, we would have the opportunity at the sentencing trial to make a public statement. It was up to us if we wanted to do it. No pressure. She suggested that we give it some thought and then decide as soon as possible. It was better, she told us, to have as much time as possible so that we could not only compose a statement but also to prepare ourselves emotionally.

My mother asked which one of us was supposed to do the talking, and Judge Gamble looked at us over the rims of her half-moons. "It doesn't make any difference. But whoever speaks, they speak for the whole family. I don't want a chorus line of differing opinions. One voice. And try to keep it brief. Five minutes, tops."

We all stumbled out of there and headed home. No one spoke. I sat in the backseat, staring out the window. When we arrived home, we pushed our way past a few waiting reporters. Only Uncle Mike wanted to stop and make a statement. Just as he opened his big, fat mouth, Mom pulled him along, nearly ripping the sleeve off his coat in the process. Fortunately we were able to drag him inside before he could speak his piece about how "the verdict will surely represent a small step for mankind, but a giant leap for justice," which was a line that he'd tried out on us during the drive home. Naturally, Uncle Mike wanted to be the one to stand up and speak in court. He felt that he had the right, or so he kept reminding us. "As Leonard's legal guardian . . ." Blah, blah blah.

The rest of us were confused about what to feel or how to proceed. Maybe we weren't used to the idea, but no one wanted to stand up in a court of law and make a big speech that would be quoted in all the newspapers and in every salon all over town. Not my mother, not Deirdre and not me. No one was that brave—or that stupid. The courtroom had been filled with many familiar faces from Neptune: my mother's customers, teachers from Neptune Senior and former classmates of Travis's. You do one thing wrong in a town like ours and that's that. You become known for it. The story sticks. You never live it down.

Over lunch my mother announced that she was glad the trial was over and she had no intention of dragging the thing out any further, because she was fed up with being depicted by failed artists who had part-time jobs working as quick-sketchers for the TV news channels.

"Who are these people? All the time, they make me look like a hag. And what kind of a job is that for a normal person? Sitting around all day making unflattering portraits of people in bad situations? I won't be party to it."

Personally, I think she was just scared about speaking in public, but either way she refused to stand up and make a statement.

Deirdre had never been big on the whole trial thing. She had agreed to come that final week because she was on a break from school, but from the very beginning, she made it clear to us that the court case and all its by-products were not going to be a priority in her life. Because she was now a student at Roberson Beauty Academy, she felt that a courtroom atmosphere wasn't consistent with her training process. Her instructor, Todd, told the class that as aspiring beauty technicians they had only one job: to learn how to create and sustain an environment of pure glamour. That was the trick, he informed them. Apparently, this is how JLo does it, as well as Nicole Kidman and other glamourpusses who'd probably never paid a visit to Asbury Park, New Jersey. In any case, by the time Deirdre did show up in court, she'd missed so many days that she wasn't able to identify who was who in relation to the case. As a designated spokesperson, she would have been useless; and more to the point, she was unwilling.

My father and Chrissie hadn't been attending the trial at all. They announced early on in the proceedings that Trenton was just too far to travel every day and they had responsibilities at work. But they were not people we would have wanted to speak for our family, since they were people who did not, at that time, speak *to* our family.

Uncle Mike had a fit when he found out that we were considering the possibility of not allowing him to speak on Leonard's behalf. He reminded us (again) that he and no one else would be speaking for Leonard.

I didn't care who did the talking, but I had plenty to say about the speech we were to make in that courtroom. But we all got into a screaming match about what Judge Gamble had told us to do, how we all had to speak with one voice. This, of course, meant that we had to come to some kind of agreement about what we actually thought.

Uncle Mike considered Travis to be beyond rehabilitation. He pointed out that "the bastard," as he referred to him, never said he was sorry, never showed any sympathy for us and certainly never demonstrated any mercy toward Leonard out on the lake. I argued with him; I said that we could not presume to know what Travis was thinking or feeling.

"It's all conjecture," I said, using a term I'd picked up in the courtroom.

Uncle Mike started yelling. He put his foot down—sometimes literally, which caused the appliances to shake and made cups and saucers rattle in the cupboard. He threw up his hands and said he'd been conjectured up the wazoo since this whole business began. He wanted it known that he was sick to death of talking about Leonard's murder as though there might be shades of gray.

"It's black and white," he kept repeating. "It's open and shut! The bastard deserves the death penalty. End of discussion."

Of course, Uncle Mike was not the only one who had been talking about capital punishment as the only acceptable outcome to this case. From the beginning all sorts of people had been claiming that if found guilty, Travis should have to pay the ultimate price: It was the only outcome that would bring closure to this whole situation.

"What's closure?" I asked.

"An eye for an eye, and all that," Uncle Mike told me. "Says so in the Bible."

I couldn't agree with him.

"An eye for an eye is just a rationalization for killing people."

Uncle Mike cut me off.

"You don't know what the hell you're talking about, and if you think Leonard's killer should go scot-free, then you're too young to understand the value of human life."

I began screaming so loud at him, I could hear the oven racks ringing.

"*Every life is worth something,*" I told him, sounding like a TV evangelist. "And what would killing Travis Lembeck do for Leonard? It's not like it would bring Leonard back from the dead. It's not like it would make us feel all happy inside afterward and allow us to go on like nothing ever happened. No. Leonard was killed. We have to find a way to live with it. We have to go on. All of us."

"But not Travis," Uncle Mike said, shaking his head and smiling out of just the bottom half of his mouth.

"Yes," I said. "Even Travis."

As I left the kitchen, I could hear Uncle Mike muttering to anyone who would listen, "What happened here? I thought we were talking this through."

TWENTY

After a long day in the courtroom and then the business with Uncle Mike, I had to go somewhere on my own to clear my head. But where? I briefly considered heading toward the beach so I could sit there, like Leonard used to say he did, watching the waves roll in and feeling his *weltschmerz*; but it was already dark, and listening to the waves just wasn't the same. I wandered up and down the side streets, thinking hard about the past two years. Soon I found myself wishing that we had never let Leonard live in our house in the first place. Then I wished that Electra and I were still best friends. Then I wished that Dad had never run off with

Chrissie Bettinger, and my parents weren't divorced. I wished Deirdre had never turned sad and sullen because of what happened between her and Dad. I wished . . . And just when I was in danger of wishing my whole life away, I found myself standing in front of St. Stephen's, the Catholic Church in town where my family goes to Mass, the place where Mom and Dad got married. I thought about stepping inside and saying a prayer or whatever, but the church was locked up tight.

Next door, however, a two-story brick building was lit up, and African music was coming from it. This was the place where Father Jimbo had lived since moving to Neptune. Though the house had originally been designed for a thriving parish that could comfortably house up to three full-time priests, two visiting novices and a live-in housekeeper, it had in recent times become home to only Father Jimbo. Constructed of tan-colored bricks and plain old concrete, it stood back from the street under a big old sycamore tree. The front steps were wide and gracious; and they led up onto a tiny enclosed porch. The heavy oak door had a gleam to it. Two very handsome stained-glass windows, one on either side of the door, silently informed trespassers and solicitors that this was no ordinary home; it was a rectory.

"Hello. Can I help you?"

I turned and saw Father Jimbo. He was standing at the foot of the stairs with his coat on and a golf club in his hand.

"Oh. Phoebe," he said when he saw me looking down at him. "It's Phoebe, isn't it?"

I nodded. And I guess he noticed me staring at his golf club, because he held it up, looked at it with a puzzled expression and then laughed out loud.

"I know. Strange thing, the golf. The nuns made a little putting green over there behind the convent. They installed lights and everything." He pointed with the club to a place I couldn't see, around the side of the house. "They made it for Father Cooper years ago. Did you know Father Cooper?"

I didn't.

"Yes, well now I have inherited his golf as well as his parishioners. But I bet you have not come to talk about golf."

Once we were inside the house, he switched off the African music and disappeared down a long corridor; he went to make me a cup of hot chocolate, and almost immediately I heard him fussing with the cups and the kettle, every sound bouncing off the highly polished floors and bare walls with a kind of brilliance. I had never been to Africa, but I couldn't help wondering how the sounds of Father Jimbo's childhood compared to the sterile clink of a single cup on a porcelain countertop or the lonely whistle of a ready kettle.

The rooms were large and spacious and seemed as if they'd been designed for the sort of elegance that the church could no longer afford. Cut-rate carpets in off shades of beige and tan clashed with the Old World fabrics of the seat cushions. Chairs that looked like they would've been more at home in a medieval play about knights and dragons hadn't been properly introduced to the Danish modern end tables. It was a mishmash of styles and patterns with only one unifying theme—thrift.

Father Jimbo had parked me in one of those ornately carved chairs in the front parlor. I sat there looking around. This was a room that seemed as if it got more use as an office than anything else. I imagined pre-Cana couples sitting down with Father Jimbo to discuss their upcoming vows, grieving widows with unpaid bills and recent converts with serious doubts. He probably leaned in to them, listened with his whole self and then gave them good advice, advice based on the very thing they wanted to do in the first place. People, as he sometimes told us in his Sunday sermons, know what's what, and what they know best is themselves. He wasn't one of those priests who push the church's agenda, rally round the Pope or stalk the altar boys; he was just one of the good guys dressed in black, doing his best to love the world at large one soul at a time.

He sat down beside me, and as I blew a few cooling breaths over my steaming mug of cocoa, he materialized a rattan coaster out of thin air. He placed it at the edge of his large heavy desk and made a gesture so that I would know the coaster was intended for me. Everything on the desk seemed to have been placed with as much care as the coaster— the blotter, the tiny calendar with each day of the month Xed off, the plastic clock with glow-in-the-dark hands, and the 1980s-type phone, the kind with a receiver attached to the base by a long curlicue wire. There was a blue ballpoint pen that had NEPTUNE SAVINGS & LOAN, SERVING THE COMMUNITY SINCE 1964 written in silver script along its side. Next to it lay a sharpened number-two pencil. A philodendron plant in a green ceramic pot spilled its shiny heart-shaped leaves over the top of the desk; and a rock the size of a child's fist with a happy face painted in Day-Glo pink sat beside it.

"Yes," he said after I'd finished explaining the situation to him. "So we have a big problem on our hands, you and I."

He went on to remind me that there is no sense arguing anything in the Bible, because people are always quoting certain passages to back up their arguments. It doesn't matter what you believe, he told me, there's always a snippet of scripture saying that you're right and the other guy's wrong. But he also pointed out that if you actually read the New Testament, Jesus kind of puts the whole eye-for-an-eye thing in perspective.

"If I am not mistaken, Jesus urges everyone to give up this business of knocking one another about and poking one another in the eyes. He told them they had to try, at least *try*, to be forgiving, even unto their enemies."

"Yeah. That's fine," I said, staring at the tiny plastic cross on his desk. "But the point is I'm afraid Uncle Mike's planning to do something totally drastic. He's definitely going to get up there in court and make a big speech about why Travis has to die."

I had already made my own position pretty clear. Even if Travis was in fact guilty, he didn't deserve to be killed. But then to press my point I added, "As Christians, we have a moral responsibility to do our best so that the jury doesn't just go for blood." I was sure that Father Jimbo would agree with me, especially since I laid the Christian thing on pretty thick. I was hoping he would volunteer to talk to Uncle Mike. But he only nodded and then gestured with his eyebrows for me to continue.

Uncle Mike, I told him, was using his voice to shout louder than anyone else in an effort to have his viewpoint be the one that mattered, and as a result we were getting nowhere fast. But, I pointed out, appealing to the jury and asking for mercy was definitely the way to go.

There was a slight pause as Father Jimbo leaned back in his chair and removed his gaze from me. He closed his eyes. I could almost hear the wheels and pullies in his brain; they were turning and clicking as he considered the options. He had the whole picture now.

"Phoebe, do you think Travis is evil?"

"I don't know. Maybe. But does it matter? He still doesn't deserve to die for killing Leonard. Does he? Isn't killing supposed to be a mortal sin?"

"It is. I do believe it is, and so does the Catholic Church, by the way. But some people, like your uncle, some people say that because Travis committed this evil, he himself must be evil; by doing away with the source of that evil, they might rid the world of more evil. They rest easier, sleep at night. For them it makes sense."

"But it's not right," I said, exasperated with Father Jimbo for taking Uncle Mike's side in the argument, even for the sake of argument. I had had enough of that for one evening.

"No. No, it is not right. Not for us. For you and for me, this is not a solution. But for others it is something definite they can do about the evil when it feels like evil is closing in around them."

"So what're you and I supposed to do? Just stand by and let them get away with it?"

"Exactly the right question, Phoebe. What can we *do*? And in my mind, that is the only question. What can we do?"

"Yeah, but that's my point, Father Jimbo. I can't exactly do anything here. I told you. Uncle Mike is dead set on doing the talking when the trial resumes."

"Yes," he said, smiling and showing me as many of his teeth as he could. "But there are days and days before that happens."

For the next half hour or so, Father Jimbo and I sat at his desk talking about good and evil. And though I'd been thinking about this stuff ever since Leonard disappeared, this was really the first time in my life that I was being asked to articulate what I thought about human beings and their enormous propensity for evil in this world. Were we truly good-natured creatures with occasional bouts of really bad behavior? Or were we all intrinsically evil with a desire to be better? I suppose it should have been some comfort when Father Jimbo told me that this was a question that had troubled some of the greatest thinkers and theologians throughout human history, and we couldn't hope to come up with an answer in one night. But really I was pissed when I noticed the time. It was after nine o'clock. More than an hour had gone by, and the only thing Father Jimbo had been able to offer me was cocoa. He still hadn't given me a game plan. I began to gather up my hat and scarf.

He grabbed his coat and walked out into the night with me. He said he had to do something inside the church and then added, "There is always something."

We paused on the sidewalk before saying good night.

"So what'll I do?" I asked him. "Will you at least talk to Uncle Mike?"

He gave a quick shrug and then, as if he had a sudden inspiration, asked me if I wanted to come inside the building with him. I looked up and saw that the church front was dark and foreboding. This wasn't one of those big swanky churches that had been built in the seventies to look like an airport terminal and to give everyone a feeling of hope about the future. This wasn't a place to which a movie star returned to get married and photographed amid the goodwill and cheers of hometown fans. (Jack Nicholson was Neptune's only movie star, and he never married.) St. Stephen's church was more of a throwback to another time. Modeled on someone's idea of a quaint village church somewhere in England before World War II, it had a tall, pointy spire, pews of dark wood, kneelers with real leather pads and a series of little arched niches where sad saints huddled in dusty shadows. With its dark-colored brick, wrought-iron railings and saturated stained-glass windows, this church always seemed to me like a hangover from an era when Catholics really ruled, like during the Crusades.

Father Jimbo was already up the front steps and unlocking the heavy front doors. He stood in the vestibule with one arm holding open the door. I could see into the darkness, but darkness was all I saw.

"Come on," he said, jerking his head toward the building. "I want to show you something."

"I really ought to get home. My mom'll be calling the police after me." But even as I said it, I was moving up the steps toward him.

"It will only take a minute."

Once we were inside, with the door shut behind us, I could feel rather than see the spaciousness of the church in front of me. A tiny lit candle flickered in the distance, but it was so small and so far off that it hardly illuminated the place; it was just a point of light. I could hear the two of us breathing, but once Father Jimbo spoke, I could also hear how big the place was. The sound of his voice carried to the far wall and then bounced back at us.

"Don't be afraid," he said. "This is what I want to show you."

"What?"

"This."

"It's dark. I don't see anything."

"Yes," he said. "Exactly. But what is darkness?"

"Huh?"

He was beginning to freak me out with this business about the darkness, his questions, his breathing. I could smell his aftershave and hear the chafing of his neck against his clerical collar as he turned to look at me in the dark. We were too close, and everything suddenly felt wrong—and scary.

"Can we say what darkness is?"

Just as I was about to turn and run, Father Jimbo flipped a switch on the wall beside him, and the chandelier lights at the back of the church went on. Instantly I could see the church, and though it seemed unfamiliar to me in this eerie half-light, it was without a doubt the place I had always come to on Christmas and Easter and on those Sundays when Mom insisted that we get dressed, go to Mass and pray for God-knows-what.

"Darkness is where light is not," Father Jimbo said, answering his own question. "Darkness is the absence of light, Phoebe. The more light there is, the less dark. It works the same with good and evil. Think about it. The more good there is, the less evil."

"So what're you saying . . . ," I asked him without exactly looking at him. "Are you saying I have to talk to Uncle Mike myself?"

On my way home, I thought about Father Jimbo's demonstration of light and dark, good and evil. I kept replaying the scene over and over in my mind, trying to figure out if it had been fair of him to lure me into the dark and use the church as a backdrop for his party trick. I wondered if he had perfected this stunt back in Africa. I pictured him as a young man traveling from village to village, astonishing whole tribes of natives. Perhaps he went around with a generator packed in the back of an open van. Maybe he had a string of lights and a big switch, so that even in a village beyond the reach of an electrical hookup, he could do his thing and mystify the crowd. *The more light there is, the less dark! It works the same with good and evil! Think about it.* I even imagined a scenario where Father Jimbo had tried his trick in a church somewhere in the United States back when he was a novitiate. I could easily picture the kind of panic it would have caused among the parishioners and the many complaints lodged with the bishop, until finally Father Jimbo was summoned to headquarters and given a stern warning not to try it again.

But how could he keep himself from indulging in such a dramatic demonstration of a question that is fundamental to our understanding of human nature, a question that has, as he put it, troubled some of the greatest thinkers and theologians throughout human history? With evil still rampant in the world and showing no signs of lessening its influence, wouldn't he feel that it was his moral responsibility to flip the switch again and again, as many times as necessary, whenever he saw the opportunity, every time someone came to him with a question? *So what'll I do?*

In my case, I was able to answer my own question. I walked over to Electra's house and knocked on the back door. Mrs. Wheeler peeked through the yellow frilled curtains, the ones that I myself had once helped to hang about a million years ago. She opened the door and grabbed me by my shoulders.

"Where you been, girl? I could just about whup you for not coming round our house. Told Electra, told that child to get herself over your house and drag your *ass* back here if she had to, but . . . What you do with your hair, girl? That's a color? Get in here this minute and let me see you in the light."

TWENTY-ONE

After a year of not being friends, there I was, once again, sitting at Electra's kitchen table on a Friday night waiting for her to come down the stairs so she could join me and we could get into some trouble. Just like always, I could hear her mother arguing with her, telling her what to do. But this time I was the task at hand.

"She came all the way over here to see you. Least you can do is go downstairs."

"And do what?"

"Say hi. Be civil. Talk to the girl. Work it out."

"And what if I don't want to?"

"Then girl, you're a bigger fool than folks take you for. Now get."

Electra appeared in the kitchen looking not that happy to see me. Her dreads were tied up in a purple scarf, and just the ends were sticking out of the top like a wrapped-up bunch of flowers. She was wearing a worn-out pink T-shirt, and her jeans were the ones that we'd stolen from The Gap almost two years ago. The moment I saw her, I realized how much I liked her, and I had to admit to myself that despite all my halfhearted efforts, no one had come close to replacing her as my best friend. I shrugged and said, "It's been like a bad year or something. For both of us. I don't even know what either of us did that was so wrong. But I'm telling you, it's not right for us to not be friends. I came to say I'm sorry. Forgive me?"

Electra shifted her weight to one hip and tilted her head way to one side. She just looked at me as if she was weighing her options or assessing my outfit. Finally, she offered me the flesh of her small round arm and said: "Lick it, bitch."

We laughed so loud, it sent Mrs. Wheeler running down the stairs and into the kitchen. When she saw us with our arms around each other, she just shook her head and glanced upward as if some explanation could be found written in the ceiling plaster. She pretended that she had been scared out of her wits by our yelping, but really I think she knew what was up and just wanted to see us happy together again.

I gave Electra a quick rundown of the situation, describing Uncle Mike's behavior and his insistence on the death penalty as a form of justice. She gasped with horror at all the right moments and reacted as a best friend should, responding to every prompt with exaggerated facial gestures and knowing nods. She understood what I was trying to say before I'd even finished saying it. Finally, she grabbed me by the hand and led me up the stairs into her bedroom. I sat on the edge of her bed as she plopped herself into a knockoff Aeron chair and began clicking away on her keyboard.

"And you're getting a computer," she informed me, without taking her eyes away from the screen. "It's ridiculous, you livin' in the dark ages. I love reading books much as you do, but you know, even *Jane Austen's* got a website now."

"I know. I know."

"No. For real. You're getting one. 'Cause if

we're going to be friends again you gotta get connected. I'll teach you."

Within minutes she had located a website devoted to the subject of capital punishment. She scooted over so that I could squeeze in beside her on the chair, and together we read what appeared on the screen. She scrolled and clicked like a master. I was amazed at her dexterity, her know-how. Obviously she'd been keeping herself busy during the past year.

"Here it is," she said.

We were shocked to learn that before the end of the month, seven human beings would be put to death somewhere in the United States either by electrocution or lethal injection. Electra read aloud the names of the condemned, along with the intended dates of their deaths and also the states where the executions were to take place.

"*Stephen Hopper—March second—Texas.*
George Mobley—March seventh—Ohio.
William Ray Smith—March eighth—
  Ohio.

Henry Wallace Jr.—March tenth—North Carolina.
William Dillard Doyle—March twelfth—Indiana.
Jimmy Ray Pollard—March fifteenth—Texas.
Julio Melendez—March sixteenth—Oklahoma."

Because neither of us could think of anything else to say, we found ourselves observing a moment of silence.

"And look," Electra said when the moment had passed. She clicked ahead to the following month. "More names in April. Same thing."

"Whoa," was all I could offer.

"Yeah. And no one notices," she remarked as she took her hand off the mouse and reached across to push the hair out of my eyes. "No one does the math. It just goes on."

"And tell me again," I said, feeling more dense than usual. "How does this help my case with Uncle Mike?"

Electra threw herself onto her bed and looked over at me like I was lame for not seeing things as clearly as she did.

"What?" I asked her.

"Nothing. It's just that up until this thing with Travis, you didn't care a hoot 'bout capital punishment. Now all of a sudden you're an activist? How'd that happen, you think?"

"I *know* Travis," I offered, though I could tell from Electra's all-knowing expression that I'd answered exactly as she expected me to. "But it's not like I don't care about all those other guys. I do. I just don't know them. Not personally."

"Ex-aaaactly!" she said as she swung her legs over the side of the bed and sat up so she could look me straight in the eye. "You got to get your uncle to *know* Travis. Somehow you got to make Travis a real, living, breathing person to him. More real than even Leonard was. Then your uncle can't possibly consider offing him."

"Right. And how am I supposed to do that?"

She let out a startled hoot and fell back onto the bed. After she kicked one leg up into the air and touched her socked toes to the canopy top, she said,

"Girl, don't look to me for the answer. You're the one who kissed the boy."

A week later, Mom decided that it was time for Uncle Mike to move out of the living room. He'd been with us since the start of the trial, and Mom was sick of coming downstairs every morning to find him hanging off the couch, half dressed and snoring like a pirate. Her solution was to give my room to Uncle Mike and move me to the rollaway bed in Deirdre's room. This was not a happy situation for anyone for the following reasons:

1. *My bed was too small for a big guy like Uncle Mike.*
2. *Deirdre wasn't thrilled with the idea of having a roommate at this point in her life.*
3. *Neither was I. And*
4. *Just hearing the word "rollaway" gave me a serious pain in my neck.*

"Why can't he move downstairs into the boxed set?" I asked Mom.

She pursed her lips and shook her head as though I'd just spit on someone's grave.

So picture me a week before Uncle Mike was to address the court, unable to sleep a wink. I'd written a long and impassioned letter to Travis, imploring him to apologize to Uncle Mike and explaining to him that his best chance for staying alive was to appeal to my uncle for mercy. I then slipped the letter to Father Jimbo in a sealed envelope. He smiled at me when he took it and promised that he would hand deliver it to Travis himself before the sentencing trial started. Because Father Jimbo was a man of God, I assumed that he'd told the truth and then followed through with his promise. But a day had passed and still there had been no word from Travis, no apology, no letter. I kept imagining the humiliation my family was soon to face when Uncle Mike stood up in court and demanded an eye for an eye. My worst-case scenario involved him playing an original song in the courtroom, a song that he'd been hammering out on his guitar in private during the week, a song that he would dedicate to the memory of Leonard. After a few hours of deliberation, the jury would return to their seats and deliver a unanimous decision, one that would involve Travis Lembeck's execution.

I must have finally drifted off at some point, because I was jolted out of a deep sleep by the sound of heavy footsteps in the hallway right outside the bedroom, followed by a pounding on my mother's door and a plea for help. I looked over at Deirdre's Hello Kitty alarm clock and watched the numbers flip to 5:17 A.M. I got up from the rollaway and pressed an ear to the door. By this time, my mother was telling Uncle Mike to calm down and shut up and what the hell was he trying to do, wake the dead? Uncle Mike was knocking some part of himself against the wall and whimpering like a wounded bear. I heard a loud plunk on the carpet. It was a wonder to me that Deirdre continued to sleep throughout the noise, which was taking place just yards from her head.

"Get off the floor, Mike! For god's sakes, get up!" my mother said in a frantic whisper. "You can't just park yourself here. It's five o'clock in the morning. Get up!"

Somehow she convinced him to go downstairs, and they settled in the kitchen. I was stationed just outside the kitchen door, which is how I heard every word.

According to Uncle Mike's account, he awoke (in my bed) to find Leonard in a ghostly form standing in the middle of the room and looking very confused. Neither of them spoke. They both just held each other's glance for a full minute, each of them considering what to do next.

"Wait. What're you doing here?" Leonard is supposed to have said. "What have you done with her? Why isn't Phoebe in her bed?"

"He *said* these things?" Mom asked Uncle Mike. "He spoke words?"

"Well," Uncle Mike replied with the kind of hesitation you usually get from a kid when he's caught in a lie. "Not exactly. More like I could feel him saying those words."

"Go on."

Uncle Mike said he just lay there staring until Leonard made the first move, a move that involved dissolving into thin air. He was gone. Uncle Mike stumbled out of the room and made his way down the hall to find my mother.

Uncle Mike was convinced that Leonard had come with one purpose—to find me. He believed that Leonard had a message to deliver, and he wanted my mother to wake me up and find out what it could be. He said we all needed to know before it was too late, before we did something that couldn't be undone.

By the time I made it back into my rollaway, the room was just beginning to lighten. Deirdre rolled over in her bed and squinted at me.

"What's going on?"

"Nothing," I told her. "Uncle Mike saw a ghost."

"Whoa," she murmured as she scratched her head. She then threw back the covers on her bed and scooted her body over against the wall, making room for me. "Come on. You might as well get in."

I did and pulled the covers over me. I could feel the warmth from where her body had just been, and I could feel the heat radiating from where her body actually was. I felt I might get some sleep after all.

"Is it late or is it early?" she asked me.

"Both," I replied.

We were in for a very long day.

Later, when I came downstairs dressed and ready for breakfast, I made buttered raisin toast, drank my orange juice and asked Uncle Mike if he'd be moving out of my bedroom anytime soon. He stared at me.

"Huh?"

"Or maybe you could move downstairs to Leonard's room," I suggested.

He shook his head no.

Nothing more was said for the rest of the week, but I felt that I had found a possible solution to my problems—not only the problem of where I would be sleeping (Uncle Mike moved back onto the couch the next night) but also to the problem of Travis Lembeck. But it wasn't until we were dressed and sitting next to each other in the backseat of Mom's car and waiting for Mom and Deirdre to join us that Uncle Mike was able to address the issue.

"I don't do much public speaking," he said. "Standing up in front of people and all. Never been my thing."

I nodded and pretended to be arranging stuff

inside my purse. The fact that he was nervous wasn't exactly news. The signs were there. He had spent most of the morning locked in the bathroom mumbling to his reflection in the mirror. Also his cologne was stronger than usual, and he had two cuts on his face from shaving. This was the morning that the sentencing phase of the trial was scheduled to begin—the phase in which Travis's fate would be decided.

"Was he wet?" I finally asked, without looking up from my purse.

"What?"

"Last time Leonard came to see me, he was dripping wet. From the lake, I guess. He looked good, though. Happy. Did he look happy?"

Uncle Mike stopped breathing, his mouth hung open.

"You seen him too?" he managed to croak.

"All the time. He's getting to be a total pest. Just like in life."

We continued to sit there in silence until my mother and Deirdre slipped into the front seat and we drove away. Once we were on the Turnpike headed toward Trenton, Deirdre, our self-designated driver, launched into a rather lengthy dissertation about the origin of the French twist, a topic that no one other than Deirdre herself cared to discuss. Uncle Mike kept looking out the window, and though he held the pages of his prepared speech furled up in his fist, he never even gave it the once-over.

We pulled into downtown Trenton, and right away we found a parking space on the street; but before getting out of the car, we arranged ourselves as best we could. We were sure to run into the same old photographers and reporters on the court-house steps, and despite the fact that we claimed not to care, we still couldn't help wanting to look our best. If Leonard had taught us anything about life, it was to always make an effort, because you never know.

Only Uncle Mike seemed unconcerned with his appearance; he just stood on the curb staring up at the clear blue sky and letting the wind make a mess of his hair. He looked wild-eyed and nervous and ashen. But then what could you expect from a person who was being haunted by a ghost?

"You all right?" I asked him.

"Just thinking."

He ran his hand over his face and pulled at his features, as if he were desperately trying to change how he felt by rearranging his expression. Then he added, "Maybe Leonard was trying to tell us something. And I've been thinking maybe I know what it is."

"Really?" I said. "What?"

"I think maybe he doesn't want me to talk today."

It had almost been too easy.

"You know," I said to Uncle Mike, "you might be right."

Then he turned toward me, placed his hand on my shoulder and said, "It's you who oughtta speak for him, Pheebs. You're the one oughtta get up and say what Leonard wants. You know what it is, don't you? He told you, didn't he? You know."

"What's going on with you two?" Mom called out from where she was standing.

"Nothing," Uncle Mike and I said at the same time.

"Well, then come on. Let's get this over with."

Once we were inside the courthouse, I surrendered to the usual grind of metal detectors and grumpy guards. As usual, I wished that I was anywhere but where I was—standing in my stocking feet on the cool linoleum flooring in a New Jersey courthouse.

"You're clear," the guard said.

When I sat down in one of the metal chairs to put my shoes back on, Uncle Mike was beside me lacing up his boots. I could feel him looking at me.

"So you're gonna do the talking, right?" he whispered.

"No prob," I said. And that was that. A deal had been struck.

TWENTY-TWO

The courtroom was packed, and in antici-pation of a sentence that would determine someone's life or death, the reporters were crammed up against the doors.

Mom glared at the courtroom sketchers as we entered and then shook out her hair so they would be sure to notice her new hairstyle. We were called to order; Judge Gamble entered and began the sen-tencing phase of the trial. Right off the bat she asked our family if we wanted to step forward and speak on behalf of Leonard. We all rose, and though I was the one who had agreed to speak, I looked toward Uncle Mike and nodded at him as though it was time for him to say something or forever hold his peace. I know it was cowardly of me, but being in that courtroom again—standing before the same jury and facing Ms. Fassett-Holt—made me realize that my plea for Travis's life might seem like the desperation of a spurned girlfriend trying to make good. Uncle Mike looked over at me as if he might lose his lunch right there in front of everyone. I shot him a don't-look-at-me look. He unfurled his prepared speech, but clearly he was lost. He managed to swallow hard, ask for a drink of water and then, after a couple of sips, clear his throat. I thought he might actually manage a few words; but just as he opened his mouth to speak, Deirdre took pity on him, lightly touched his arm and stepped forward.

"Your honor, if it's all right, I'd like to speak for my family. But um, if there's no objection, I'd like to say it directly to Travis. I mean, if that's all right?"

Judge Gamble looked around the room, took the temperature of everyone present and then indicated with a quick nod that it was fine. She gave her gavel a single bang to quiet the rustles and whispers. Deirdre then turned her body to face Travis, who was sitting at the defense table. She addressed him directly.

"Hey, Travis."

He looked up, startled by the sudden attention. It seemed that for the first time since the trial began, he actually looked like a human being; and maybe that was because for the first time since the trial began, someone was speaking directly *to* him instead of just *about* him. It was kind of genius, and I think everyone took notice. Suddenly he was just Travis Lembeck, some kid Deirdre had gone to school with, someone you could pass on the street and say "hey" to. But then as if the pressure of being ordinary was too much for him, Travis turned and looked away.

"Look, I don't know how to do this, so . . ." Deirdre fussed with her hair and let out a nervous little laugh. She was wearing a gray sweater hoodie and a black pleated skirt. She was actually wearing knee socks, her Adidas running shoes and, though she didn't really have enough hair to warrant it, a headband. It was as if she had dressed to please just about everyone in the courtroom. On top of all that, her nerves had added a deep and sudden blush to her cheeks. She looked stunning. "Anyway, I just wanted to say that I don't think anyone in this courtroom can excuse or pardon you for what you've done. No one in the world can do that. I guess maybe that's God's business. And really, for us, for my family, no punishment on Earth could ever make up for the loss of Leonard Pelkey. You know that, right?"

Travis didn't respond. In fact, he wasn't looking at her, not even close. He'd fixed his gaze across the room where the wall and the ceiling joined; he was squinting hard as if desperate to read a message that had been written there for him in invisible ink. Unfazed, Deirdre continued.

"And y'know, as much as I hate to admit it, if that's true . . . I mean, if it's true that no one can pardon you, then I guess it's also true that no one has the right to condemn you to death either."

She paused here to yank up one of her socks, but really, I suspected her of pausing for dramatic effect. In either case, she accomplished both and then went on.

"Honestly? My whole family, I think we all wanted to see you die a slow and painful death. I mean, at first. We were *that* angry. But even Uncle Mike here, who's been dead set against you, has kind of come round to another way of thinking in the past couple of weeks." Uncle Mike snapped his head around at that and looked at Deirdre with an expression that said, *Who me?* "We all realize that maybe it'd be better if you were forced to live." Mouths dropped open at this. "I mean, because that way, you'll be forced to wrestle with your own conscience every single day for the rest of your life." Murmurs of astonishment came from the crowd and a knock from the gavel. "But my one big hope, Travis? *Our* hope is that in that struggle, your conscience'll beat the crap out of you every time. Some people complain that this kind of thinking allows killers to, literally, get away with murder. They say stuff like, 'A killer has *no* conscience to wrestle with.' And until recently maybe I was thinking that too. But then, you want to know what made me change my mind?"

Once again, Travis didn't respond. He just sat

there staring off into space. Deirdre waited for him to at least look over at her. He didn't.

"Travis? I said, you want to know what made me change my mind?"

More waiting as we all sat there watching Travis, knowing that he knew we were watching him. It was so painful, I thought the clock on the wall was going to explode into a million pieces. You could hear the pencils against papers as the courtroom sketchers made a mess of Deirdre's beautiful face. The court stenographer stopped working her tiny machine. We all waited. But Deirdre wasn't about to say another word until Travis made a move; and it was clear that he'd made up his mind to not make a move.

Judge Gamble opened her mouth to say something, perhaps to demand a response from him; but before a bubble of sound could form in her throat, Travis turned toward Deirdre and was saying in his most defiant voice ever, "What?"

Hearing Travis speak was a shock. And I think not just for me, but also for everyone. For the first time since this whole thing began, he was a participant in his own trial. That one word was enough to satisfy Deirdre and allow her to go on.

"My sister. Phoebe. It turns out she was kind of in love with you."

Here she turned and looked over at me. Just her expression was enough of an apology for dragging me into it all over again. I could tell she was genuinely sorry to say my name aloud in court. But there it was. Meanwhile, I wished I could be anywhere else in the world but where I was. My mouth was as dry and dusty as a bag of Cheetos puffs, my shoulders had hunched and tightened and even my hair was feeling the pressure of being stared at by strangers. To make matters worse, big gobs of shafty sunlight were streaming in the window like God had nothing better to do than make special effects.

"Sorry, Pheebs. But . . ."

Despite the fact that my face had probably turned a shade of beet and my body temperature was about ten thousand degrees above normal, I was cool with everything she'd said so far, and I'd live with anything she was about to say. For the first time in years, I actually felt like Deirdre and I were sisters again. But more than just blood bonded us together, it was the fact that now both she and I had been through something—again—that had left us irrevocably changed. I nodded so she could see in my eyes that she was my hero, she'd always been, would always be. She nodded back and then turned her attention to Travis.

"And I figured if someone as good and kind and smart as my kid sister could find something to love in a loser like you, then maybe there's something in you worth saving. Okay, so maybe most people can't see it, or don't *want* to see it, but that doesn't mean it isn't there. Some spark, some, I dunno, some goodness or whatever that's buried deep. At first, I couldn't figure out why Phoebe could see it when no one else could. I mean, she fought tooth and nail for your life. You should know that. But then after this morning here in court, I dunno, everything suddenly added up, because I saw it was love. What else could explain it? And maybe that's why she's able to see the good in other people too, why she was the first to make friends with Leonard when he came to live with us. Sure, she may've wanted to kill Leonard. We all did every once in a while. He could get on your nerves. But make no mistake—Phoebe loved Leonard. She loved him, and because of that, she was able to see what everyone else couldn't. Same with you, Travis. You might not've deserved her love, but you got it anyway. That's just the way it works."

She came to a full stop here and appeared to be chewing the inside of her cheek. This was one of the oldest tricks in her book. I knew it from our childhood. Chewing her cheek was what she'd always done to keep herself from crying. I figured she was probably thinking about Dad. No matter what had happened between them, he was her father, always had been, always would be. And even though he didn't deserve her love, she loved him anyway. That's just the way it worked.

Finally she cleared her throat and started up again. But as she did, it was obvious that she wasn't just talking to Travis anymore; she'd turned her attention toward the whole room.

"Over the past few weeks, our house's seen some pretty lively debate about all this. But it was basically the same fight over and over. There was a lot of talk about justice and an eye for an eye and all that shit—sorry, your honor—and there was plenty of hate in the room. My sister, she kept arguing for more love, really. More mercy. And finally, I think for me it all came down to which side of the argument I was on—the hate side or the love side. I didn't mean to make a big soapbox speech here today, I just wanted to say that in the argument, y'know, between hate and love, it's really up to each one of us. In our hearts or wherever. Each of us has to take a stand every single day and say which side we're on. And I dunno for sure, but maybe the whole purpose of evil in this world is to get people who aren't really good and who aren't really bad to stand up and, y'know, be better. Maybe without evil, the just people of the world who happen to be just going along, living their lives and minding their own business—like the Hertle family, for example—maybe without evil, they'd never find the courage to come forward and do the right thing."

She paused here and looked down at her running shoes, but I knew her so well. Her attention was so clearly on the room. She seemed to be aware of the effect she was having on the crowd, on the jury, on me and, yes, even on Travis. Who could blame her if she wanted to savor it for a moment before moving on to the next thing? But she'd said enough, and like any great performer who knows how to accurately take the pulse of the audience, she knew it was time to wrap it up.

"I guess that's all." Then a thought occurred to her. "Oh. Except, one more thing. I'm really sorry Leonard isn't here with us. He would've loved all the theatrics. He would've had plenty to say about it all. He was like that. Mouthy. But since he couldn't be here, I figured it was up to me to speak up."

She then turned to face the ladies and gentlemen of the jury.

"Look. All I'm saying is this: When you're back there deciding whether Travis Lembeck should live or die, all you have to do is think about it in your hearts—and choose between hate and love."

When we finally left the courthouse that day and walked out into the late-afternoon sunlight, I noticed that everyone was leaning in, trying to get a good look at us. The usual gaggle of reporters and photographers was there, all of them tripping over themselves and tipping their mikes and cameras toward me or Deirdre or Mom while at the same time nagging us for a comment or attention. But there were also ordinary folks who had attended the trial and were now waiting for a glimpse of us. A woman with everyday hair was wearing a raincoat over her sweats and running shoes and yelling, *"There she is! The girlfriend."* A guy in a leather bomber jacket, cheap jeans and a gold chain around his neck was calling out Deirdre's name like she was supposed to know him. A tangle of high school girls who looked like me two years ago, which is to say innocent and with coordinated outfits, kept jumping up to see me over the heads of other people. *"I saw her!"* one of the girls said to the others. *"I saw her!"* But I couldn't tell whether they were referring to me, Deirdre or Carol Silva-Hernandez, the newswoman from NEWS 5.

Of course, several of Mom's customers were there as well; they stood in a row with their arms interlocked and their faces set. I'd never seen them look so determined, so serious. It took me a minute to realize that they had positioned themselves between the heaving crowd and us. They were standing nearby, moving along with us, and quietly protecting us from the crush of thrill seekers and rubberneckers until we were down the stairs and in the clear.

"You'll be okay from here," Mrs. Liggeria said to my mother. "You get into any trouble, you got my cell, right?"

Mom nodded and thanked them all, said she'd see them all back at the salon. I tried to thank them as well, but Deirdre took hold of my arm and pulled me along. I looked back, and I could see the women standing there—Mrs. Liggeria, Mrs. Kavanaugh, Mrs. Mixner, Mrs. Trabucco, Mrs. Landis, Mrs. Grig—all of them stared after us as we moved along. When I lifted my arm to wave them good-bye, I felt like a stranger, not only to them, but also to myself.

TWENTY-THREE

On a bright afternoon in the spring of my senior year, I came home from school to find an actual letter waiting for me in our mailbox. We rarely ever got snail mail, so a letter with a handwritten name and address was something I would notice. We got birthday cards, of course; the occasional postcards from one of Mom's regulars announcing the weather conditions in Tampa or the fact that her eczema had unexpectedly cleared up; and sometimes a customer who remembered me for giving her a good set and perm sent me a Christmas greeting with a five-dollar bill enclosed. But mostly my family's daily post (as Jane Austen might have said) was made up of bills and advertisements. As soon as Electra hooked me up to my computer and connected me to the Internet, I was busy night and day receiving emails, checking my MySpace account and IMing people I'd met online. The only reason I bothered to flip through the mail each day was because I hadn't yet heard that I was accepted at any of the three colleges to which I had applied.

The letter was addressed to me in shaky hand-writing that I didn't immediately recognize. But even before I opened it, I knew it was from Travis. Who else would be writing me from a state prison? I stood there in the hallway, weighing the envelope, examining the postage and wondering where I should go to open it.

There was a time not that long ago when I would've clutched the letter to my heart, taken the stairs two at a time, thrown myself down on Deirdre's bedspread and forced her to open and read it because I was too excited. Together we would have examined the boy's penmanship, speculated what his dotted *i*'s revealed, discussed what was written between the lines and devised a suitable response.

Travis would've become one of our projects, like but- terfly collecting or candle making, projects that we took up with relish only to realize a month later that we had abandoned it for the next thing.

Deirdre and I used to tell each other everything. We were, after all, sisters; we had lived together under the same roof with the same set of parents, shared the same hairbrush and showered with the same bar of soap. But so much had happened to us over the past few years, and so much of what had happened had happened to us separately, that we had quietly mislaid our common language. Following the trial and her amazing eleventh-hour performance, she and I had begun to once again live in the same universe; but it was a universe that was still new to both of us, and we were taking it slowly. Also, Deirdre graduated Roberson's Beauty School and then started a new job answering the phones and booking appointments at a salon over in Asbury Park called P.S. Love Your Hair. She was working full-time, and the job had become her life. She was never home. After all that had happened, she was eager to get on with things and appear as normal as possible. And who could blame her for wanting that?

Sharing the contents of the letter with my mother would have been just as complicated, but for different reasons. She was at least on the premises, but she did not approve of any discussion involving Travis Lembeck. After the trial was over, Travis's had become just one of the names we didn't mention in her house, along with Dad's. Once when Father Jimbo suggested that we all pay a visit to Travis in jail, Mom responded by sighing, grabbing hold of the countertop and saying, "No way are we going anywhere near that boy. We've had enough in that department." She then walked Father Jimbo to the front door, and that was the last I ever heard about the possibility. Just as well. As recent as a few months ago, I wasn't yet ready for face time with the person everyone in Neptune had characterized as pure evil, even if that face happened to be on the other side of bulletproof glass.

I thought about going downstairs to open Travis's letter in private, but six months earlier, a flood had ruined everything down there and we'd had to trash most of the stuff. Waterlogged books and clothes got crammed into big black bags and then dragged out to the curb on trash night. The last of Nana Hertle's belongings, the Sierra Club posters and the locomotive garbage can, all became things of the past, literally overnight. The boxes were gone and every trace of Leonard was removed. We were moving on, and my mother sent everything into an unsuspecting world by way of various charities that specialized in junk with no questions asked. She wanted a new look downstairs, one that involved a freshly painted concrete floor and plenty of wide-open space. After it was all gone, we listened as she verbally decorated the place over and over. A game room would be nice, or maybe a family entertainment center, or how about an exercise area. We offered no suggestions. For me, whatever it ended up looking like, the place would always belong to Nana and Leonard. But without their actual stuff, the basement no longer seemed like a viable location to me; it became just one of the many spaces on this Earth that I would pass through on my way to somewhere else.

Alone, I sat on the front stoop of our house and opened Travis's letter. Like the handwriting itself, the message was simple and straightforward.

Dear Phoebe,

How are you doing? I hope you're enjoying school and everybody in your family is doing good. I'm adjusting to life in prison here as best I can. I wake up way too early, the food is crap and the noise drives me fucking nuts, but other than that prison life is not so bad as I thought it would be. Don't get me wrong. It totally sucks. But I can't complain. I mean, considering. I know I got no right to ask, but I'm wondering if maybe you'd think about coming to visit me sometime. No big deal, if you're not into it. I wouldn't blame anyone for wanting to stay as far away from this place as they can get. Even the lighting in here is a buzz kill. But if you'd come, I could see you and that would be nice. Whatever happens, take care of yourself.

Sincerely,
Travis Lembeck

P.S. A special hello to my girl Deirdre.

I folded up the letter and tried to imagine myself sitting in a maximum-security-prison visiting area. I just couldn't do it. What would I wear? was the first question that occurred to me. And then there was a series of many other questions that were more serious, like what would Travis and I actually talk about, how would I be able to look him in the eye and finally who would drive me to Trenton?

I did have a driver's license by that time, but without a car, a license wouldn't have done me much good. Public transportation was always an option; but considering the situation, I thought it would be best if I had someone with me. Deirdre was out of the question. Like I said, she was busy with her new life.

My mother remained dead set against the idea of me going to Trenton. She said it was wrong and possibly dangerous. I reminded her that as an aspiring writer, I needed life experience. Think of it as research, I told her. I could write an article for the school paper and get extra credit. She shot me one of her killer sideways glances, the kind that seemed to say, "Don't start in with me." Then I asked her if she thought the mothers of writers like Norman Mailer and Truman Capote ever prevented *their* children from doing what had to be done, because both of them spent time with hardened criminals so they could write books. She replied by saying, "I don't know what you're talking about. But if the mothers of those writers let their kids hobnob with killers, they oughtta be ashamed of themselves."

"Is it because I'm a girl?" I suggested with more than a little attitude. "Is that it?"

She looked at me straight in the face and said, "Yeah. Call it that. And if you'da stuck with the ballet classes like I told you, this never woulda happened."

My father was, under the circumstances, no longer in the running. He'd moved away to Las Vegas so Chrissie could pursue her dream of becoming a croupier. Not long after he moved, he sent us a picture postcard of a fake Eiffel Tower with his new address scribbled on the back. I felt sad whenever I allowed myself to think about him.

I decided that the best person to give me a ride

was Officer DeSantis. I knew for a fact that Chuck and his life partner, Craig, went to Trenton a lot on Saturday mornings to make the rounds of the local thrift shops, poke through old stuff, have lunch at their favorite diner and treat themselves to a pedicure before going home. They had even asked me if I'd like to tag along sometime.

The fact is that after all the hoopla about the trial had blown over, I began spending time with Chuck and Craig. I liked them. They were such a funny couple, especially when they started to bicker. It wasn't like they were serious about their disagreements, and it wasn't as if they disagreed about anything earth-shattering. Usually, their arguments were about stupid stuff like whether a piece of fabric was plaid or madras or who said what to whom and why. But no matter how heated they got, I never had the feeling that anything bad was about to happen or that one of them was going to haul off and hit the other. And that was probably a good thing, because they were both pretty large.

At first, I was confused. I had never (to my

knowledge) met such big gays. Craig told me that he and Chuck were considered to be "bear" types.

"By who?" I wanted to know.

"By *whom*?" he said, correcting me without bothering to turn around in his seat.

Craig was a freshman-year English teacher over at Manasquan High, but even when he was off duty, he remained a stickler for grammar. He was not as big as Chuck, but he seemed to make up for this slight disadvantage by upping his volume whenever he spoke and by taking up more space wherever he went. I wouldn't say that he was exactly handsome; his features were a bit too spread out across his face and his ears were tiny, giving him a look that was more otter than bear.

Just in case you don't know, bears are a subset of the homosexual experience, a group of men who can be easily identified by their burly frames, facial hair and beer bellies. Once the whole thing was explained to me, I had to agree that Chuck and Craig pretty much fit the profile. But I was still unclear about how to distinguish a bear from an average big guy on the street.

"I mean, how do you know?"

"I can just tell," Craig said, turning to me and giving his beard a smoothing.

"Signals," Chuck added.

"Like . . . ?"

"Like, I don't know, clues. Clothes," Craig said. And then he added, "Well, not the clothes exactly, but the way we wear them."

This conversation took place last Sunday while they were driving me to visit Mrs. Kurtz. Mrs. K. had been having a hard time taking care of herself, and people were saying that something ought to be done before there was an accident. Then there was an accident. First her space heater caught fire, and then her dog, Joey. The dog didn't make it, and though her house suffered only some minor smoke damage, a meeting was called and a decision was made to move Mrs. K. into assisted-living quarters in Sea Crest. Everyone agreed that it was the best course of action. Everyone except Mrs. K.; she thought it was the worst idea she'd ever heard of, and she adamantly refused to go.

Before she'd even stepped foot onto the property

of the Bonnie Dunes Assisted Living Center, there had been a lot of crying, some hysterical carrying on and a broken figurine. But once she was settled in, Mrs. K. came around to the idea of making a new life for herself in a minimum-security holding environment. To help with the transition, many of her friends and neighbors agreed to visit her, at least until she got familiar with the place. Somehow I got roped into sleeping over once a week and reading aloud to her.

The minute Chuck and Craig dropped me off and I was waving good-bye to the taillights of their car, I realized that I'd forgotten to ask them for a ride to Trenton. Oh, well, I told myself, it's not like Travis is going anywhere. Life without parole is a very long time. And maybe I just wasn't ready; it would take a while.

Mrs. K. and I were still in the middle of reading *Great Expectations*, a novel by Charles Dickens about this guy named Pip and his trials and tribulations as he grows up and, of course, ends up with the girl he loves. My rule is: If Mrs. K. starts snoring loudly, I stop reading. I'm not about to compete with her. I figure at the rate we're going, poor Pip might never make it to adulthood.

But this particular evening, Mrs. K. had been unusually alert. We'd just finished reading the final few paragraphs of chapter 47 when her hand with the rag reached over and touched me. She said, "Oh, by the by. I almost forgot. I got something for you." She pulled herself up from her chair and hobbled into her bedroom. I heard her rattling around in there and then the sound of something like boxes or papers toppling over.

"You all right?" I called out from where I was sitting.

I was just about to press the panic button, which would alert the facilities manager and automatically contact the paramedics, when she came back carrying a spiral notebook and brushing some dust off her housecoat; the book had a green, dog-eared cover. I'd seen the thing before. It had belonged to Leonard once upon a time. She handed it to me and said, "I've been meaning to give this to you. He left it at my other place, back then, y'know, before . . . before the fire and everything. I packed it up and took it with me, but, well, I don't have room for an extra toothpick in this place, so you have it."

"Thanks," I said, and took the notebook from her and tucked it in my backpack. Mrs. K. turned on the TV. I closed *Great Expectations* and placed it on the end table, where it lives when it's not being read. We were clearly finished for the evening.

After a while, Mrs. K. called it a day and went into her bedroom. She was supposed to be asleep, but I knew she was probably just lying there, because she told me once that sleep doesn't come as easily to her as it once did and sometimes she has to wait many hours before it takes her. She said she gets afraid at night. She can't tell me what scares her, but she claims it's there, the terror, waiting. She can feel it sometimes hovering at the foot of her bed, sometimes under it. Personally, I think she scares herself. But just so she doesn't wake up screaming and frightening the other Bonnie Duners to death, I stay overnight with her and sleep on a pullout sofa that smells of dog and hot soup. I stayed up way later than I should have that night watching TV, reading, writing, doing whatever.

Later I remembered Leonard's notebook. I pulled the old thing from my backpack. I was surprised to discover that I was afraid to open it, afraid that I would turn the pages and suddenly come across an original poem by Leonard Pelkey, or a short story that he'd written, or an unfinished letter. I knew that if anything like that happened, my heart would break. At the same time, I was scared that I might find only unsolved math problems, mindless doodlings in the margins and an unfinished composition on the subject of the history of the tomato or a brief biography of Cotton Mather. That too would break my heart, but for an altogether different reason.

An envelope slipped out and fell into my lap. It was an ordinary business envelope, a white one with a flag stamp in the corner and Leonard's name and our address written in a shaky hand that I instantly recognized. There was no return address. I opened it and pulled out the single sheet of ruled paper that had been torn from a spiral notebook.

Leo,

Just wanted to thank you for the money clip. It was stupid giving it to me. I

lose shit like that all the time. And I know
how much it means to you since it belonged
to your mother and all. So I'm going to try
and take care of it. Anyway, thanks.

> *Your friend,*
> *Travis*

In the morning I woke up and made breakfast in Mrs. K.'s cramped kitchenette. Over frozen
waffles and coffee, she and I discussed the night
and the state of her hair. As usual, I reminded her
to take her pills, and as she downed them one by
one, she told me for the umpteenth time that when
she was my age, she didn't have the opportunities
I have now. She told me not to waste my time and
to make the best of everything. She told me about
the boys she had crushes on back in the Bronx
where she grew up. She said their names and then
discussed their looks and habits as if they still lived
next door and she would see them later at a karaoke
sing-along.

The letter was in my pocket the whole time. I
would have to wait until I got home in order to

compare it with the other letter, the one Travis had sent to me. Just to be sure. But eyeballing it was enough to convince me that Travis had written the note. And that sent things spinning: the fact that Travis and Leonard had enjoyed some kind of friendship, the fact that their friendship had never made it onto anyone's radar, the fact that Travis had been telling the truth about how he came to own the money clip. All these facts seemed to vie for my attention, as if they were trying to outshout the single unchangeable fact that Leonard Pelkey had been brutally murdered by Travis Lembeck.

A car horn honked. I quickly gathered up my belongings, kissed Mrs. K. on the forehead and rushed out of her unit. Once on the street, I was ashamed at how thrilled I was to be out of there, free of that tiny, shrinking world, and with my day stretched out before me.

Electra was sitting behind the wheel of her used gunmetal Geo Prizm. She didn't have her license yet and technically she wasn't supposed to drive without a licensed driver, but she did anyway and her parents were unable to stop her.

"Hurry it up," she yelled at me. "We're late!"

As I slid into the passenger seat, she explained that she was in no mood. She'd had to drive her brother to physical therapy, which meant she'd been up since the crack of Jesus and was tired as hell. She didn't want to be late for school and spend the morning in detention.

"Calm down," I said to her. "We're seniors. What can they do to us? We're gods."

"Goddesses," she reminded me. And then she launched into a debate about college life, and should we be submitting ourselves to four more years of mental slavery or should we just chuck everything and head for Europe.

I wasn't listening. Not really. I'd heard it all before. Every day, in fact. And besides, I was thinking about the letter.

"I got a letter from Travis."

She gave me a sidelong glance and sucked air between her teeth as a way of signaling her disapproval. I was about to ask her if she would consider driving me to Trenton some Saturday, but she interrupted.

"What'd I tell you? Didn't I tell you?"

"He wants me to visit him," I said.

"No," she replied, point-blank.

"It's just that he's got no one."

"No."

"He needs someone to talk to. Someone on the outside."

"Someone?" she said, as if I had just insulted her and her whole family. "Someone?"

The car came to a dead stop at the intersection. She leaned over and spoke directly into my face. "Tell me right now, Phoebe Hertle, that you are not, not, not seriously considering this. That boy is pure evil through and through, and I am not moving from this spot till you give me your honest-to-God word of honor that you will totally steer clear of him."

I looked at her and I remembered a time when everything was different, a time when everything was pure and it was easy to steer clear. My world made sense and everything was absolutely bright. Trenton was just a dot on a map and we weren't connected to it at all, except through the occasional news story. We knew no one who lived there, and certainly no one in a maximum-security prison. Mom and Dad were still together. My older sister was perfect and so was Winona Ryder. My best friend didn't have opinions that were the opposite of mine.

In those days, if evil had a face, it was just some girl I hardly knew who was saying mean things behind my back, or it was someone I didn't know at all living in some other town or in a far-off country. Evildoers might be sitting right outside my house in a parked car, but back then I didn't know their names or where they lived or what they had in mind.

"Pheebs?" Electra said, as we idled at the corner waiting for the light to change. "You aren't saying anything. You have to promise. You have to say it."

But what could I say? I couldn't promise Electra anything, because I knew that steering clear was no solution. She didn't understand, not yet, that Deirdre was right—every day you have to stand up to evil. You might even have to risk getting in a car and driving all the way to Trenton. You might have to sit with it in an airless room and look it in the eye until you can see its all-too-human face. And then someday, if you should ever find yourself in the grip of evil, tied up and sinking down to the bottom of a lake, you can remember that, once, you saw a glint of goodness in that same evil eye, and without you, it never would have been there.

The car behind us gave us a toot, urging us forward.

"Just go," I told Electra, nodding in the direction up ahead. "Just go."